The Da Capo History of
Western Classical Music

The Da Capo History of
Western Classical Music

JOHN BAILIE

DA CAPO PRESS • New York

Publishing Director: Laura Bamford
Executive Editor: Mike Evans
Editor: Michelle Pickering
Production: Joanna Walker
Picture Research: Liz Fowler
Art Director: Keith Martin
Art Editor: Geoff Fennell
Book Design: Birgit Eggers

The author wishes to thank
Joanna Bailie for her advice and
assistance in writing this book.

First published in the United States in 1999 by
Da Capo Press
A Subsidiary of Plenum Publishing Corporation
233 Spring Street, New York, N.Y. 10013

First published in the United Kingdom in 1999
under the title THE HAMLYN HISTORY OF CLASSICAL MUSIC by
Hamlyn, an imprint of Octopus Publishing Group Limited
Michelin House, 81 Fulham Road, London SW3 6RB

Library of Congress Cataloging-in-Publication Data
Bailie, J. M.
   The Da Capo history of western classical music /
   by John Bailie.
     p. cm.
   Published in the United Kingdom under title:
   The Hamlyn history of music.
   Includes index.
   ISBN 0-306-80885-4 (alk. paper)
   1. Music—History and criticism. I. Title.
ML 160. B107 1999
780'.9—dc21
                                      98-40010
                                      CIP
                                      MN

Printed in China

Contents

the origins of
western
music

e origins of Western music can
traced back to ancient
sopotamia. This limestone relief
m the palace of an Assyrian king
cavated in Nineveh shows army
sicians playing stringed and
rcussive instruments. It dates
m the 7th century BC.

Music has formed an important part of human life since the earliest recorded history. There are many theories about how it began: as a means of communication, as an accompaniment to religious ceremonies or to the rhythmical pattern of work in the fields, or as an adjunct to singing and dancing and other social activities. Music played a significant role in the early civilisations of the Indian subcontinent and China. However, the origins of Western music are to be found in Mesopotamia in the fourth millennium BC.

3500 BC –
200 AD

The earliest civilisation began in the fertile lands beyond the shore of the eastern Mediterranean about 3500 BC, with the foundation of the Sumerian city-states. Music appears to have had an important role in the lives of the Sumerian peoples from the very earliest times. Illustrations on clay tablets from around 2800 BC depict a three-stringed harp. Later examples have six or seven strings. Of equal importance was the lyre and there are many representations on cylinder seals of lyres. The only other instruments from this early period were simple percussion ones. Religion was a dominant force in Sumerian society and music was chiefly associated with worship – professional musicians sang and played in temples. There is also, during the Akkadian period, evidence of the use of antiphonal music, in which two groups sang alternate parts. From about 2350 BC Sumer came under the rule of a succession of powerful dynasties, but its culture was to have a profound influence on later civilisations of the region. The Babylonians introduced a smaller, more portable lyre and the angled harp, an instrument resembling a lute, drums of various sizes and a variety of wind instruments. The Assyrians were also renowned for their use of music as an accompaniment to festive occasions and celebrations. Reliefs show musicians, both men and women, playing instruments, including double-pipes, frame drums, harps and trumpets. The new peoples who conquered Mesopotamia absorbed the musical traditions of those before them and introduced their own. Yet during a period of 3,000 years it remained primarily a religious activity.

The Egyptian contribution

Civilisation in Egypt began some 500 years after the founding of Sumer. Reliefs, paintings and illustrations on pottery and utensils provide a precise description of the types of musical instruments employed and their evolution. During the period of the Old Kingdom (2700–2200 BC) musicians were depicted playing harps and flutes to accompany the chanting of priests, and also for dancing. The period of the Middle Kingdom (2050–1750 BC) saw refinement of instruments and introduction of new ones, notably the sistrum, a kind of rattle, and a cylindrical drum. The New Kingdom (1550–1050 BC) witnessed a remarkable expansion of Egyptian power, and was an era of cultural achievement in which music played an important part. New forms of harp and lyre appeared and a lutelike stringed instrument was introduced from Mesopotamia. Wall-paintings illustrate the variety of musical instruments available, including the trumpet. Music had an important role in religious ceremonies, but was also played at funerals and banquets, where female musicians were prominent. There is evidence of ensemble playing, with pictures depicting a singer, perhaps leading a group of instrumentalists using hand signals. This aid to performance seems to disappear later, suggesting the existence of notation, although there is no conclusive evidence. The specifics of tuning systems and melodic patterns also remain mysterious. At the end of the New Kingdom Egypt became subject to foreign invasions creating a climate in which the arts could no longer flourish.

Music flourished under the Ancient Egyptians and played an important role in both social and religious celebrations. Musical instruments, such as the nine-string harp being played in this Theban music room, became increasingly sophisticated.

The era of the New Kingdom (1550–1050 BC) ushered in the golden age of Ancient Egyptian cultural development. These wooden clappers, or drumsticks, date from the 18th dynasty, in the 16th–14th centuries BC.

The Hebrew legacy

The Old Testament provides a description of the singing and dancing
which accompanied the Jews as Moses led them out of Egypt. King David
first appears in the Bible as a musician, composer and performer at the
court of King Saul, where he helped to soothe the king's depression with
his playing – an example of the healing powers of music. As king, David
put Hebrew music on a firm foundation, encouraging both vocal and
instrumental performance in divine worship. The singing of psalms
became an essential feature of services in the Temple of Jerusalem and
the instruments included the kinnor, the nevel (a kind of harp) and
cymbals. Music was also played on other occasions – weddings, festivals,
funerals and military celebrations. The trumpet and the shofar or ram's
horn were used for ceremonial and ritual purposes. A blast of trumpets
helped bring down the walls of Jericho, illustrating another of music's
miraculous powers. There is also evidence for the development of
antiphonal singing, in which a solo voice is followed by a response by the
whole congregation. This was later adopted into the liturgy of the Early
Christian Church and provides a vital link between Jewish music and the
evolution of Western music in general.

**King David first appears in the Bible as a musician, composer and
performer at the court of King Saul, where he helped to soothe the king's
depression with his playing – an example of the healing powers of music.**

An illumination from a 9th-century
psalter showing King David playing
a stringed instrument in the
company of a pair of drummers and
dancers. David encouraged both
instrumental and vocal music to be
used in worship and the singing of
psalms became an essential
feature of religious services.

This Greek marble statuette depicts a harp player. The Ancient Greeks believed that the emotive power of music could incite the listener to both good and evil actions, depending on the particular qualities of the music.

This Greek dish shows female dancers and musicians. Music and dancing played an important part in processions, festivities and religious worship. A wide range of instruments were played, including rattles, lyres, aulos and kitharas.

The significance of Greek music

The first great European civilisation began in Crete at the beginning of the third millennium BC, reaching its peak around 1500 BC. Illustrations on vases show lyres, rattles and reed pipes, similar to those in Egyptian paintings. The Minoan culture of Crete was eventually overwhelmed by that of Mycenean Greece, which in turn fell to the Dorians, who brought the so-called 'Dark Age' to Greece. The poems of Homer (9th century BC) were probably sung to the accompaniment of a lyre. In the *Iliad* and the *Odyssey*, Homer mentions such instruments as the phorminx, resembling a lyre but larger, the panpipes or syrinx, the salpinx, a trumpet, and the aulos, a double-reeded pipe with reputedly wild intonation.

In Ancient Greece the term 'mousike' included not only music but also poetry and dancing. In fact, for the Greeks the concepts of music and poetry were inextricably mixed and through the centuries music was to have an increasingly dominant role in the shaping of Greek civilisation. In Greek mythology music was invented by the gods, with particular music being associated with particular gods. The lyre was the instrument most favoured in the cult of Apollo. The aulos was used in honour of Dionysus, the god of wine, to accompany the singing of the dithyramb, a poem set to music and sung by a chorus. These choruses were the forerunners of the age of Greek drama, where poetry, music and dance all played a part.

The aulos and the kithara, an elaborate kind of lyre with up to 11 or 12 strings and a large wooden soundbox, were the two most important instruments. The aulos' piercing tones accompanied processions, dances, soldiers, choirs, marriages and funerals. The kithara was played as an accompaniment to singing or the recitation of heroic poetry. Both aulos and kithara also featured as solo instruments and contests were held to judge the best performers.

The development of a theory of music really began in the 6th century BC with the work of Pythagoras, a philosopher and mathematician, who believed that numbers were of supreme importance in understanding both music and the universe itself, culminating in the notion of 'the music of the spheres'. It is to Pythagoras that the discovery of the mathematical basis of musical intervals is attributed, although he may have learnt this from the Babylonians.

The philosopher Plato thought that music should form an essential part of education and that, carefully selected, it could have a permanent and beneficial influence upon a person's character, among other things enabling him to distinguish instinctively the beautiful and the good from the ugly and the evil. Aristotle, too, believed in the ethical qualities of music. Since music had a direct appeal to the emotions, listening to a certain kind of music played on the appropriate instrument would help one to acquire the qualities associated with it. Exposure to the wrong kind of music would have disagreeable consequences.

The Greeks based their music on scales called modes which were derived from different kinds of tetrachords (a tetrachord consisted of four notes, the interval between the first and last being a fourth). Tetrachords could be joined together to make a longer scale. As far as is known Greek music was monophonic, consisting of single melodic lines. There is evidence of the existence of heterophony in ancient Greek music, where the vocal line is accompanied by a free and often elaborated version of the melody on the lyre or aulos. However, this development constitutes more an increase in melodic sophistication than the presence of harmonic or contrapuntal practice. Music was improvised and its rhythms were closely linked with inflections of the spoken language. Aristoxenus, a musician of the fourth century BC, endeavoured with some success to assimilate the various theoretical writings about Greek music, mentioning both the systemisation of microtonal intervals and the existence of musical notation. Greek music was ultimately to have a profound influence on the evolution of Western music in general.

A copy of a 5th-century BC Etruscan fresco in the Tomb of the Leopard at Tarquinia showing wind and stringed instruments. The musical traditions of the Etruscans were absorbed and adapted by the Romans after their conquest.

The Roman inheritance

From the very earliest times music played an important role in Roman life, both as an integral part of religious worship and in social activities. The Romans absorbed many musical traditions from the people they conquered, notably the Etruscans, the Greeks and the Hellenistic kingdoms of the eastern Mediterranean. Musical instruments included the tibia, similar to the Greek aulos. Its players, known as the *tibicines*, took part in religious and military ceremonies and when the influence of Greek drama began to be felt, they also played in the theatre.

The Romans developed a number of brass or bronze instruments adapted from Etruscan models, notably the tuba, a kind of trumpet, and three types of horn: the buccina, the cornu and the lituus. They were heavily indebted to Egypt and the Middle East for instruments – especially the hydraulis, a primitive form of pipe organ, the sistrum, cymbals, foot-clappers and frame drums. The kithara became the principal stringed instrument. The lyre, too, was adapted to suit Roman tastes.

In Rome as in Greece musical performance was generally improvised. A form of musical notation existed, but was seldom used. Nothing is therefore known for certain about the sound of Roman music. However, apart from its popularity with ordinary people, music had a vital role to play in the educational system, and both poets and philosophers discussed its applications in such diverse subjects as oratory and medicine. Yet Rome's most important function was to pass on to the medieval world the priceless Greek musical heritage.

music in the early
christian church

Cadelanonis urba deriuat̃. arrogans ṽtani fidei exprimitur.

The Roman Empire reached its greatest extent at the beginning of the second century AD, but in the space of 50 years there began a slow but inexorable decline. At first Christians suffered intermittent persecution from the Roman authorities, but by the third century Christianity had spread to all parts of the Empire. In 312 the emperor Constantine became a convert and the Christian faith was officially acknowledged as the state religion in the year 380. The Church grew in authority and influence and, with the collapse of the Western Roman Empire, became a uniquely civilising force in an age of turmoil and uncertainty. Monasteries were now virtually the sole repositories of all forms of learning, and safeguarded the cultural heritage of antiquity, including, of course, its music.

300 AD – 12th century

The late fifth century onwards was a period of upheaval, as barbarian tribes invaded Europe and North Africa. Visigoths, Franks, Moors, Vikings and others carved out new lands for themselves, replacing the Roman imperium with a patchwork of rival kingdoms. In the east, however, the Byzantine empire, centred on Constantinople, lived on for another 1,000 years. The attempt by Charlemagne to re-establish the Western Roman Empire in the ninth century was doomed to failure but paved the way for the foundation in 962 of the Holy Roman Empire – a vast territory covering Germany, Austria, northern Italy and part of France. In the 11th century the Normans conquered England, the Spanish began to drive out their Muslim overlords and the First Crusade was launched. Populations increased, towns sprang up, universities were established in Bologna, Paris, Oxford and Cambridge, and literature began to appear in the vernacular languages.

The music of the early Christians

The music of the early Christians was strongly influenced by the liturgy of the synagogue, notably in the chanting of the scriptures and in the unaccompanied singing of psalms and hymns. At a later stage, responsorial singing, a part of the Jewish liturgy in which a choir sang alternately with a soloist, was introduced into Christian worship. It was probably in Syria, one of the earliest centres of Christianity outside

This 12th-century illustration shows Pope Gregory I dictating to his scribe. Gregory I began the work of organising and codifying the melodies used in Church music. The monophonic Gregorian chant was named after him.

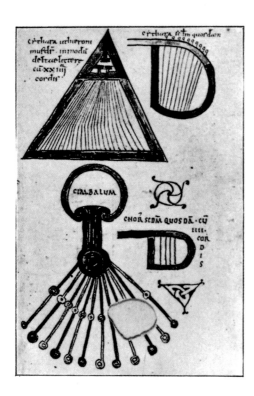

A page from Boethius' musical treatise 'De institutione musica'. Boethius was a Roman philosopher and writer whose treatise summarised Greek musical ideas, including those of Pythagoras. His work was extremely influential on the musicians of the Middle Ages.

Jerusalem, that antiphonal chanting, in which two choirs sang alternately, first developed. The Syrian Church was also noted for its psalm singing, but especially for the popularisation of a new kind of hymn which led to the flowering of the Byzantine art of hymnology. Although the Church in the Eastern Roman Empire never provided the dynamic impulse of its counterpart in the west that led to a great outpouring of musical culture, it gave western Europe both the rudiments of its tonal system and certain basic forms of notation.

Ambrosian and Gregorian chant

The fourth century was a period of reform in both the liturgy and Christian music. Greek, the liturgical language of the Church, was replaced in the west by Latin. Local churches in western Europe enjoyed considerable independence and varied in both forms of worship and accompanying music. In Milan, an important centre of Christianity which had strong links with Byzantium, there developed the Ambrosian or Milanese chant. It was named after St Ambrose, a bishop of Milan, who is credited with the introduction of the antiphon into the liturgy of the Western Church. However, since the earliest surviving examples date from the 11th–12th centuries, it is possible that it was established as late as the ninth century.

Visigothic Spain established its own independent liturgical music (later, under Arabic rule, known as the Mozarabic chant), which remained in use until the 11th century, when it was replaced by the Roman rite. It has resemblances to both Ambrosian, Gallican and Gregorian chant. In France the Gallican chant enjoyed a briefer existence. Established in the fifth century, it was suppressed by Emperor Charlemagne in an attempt to bring about a common Christian liturgical practice. Rome remained the most important centre of church music, and the repertory known as the Old Roman chant can be dated back to the eighth century. It was finally replaced by the Gregorian chant, which became an important unifying factor in the Western Church. The work of codifying and organising the melodies used in Church music was begun, according to tradition, by Pope Gregory I (540–604), after whom the Gregorian chant is named. He is also credited with the establishment in Rome of a *schola cantorum*, to train musicians.

The evolution of plainchant

Both the Gregorian chant and its predecessors are forms of plainchant, or plainsong. Plainchant is the music to which the texts of the Roman Catholic liturgy are sung. It is monophonic, that is, it has only a single line of melody, and was originally sung unaccompanied. The melodic range is quite limited and is in accordance with one of the eight church modes. During the ninth century the repertory of plainchant was enriched with the appearance of tropes and sequences. A monk at the Swiss monastery of St Gall, Tuotilo (died 915), is credited with the invention of troping, which originally meant an additional melody. New words and music or new text were added to a passage in order to give emphasis to the text. It was applied to many different categories of Church music and became extremely popular during the 10th and 11th centuries. A trope consisting of a brief, dramatised dialogue, added to the introit of the Easter mass and performed in church during the service, later evolved into a series of dramatic episodes. Eventually ecclesiastical authorities banned these increasingly worldly musical dramas from performance in church. Moving into the open, they were transformed into miracle or mystery plays, with spoken dialogue taking the place of music.

The sequence, which could be classified as a kind of extended trope, was originally a new text set to the music sung to the long melisma on the final 'a' of the alleluia of the mass. In the course of time it became more elaborate, new music being added. The best known creator of sequences was a German monk, Notker Balbulus (c.840–912), who also lived at St Gall, which had become a centre of musical development. The sequence enjoyed great popularity, stimulated creative activity and was even adapted for the secular music of the trouvères. In its religious form it eventually suffered the same fate as the trope, most sequences being banned by the Council of Trent in the 16th century.

Musical theory in the Middle Ages

St Augustine (354–430) wrote a long but unfinished treatise on music. He believed that it had the power to inspire lofty ideas and to influence its listeners in the direction of good or evil. The general opinion among ecclesiastical authorities was that music which brought men closer to God should be heard in church. Elaborate music, instruments, singing and dancing were associated with pagan entertainments. Boethius (c.480–524), a Roman philosopher and writer, wrote the treatise *De institutione musica*, which provides a useful, if not always accurate, outline of Greek musical ideas. Boethius himself believed music to be firstly a force pervading the whole universe (*musica mundana*), secondly an element which controls the union of body and soul (*musica humana*) and lastly music which can be heard (*musica instrumentalis*), the music produced by certain instruments, including the human voice.

Guido d'Arezzo's device for showing his six-note scale system. d'Arezzo developed a stave of four lines on which pitch could be recorded accurately. This allowed singers to learn a piece of music without the aid of a teacher. He also introduced the practice of designating the notes of a scale by syllables, known as solmisation.

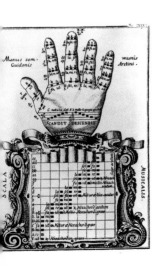

Notation

The systematic transcribing of aural music or as a set of instructions for performance began with the Greeks and was adopted by the Romans. A notation system intended to assist the singing of liturgical texts existed in the Eastern churches and in Jewish synagogues. However, in western Europe plainchant melodies could only be passed on by singers themselves so some method of recording them became vital. This began with neumes in the seventh century. These consisted of symbols written above the text of the music, indicating an ascending or descending melodic line. The earliest neumes carried little indication of the pitch or length of a note and a single neume could represent up to four notes. There is evidence from the German writer 'Anonymus Vaticanus' that neumes could also carry durational value and he mentions the existence of brevis and longa. He also alludes to the building up of these neumes into more complicated melodic patterns. In his *De harmonica institutione*, the first systematic treatise on Western music theory, the Frankish monk Hucbald (c.840–930) evolved a notation to indicate changes of pitch. Neumes became more sophisticated: the height of a neume above the text was an indicator of pitch and points and diagonal lines were added to them to represent long and short notes and form so-called 'compound neumes'. By the 11th century coloured lines were used to indicate a pitch. The monk Guido d'Arezzo (died c.1050) developed a stave of four lines, enabling pitches to be noted with accuracy and making it possible to learn a melody without a teacher. He also introduced solmisation, in which the notes of a scale were designated by syllables (the familiar ut, re, me, ta, so, etc). His system was based on hexachords (six-note scales) and replaced the Greek tetrachord (four-note scale).

Early polyphonic music

Polyphony is music in which two or more independent melodic lines are heard simultaneously. Polyphonic music emerged only gradually and existed alongside the monophony of plainchant over a long period. The earliest examples are found in the *Musica enchiradis*, an anonymous manual for singers, probably dating from the early ninth century, in which the original plainchant melody (*vox principalis*) is accompanied by a second voice (*vox organalis*). Each line moved in parallel to the other. Later other voices were added an octave below the original melody or an octave above the second voice. This primitive form of polyphony, known as organum, soon became more elaborate. In his treatise *Micrologus*, Guido d'Arezzo describes organum in which the second voice gained greater independence and an interval of a third (three notes) appeared. A more elaborate form of organum developed during the next 100 years, notably at the abbeys of Saint-Martial at Limoges in France and Santiago de Compostela in northwestern Spain. The lower voice (tenor) or cantus firmus was given the basic plainchant, while the upper voice, known as the duplum, enjoyed freedom of expression with an ornamented melody, the so-called melismatic organum.

An illumination showing the Coronation of the Virgin from a Notre Dame Book of Hours, a book of prayers that were to be chanted at set hours of the day. The School of Notre Dame was the main centre of musical activity in western Europe in the early 12th century.

The School of Notre Dame

In the first part of the 12th century the School of Notre Dame became the main centre of musical activity in western Europe and a new generation of composers achieved prominence. Léonin (c.1163–90), about whom nothing is known for certain, may have held an official appointment, possibly as choirmaster, at the cathedral of Notre Dame, then in course of construction. An anonymous musical theorist writing over a century later describes Léonin as the greatest composer of organa and names him as the author of the *Magnus Liber Organi* ('Great Book of Organum'), a collection of organum music for the entire church year, containing settings of plainchant for two voices. The original book is no longer in existence, but its contents, including revisions by Pérotin (c.1160–1225) of Léonin's work, are preserved in manuscripts dating from the 13th century. Pérotin and Léonin are the only members of the School of Notre Dame known by name. Pérotin is remembered for his expansion of polyphonic music, writing compositions for three or four voices, skilfully interwoven to create works of remarkable power and beauty. The anonymous writer who praised Léonin for his organa considered Pérotin the best composer of discant, a style of organum in which all the voices move in a strictly note-against-note style. Pérotin also originated other forms of music, including the conductus a polyphonic setting for three or four voices of a monophonic piece. Works by Pérotin which are still played today include two four-part works, 'Sederunt principes' and 'Viderunt omnes'.

The motet

The motet (from the French *mot* 'word'), which first emerged in the 13th century, became one of the main forms of composition in the Middle Ages and, having undergone various transformations, remained in vigour until the mid-18th century. It originated at the School of Notre Dame with the addition of text to the wordless upper voice part (the duplum) of short sections of organum. Later a third part, the triplum, was added. Each part was sung at a different speed, sometimes using different words. The earliest motets were intended for religious services, but a secular element gradually crept in. The new texts were in French rather than Latin and popular songs provided a source of inspiration, indicating the growing influence on each other of sacred and secular music.

Hildegard of Bingen

Born in 1098, she was educated by a group of nuns attached to a Benedictine convent near Bingen in Germany. Founding her own convent, at Rupertsberg, she became abbess. Later she experienced mystical, prophetic visions, which she expressed in literature and music. She also wrote on medicine and natural history, and composed lyrical and dramatic poetry. Her *Symphonia harmonie celestium revelationum*, which comprised over 70 lyrical poems with their music, made her one of the major medieval composers of chants. The music is made up of a fairly limited number of melodic patterns, but shows remarkable individuality.

Detail of a 13th-century illumination showing Hildegard of Bingen recording one of her prophetic visions. Hildegard was a German abbess who expressed her visions in poetry and music. She was one of the most prolific composers of plainsong chants in the medieval period.

The music of the troubadours

The earliest recorded secular music is that of the 'goliards', wandering students and itinerant churchmen who roamed the land singing boisterous songs in Latin on the subject of wine and women and satirical verses often targeting the higher clergy. Another group, which appeared in the ninth–tenth centuries, was the 'jongleurs' or 'ménestrels' (minstrels), professional travelling musicians and players (men and women) who earned a living singing, dancing and displaying acrobatic skills. Despite the hostility of the ecclesiastical authorities, they gradually improved their status and formed guilds of musicians, providing professional training for their members. Some even obtained positions in noble households. They also sang the 'chansons de geste', long epic poems describing heroic exploits, in which the music consisted of a simple melodic phrase constantly repeated. The most famous was *The Song of Roland*.

The 12th century witnessed a remarkable cultural phenomenon. This was the emergence in the south of France of the troubadours, poet-musicians who sang of courtly love. The language of this poetry was not Latin but the vernacular *langue d'oc* and the troubadours were drawn from the middle and upper ranks of society, although one of the most prominent, Bernart de Ventadorn (c.1130–90), was of humble birth.

Many of the poet-musicians composed and sang their own songs, which often displayed considerable complexity and variety in their structure. The courtly love songs were most popular, but there were also poems with music intended for dancing such as the 'ballade', the 'pastourelle' and the 'alba', or morning song.

The trouvères, the northern French equivalent of the troubadours, came to prominence in the 12th century. There are parallels between the two groups: trouvère poetry was essentially courtly and the poet-musician generally moved in aristocratic circles. Trouvères, too, used a variety of musical forms and sometimes adapted ecclesiastical chants, substituting secular words for sacred texts. The most famous of the trouvères, Adam de La Halle (c.1237–c.1285), composed both monophonic and polyphonic music at a time when most secular music was still monophonic. He is best known for his musical play *Le Jeu de Robin et de Marion*.

It was not until the development of more complex forms of polyphony that instruments began to play a part in the liturgy of the Church, many of them brought to Europe by crusaders.

Musical instruments

In the ancient world instrumental music was an art in itself and not merely an accompaniment to the human voice. However, in early Christian Europe the Church disapproved of instruments in religious services because of their association with pagan antiquity. It was not until the development of more complex forms of polyphony that instruments began to play a part in the liturgy of the Church, many of them brought to Europe by crusaders.

Among the most common instruments in the Middle Ages were the psaltery, a type of zither and ancestor of the harpsichord, the transverse flute and the shawm, which was a double-reeded woodwind instrument and an early form of the oboe. The bagpipe, whose history went back to remote antiquity, was the instrument of minstrels and strolling players.

An illustration from a 13th-century Spanish songbook. Biblical events were often expanded into dramatic stories and each scene set to music. It is from these humble beginnings that the traditions of European drama developed.

The organ was reintroduced to Europe in the eighth century when the emperor of Byzantium sent one as a gift to Charlemagne. For a long time it was the only instrument approved by the ecclesiastical authorities.

The harp, another ancient instrument, spread from Ireland and Wales to Europe in the Middle Ages. It enjoyed considerable popularity played by minstrels, who also favoured the vielle, a type of violin, and the gittern, a form of guitar. The rebec, a small bowed instrument from North Africa and, like the vielle, a forerunner of the violin, was used to accompany singing and dancing. While the vielle was played sitting down the rebec was placed under the chin. Another stringed instrument, the rather strange organistrum, was played by turning a wheel causing the strings to vibrate. Additional lower strings provided a drone sound. It was later simplified and evolved into the hurdy-gurdy. The lute was known but not widespread until the Renaissance. As with other instruments it was of Middle Eastern origins and reached Europe by way of Moorish Spain. Trumpets were played by musicians and percussion instruments, including various kinds of bells and the tabor, a two-headed cylindrical drum of Arabic origin, were used to beat time for singing and dancing.

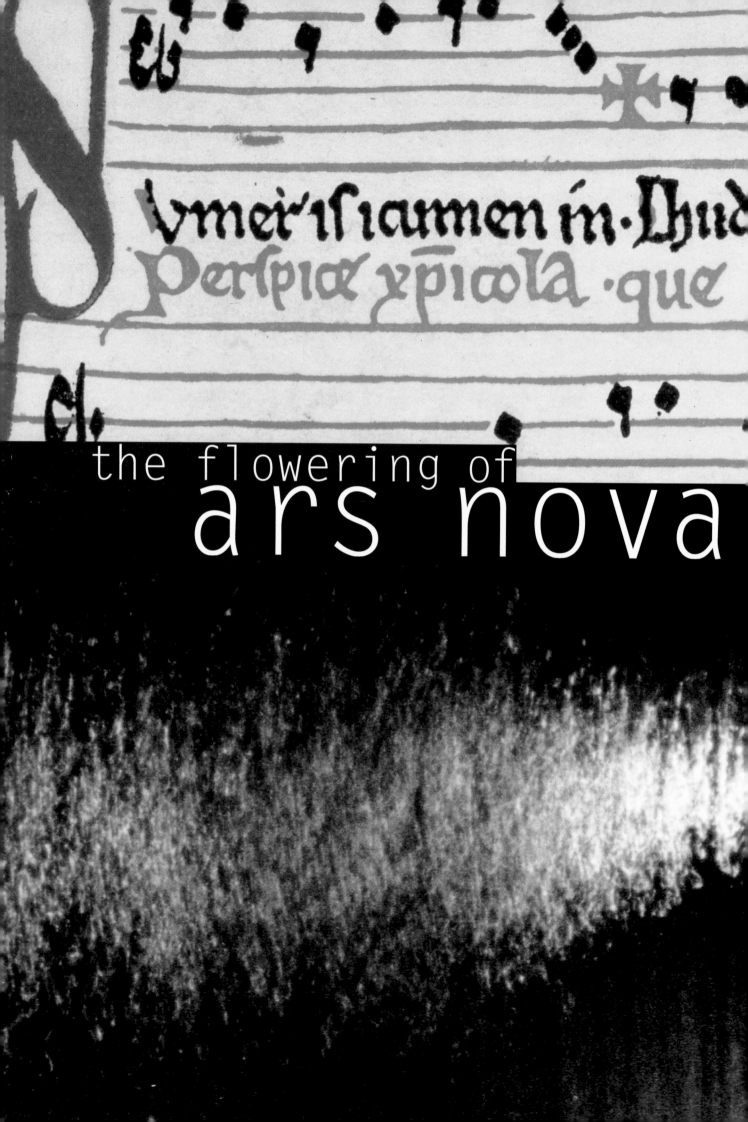

page from 'Le Roman de Fauvel', an allegorical satire in verse on the Roman Catholic Church. The book contains five polyphonic motets that have been ascribed to Philippe de Vitry, the first composer to use the expression Ars Nova, 'New Art'.

The 12th and 13th centuries were comparatively peaceful times, but the 14th century ushered in a period of unrest. The authority of the popes was increasingly called into question and the papal court was compelled to move from Rome to Avignon in southern France. The Hundred Years War, a series of conflicts between England and France, began in the 1340s. In the same decade the Black Death reached Europe and brought about a catastrophic loss of population (as many as 25 million people died). This, together with a succession of bad harvests, led to peasant uprisings and was also the cause of much urban discontent.

13th – 15th century

Pope John XXII, the second of the popes to reside at Avignon, was hostile to Ars Nova, preferring musicians to sing in the old manner. His hostility indicates that music was moving away from the orbit of the Church and that composers were beginning to see themselves as individual artists.

Among important figures in the late 13th century who to some extent foreshadowed the musical innovations of the early 14th century were the theorist Franco of Cologne, who in his *Ars cantus mensurabilis* ('The Art of Measured Song') codified the newly established system of rhythmic notation, and Petrus de Cruce (active 1370–90), whose motets were notable for their elaborate rhythmic lines.

Ars Nova ('New Art') was the great flowering of new music in France in the 14th century. The expression was first used by the composer, musical theorist and ecclesiastic Philippe de Vitry (1291–1361), as the title of a treatise written around 1320. Ars Nova was essentially a liberation of musical form from the constraints of Ars Antiqua ('Old Art'), as the music of the 13th century came to be called. Among its most important features was the use of more varied rhythmic patterns: traditionally music (with the exception of plainchant) had been in triple metre; now the division of note values into duple metre became acceptable. Another innovation was the introduction of the minim (from the Latin *minimus*, 'least'), which became the note with the shortest time value in medieval music of this period. De Vitry is also associated with the use of isorhythm ('the same rhythm'), in which a voice part, usually the tenor, is built around a rhythmic phrase repeated at intervals. Although isorhythm had been employed before, de Vitry's motets display the use of this technique on a larger, structural scale as the unifying basis for an entire piece. The isorhythm often involved a somewhat complicated interlocking of pitch ('color') and rhythmic ('talae') patterns that could be of the same length or of differing lengths.

Unfortunately, much of de Vitry's creative output has been lost. Five of his polyphonic motets, however, found their way into *Le Roman de Fauvel* ('The Story of Fauvel'), an allegorical satire in verse on the Roman Catholic Church. These provide examples of the use of isorhythm and display an original approach that allows the tenor to move slowly against the faster notes of the upper voices.

Guillaume de Machaut

Guillaume de Machaut (c.1300–77) was a leading exponent of Ars Nova, who followed the guidelines set out by Philippe de Vitry in his treatise, adding his own creative genius. His four-part setting of the Ordinary of the Mass, the *Messe de Notre Dame* (c.1364), was one of the earliest completely polyphonic masses and one of the first written by a single composer. Its isorhythmic techniques proved a landmark in the evolution of the mass as a musical form. Not only were the five separate texts of the Ordinary treated as an entire structural unit to be performed as a whole, but the mass was unified musically through the use of only two key centres, common isorhythmic techniques and general musical style.

Although the Ordinary was perhaps the best-known composition of the age, most of Machaut's music was not destined for the Church. His prolific output included ballades, motets, rondeaux, virelais and lais. Some of it was monophonic, following the trouvère or troubadour tradition, notably the lais and virelais, which were generally unaccompanied songs. His ballades, however, demonstrate a new approach: they were written for two three or four voices and for various combinations of voices and instruments, the most typical being a vocal part accompanied by two lower instrumental parts. His three-part motets are characterised by the use of isorhythms in all three voices. The rather unusual 'Hoquetus David' whose rhythmic pattern looks back to the style of the 13th century, was probably meant to be performed on instruments only and must therefore be considered one the first purely instrumental pieces in Western music.

One of Machaut's rondeaux, entitled 'My end is my beginning and my beginning my end', displays both flair and ingenuity. The lower voice has the same notes as the upper one but in reverse order, while the second half of the melody, sung by middle voice, is the reverse of the first half. Machaut is widely acknowledged as the first great composer and in his music we can see the emergence of the artist as an individual and not simply as an instrument through which the voice of God is heard.

A 14th-century French miniature depicting an allegorical scene in which Nature offers Guillaume de Machaut three of her children. Machaut is widely acknowledged as the first great composer.

Italian secular music

In Italy the first flowering of secular music came early in the 14th century. In 1318 Marchetto of Padua, who composed motets but is best known as a musical theorist, published his *Pomerium musicae mensuratae* ('The Fruits of Measured Music'), in which he provided a system of notation for aspiring musicians.

The leading Italian composer of the 14th century was Francesco Landini (c.1335–97). He was a prolific composer who wrote only secular music; those of his works which have survived include ballate (more than 140), madrigals and one caccia. His compositions contain beautiful harmonies using the fifth and third or sixth and third as opposed to the seconds and sevenths in parallel motion that were prevalent in the music of the previous century. Landini was also innovative in his composition of cadence points (the musical/harmonic equivalent of punctuation marks), with the so-called 'Landini' and 'double leading-time' cadences.

The ballata was one of the three chief musical forms in 14th-century Italy, along with the madrigal and the caccia. It was originally a song intended to accompany dancing and the name is derived from *ballare* ('to dance'). Most of the surviving ballate are for two or three voices and it was in these that Landini excelled. The madrigal, which should not be confused with the 16th- and 17th-century musical form, was a polyphonic composition, usually for two voices, set to a text of several three-line stanzas on pastoral, amorous or satirical subjects, followed by a *ritornello* or refrain in a different rhythm and with different music. Madrigals are notable for the fairly melismatic upper voice supported by a much less elaborate lower one. Leading exponents of the madrigal were Giovanni da Cascia and Jacobo da Bologna, whose beautiful 'Fenice fù' is an outstanding example of the genre. In the caccia (literally, 'hunt' or 'chase'), two voices in unison canon sing a text describing hunting scenes or a similar lively scenario, the caccia referring both to the idea of one voice chasing another and to the pursuit by the huntsmen.

From about the middle of the 14th century Italian music began to absorb some of the characteristics of the French Ars Nova. The papal court at Avignon was a flourishing centre for composers and when the pope returned to Rome in 1377 the French influence on Italian music became more pronounced. Moreover, in the late 14th century composers from northern countries began to settle in Italy and to take up important posts. Among the first of these was Johannes Ciconia (c.1340–1411), who was born in Liège, then part of France, and who became a cantor at Padua cathedral. His secular compositions included ballate and madrigals, but most important were the motets, intended to celebrate historical events or to eulogise prominent people. His music combines elements of the later French Ars Nova and the more effusive, contemporary Italian style. Ciconia, who was also the author of two treatises on music, had considerable influence on composers of the following generation.

John Dunstable and the English school

Little is known about English music in the early Middle Ages. The famous 13th-century canon or rota 'Sumer is acumen in', in which four voices take up the melody in succession over a two-voice ground bass, is the earliest known example both of a canon and of a piece for six voices. Knowledge of 14th-century music comes from a collection of manuscripts from Worcester cathedral containing over 100 polyphonic compositions. These include two-voice settings of tropes, motets and rondelli (a type of three-voice motet). English music of this period is characterised by its use of full harmony and the favouring of 'major' tonalities. Sequences of parallel harmonies containing thirds and sixths become prevalent in English music of this time, a style of composition known as 'faux bourdon'.

John Dunstable (c.1385–1453) was the first English composer to achieve recognition in Europe. Many of his surviving works, some 60 or 70 in all, appear in Italian manuscripts. They include polyphonic masses, settings of individual movements from the mass and isorhythmic motets, notably the

The gravestone of Francesco Landini, the foremost Italian composer of the 14th century. He wrote only secular music, including over 140 ballate, and was much respected by his contemporaries, who admired his gift for creating beautiful harmonies.

'Veni sancte spiritus'. His three-part sacred pieces – settings of antiphons
and other liturgical texts – are also important. As far as is known he
composed few secular works, but these include the lyrical 'O rosa bella'.
Dunstable's influence on the evolution of European music lies above all in
his harmonies and his remarkable ability to create sonorous melodies.

Instrumental music

Little instrumental music survives from the early Middle Ages, although
literary sources and the depiction of instruments in paintings indicate that
they must have played an important part in social activities. Information
about instrumental music becomes a little more accessible in the 14th
century, but it is not always clear whether a particular part is instrumental
or vocal, since music manuscripts frequently fail to specify. A considerable
array of instruments was available. The so-called 'high' ensemble referred
to the louder instruments such as shawms, slide trumpets and cornetts
(small wooden horns), which were appropriate to festivals or dancing. The
'low' ensemble included vielles, harps, psalteries, flutes, recorders, small
organs and cymbals and was used on more intimate occasions.

In the later Middle Ages the ecclesiastical authorities began to relax
their attitude towards the playing of musical instruments in church. Bowed
instruments, such as the vielle and the rebec, were in use from the 12th
century, later followed by wind instruments, such as the members of the
flute family and the distinctly loud shawm, and the harp and the psaltery.

The precursor of modern notation was the French system, which subdivided the main note values – the long, breve and semibreve – into either two (imperfect) or three (perfect) parts. The combination of subdivisions set what were termed the mode, time and prolation of the music. Time signatures consisted of a whole or half circle to indicate whether the 'time' was perfect or imperfect and the presence or absence of a dot inside the circle to represent major or minor prolation. The modern-day symbol C for common, 4/4 time originates with this system of notation. As shorter note values, such as the mimim and semiminim, came into use, so the various symbols for note durations were modified. Longer values were represented by empty, white noteheads and shorter ones by black noteheads, with a series of flags for durations of even smaller value.

The new 'filling out' of harmonies with thirds and sixths led to new rules and theories concerning harmony, especially since the cadence 'musica ficta' involved the sharpening and flattening of certain notes to improve the melodic line, avoid tritones (a dissonant interval of three whole steps) and emphasise cadence points. Its name comes from the introduction of semitonal relationships other than the most common B/C and E/F ones (part of the so-called 'musica vera' or 'musica vecta').

In 1477 the Franco-Flemish theorist Johannes Tinctoris (c.1435–c.1510) codified harmonic practices, especially the treatment of consonance and dissonance, in his *Liber de arte contrapuncti* ('A Book on the Art of Counterpoint'). Unfortunately, the Pythagorean tuning system could not cope with the wider range of intervals in use and thirds and sixths were out of tune. A system known as 'just intonation' increased the number of harmonic ratios employed in the tuning of notes and thus rectified the problem of unacceptable thirds and sixths. However, just intonation had its drawbacks when used in 'distant' keys and was eventually supplanted by other methods.

Right: A page of musical notation produced at the Florentine monastery of Santa Maria degli Angeli in the early 15th century.

Far right: A page from Bartolomeo Ramos de Pareja's treatise 'Musica Theoretica'. The 15th-century Spanish theorist shows the division of the main note values into two (imperfect) and three (perfect) parts. This system originated in France and is the precursor of the modern notation system.

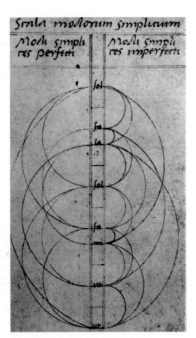

renaissance
music

The period from the beginning of the 15th century to the end of the 16th was one of the most eventful in European history. It began with the early flowering of the Renaissance in the cities and ducal courts of Italy. There was a new spirit of enquiry afoot and the invention of printing helped to spread the humanist ideas of the time. There was also increasing discontent within the Catholic Church, leading ultimately to the Protestant Reformation. The new religion found fertile ground in Germany, Holland, France, Switzerland and Scandinavia, and, after Henry VIII's break with Rome, in England, too. The Counter-Reformation was successful in checking the further spread of Protestantism, but Europe was now permanently divided into two religious camps.

15th – 16th century

Philip the Good, duke of Burgundy from 1419 to 1467, maintained one of the most prestigious musical establishments in Europe. His musicians were much in demand – at the princely courts of Florence and Milan, in the papal chapel in Rome and in the court of the Holy Roman emperor in Austria.

From the late 14th century the duchy of Burgundy in south-central France was under the control of a series of strong rulers who, through marriage and diplomacy, acquired enormous tracts of territory including northeastern France, Flanders and the Low Countries. The prosperous Burgundian court was renowned for its patronage of the arts and became a focal point for cultural activities of all kinds in northern Europe. From the region now divided between Belgium and northern France came many of the composers of the Franco-Flemish school, who were to exert such a profound influence on the development of music in Europe in the 15th century. The late 14th century saw the establishment of chapels at various European courts. These consisted of groups of salaried musicians who provided music for religious services and also for secular occasions. The Burgundian rulers maintained one of the finest musical courts in Europe; its prestige was such that its musicians were in demand all over the continent.

The Franco-Flemish composers

Guillaume Dufay (c.1400–74) was acknowledged as the leading composer of the Burgundian court. He was not a great innovator, but he managed to achieve a fusion of the traditions of the Ars Nova of his native France and the early Renaissance styles which he absorbed during his travels in Italy. One of his most important contributions was to church music, notably the evolution of the mass.

This illustration from a 16th-century royal songbook depicts Johannes Ockeghem conducting a choir singing the Gloria. Ockeghem was a renowned Flemish composer of the 15th century, particularly admired for his beautiful melodies.

He was the first to compose entirely polyphonic settings of the mass as a complete cycle of movements, using both sacred and secular melodies as a basis. Among his most outstanding settings of the mass are the 'L'Homme armé', whose cantus firmus is taken from a popular song and 'Se la face ai pale', which is derived from one of his own ballades. His greatest mass was, however, the 'Ave regina caelorum'. His motets were mostly written to celebrate ceremonial occasion and include the famous isorhythmic 'Nuper rosarum flores', composed for the consecration of the dome of Florence cathedral. Dufay's secular chansons were also important. They were generally solo songs in the form of rondeaux or ballades accompanied by one or more instruments and usually dealing with the subject of love. Dufay's distinction as a composer lies in the high artistry and broad scope of his output. His characteristically Burgundian style provides a link between the music of the late Middle Ages and that of the Renaissance.

Gilles Binchois (c.1400–60), together with Dunstable and Dufay, ranks as one of the leading composers of the first half of the 15th century. He was probably born at Mons, now in Belgium, and joined the Burgundian court chapel in the 1420s. He wrote some notable sacred music, including many mass movements but no complete cycle. He is chiefly remembered for his chansons, mostly rondeaux for three voices in which the top voice carried the melody. A typical example is the 'Filles à marier', a lively exhortation to girls of marriageable age not to allow themselves to be tied by the bonds of wedlock.

Johannes Ockeghem (c.1430–c.1495) was born in Flanders but lived most of his life in France, undertaking occasional visits to Spain and Bruges. Ockeghem's work includes masses, motets and chansons, of which the masses are the most important. Now generally written for four parts, they shifted the melody away from the tenor line, giving equal weight to the other voices and shifting the bass voice to a deeper register. He succeeded in sustaining long melodic lines of remarkable beauty, achieving this by allowing the dovetailing of voices. Ockeghem was also noted for his use of complex but subtle canons and sophisticated contrapuntal technique, as in his masses 'Missa prolationum' and 'Missa cuivis toni', or 'mass in any mode'. In the latter, using a different combination of clefs for the various parts, the mass can be transposed into any of four different modes. His ten existing motets also display an inventive use of canon. His chansons (numbering more than 20), written chiefly in the rondeau form of courtly poetry, were extremely popular.

Another northern composer active in the second half of the 15th century was Antoine Busnois (c.1430–92). Born at Béthune, France, he spent most of his life at the Burgundian court. He is remembered for his chansons, mostly rondeaux for three voices and including the well-known 'Bel-acueil'. These employ a variety of contrapuntal techniques and are noted for their melodic beauty and rhythmic subtlety. Busnois' most celebrated motet, 'In hydraulis', was written in homage to Ockeghem. His masses, 'L'homme armé' and 'O crux lignum', are for four voices.

Josquin Desprez (c.1440–1521) was undoubtedly the greatest composer of the Franco-Flemish school and one of the supreme musical talents of the Renaissance. He was born in northern France, in the province of Hainaut, in what was at that time Burgundian territory. He spent most of his life working in Italy, returning to France in 1504.

In Josquin's work and that of his contemporaries music begins to lose some of its more abstract qualities and to express a wide range of human feelings. Josquin was a prolific composer of both masses and motets but it is his motets which display his musical genius to greatest advantage. His earlier motets are more traditional in structure but his later music shows a greater adaptability and fluency of style. Perhaps his most beautiful motet was the 'Ave Maria ... virgo serena' for four voices. He was, in addition, one of the first composers to use the psalms and other passages from the Old Testament as a textual basis for his motets.

Some 18 of Josquin's many masses have survived in complete form: they mostly use a secular tune for the cantus firmus and employ a number of ingenious compositional devices. The 'Missa Hercules Dux Ferrariae', for example, uses a subject that is derived from the vowels of the title and their corresponding pitches from the solmised hexachord. The beginnings of the parody mass, a form that was to gain favour in the 16th century, can be seen in the mass 'Malheur me bat', where the original borrowed material is used both in a fairly complete form but also subjected to various transformations and developments. His most famous masses were 'Missa pange lingua' and 'Missa de beata virgine'.

In his chansons (about 70 in all), as in his motets, Josquin frequently used four-part settings, some of them based on already existing melodies. His treatment of traditional forms was freer and he was possibly the first to discard the strict forms of the rondeau and ballade, achieving both great depth and richness of tone and showing great contrapuntal skill in

IOSQVINVS PRATENSIS.

Josquin Desprez was the greatest composer of the Franco-Flemish school. He synthesised all that was best in late medieval music and introduced a style of composition that was to provide a pattern for the later Renaissance.

A portrait of Jakob Obrecht, painted in 1496 during his lifetime. Obrecht, an imaginative composer in the Franco-Flemish tradition, is known mainly for his sacred music though he also wrote secular songs.

pieces for up to six voices. Among his best-known chansons are the 'Mille regretz' and the lamentation on the death of Ockeghem, whose pupil he had probably been.

Josquin is of particular importance in the contribution that he made to creating a better relationship between words and music. The text was more audible and the accompanying music more suited to it in terms of its shape and stresses. Josquin even composed declamatory homophony in his motet 'Tu solus, qui facis mirabilia' and in other places exhibits a manipulation of chromaticism and contrast in order to bring out the meaning of the words.

Jakob Obrecht (1452–1505), another important figure among the Franco-Flemish composers, worked mainly in the Low Countries but also spent some time in Italy. He wrote mainly sacred music and is best known for his masses, of which nearly 30 survive, written mainly for four voices. In most of them he makes use of cantus firmus taken from both secular music and plainchant. Obrecht's skill lay in the imaginative treatment he gave to the material he borrowed. The melody may be repeated in its entirety in every movement but is most often divided into sections, which are introduced in successive movements. His motets were of similar high quality and his secular music includes songs in French, Italian and Dutch.

Heinrich Isaac (c.1450–1517), another contemporary of Josquin Desprez, was probably born in Flanders but lived and worked in Florence and Austria. Isaac absorbed influences from Italy, Germany and the Low Countries into his music. Among his sacred compositions are more than 30 settings of the Mass Ordinary, which use a mixture of borrowings from secular music and from plainsong. His most famous work is the posthumously published three-volume *Choralis Constantinus*, a collection of nearly 100 polyphonic settings for the Proper of the Mass.

Isaac's versatility as a composer was amply demonstrated in his secular compositions. He wrote over 80 songs, including French chansons, German lieder and Italian frottolas, and also some instrumental music. The lieder are polyphonic and frequently based on a borrowed melody, which is usually in the tenor part. The most famous of Isaac's lieder is the 'Innsbruch, ich muss dich lassen' ('Innsbruch, I must leave you'), which was later reworked by J.S. Bach and others. The Italian frottolas, usually for three or four voices, are simpler in style, with the generally clear-cut melody in the top part. Isaac also wrote 'canti carnascialeschi' (carnival songs) for festive occasions in Florence, but unfortunately none of these has survived intact.

The madrigal

At the beginning of the 16th century, thanks to the wide influence of the preceding generation of Franco-Flemish composers, vocal music presented a generally uniform appearance. However, the international idiom was gradually superseded by distinctive national styles and this was particularly true of Italy. Moreover, music was now an indispensable social accompaniment and new musical techniques were rapidly passed from one country to another, aided by the development of printing. Much more secular music was now being written and, since it was more flexible than church music, allowed considerable scope for experimentation.

A 16th-century portrait of Petrarch, the 14th-century Italian poet laureate, considered by many to be the father of modern poetry. In the 16th century some of his poems were used as the texts for the new form of madrigal, which became the leading genre in Italian secular music.

In Italy the madrigal was to become the most important vocal music of the 16th century. It bore no resemblance to the 14th-century genre of that name with two or three voice parts, but was a setting of a poem on a serious subject, for which the contemporary frotolla was considered too frivolous to be suitable. Many of the texts were by famous poets such as Petrarch and Ludovico Ariosto and the music was written to convey the profound emotions of the poetry: words and music were now, in fact, in harmonious conjunction. Madrigals, which were sung unaccompanied, were usually written for three or four and later five voices, employed both homophonic and imitative contrapuntal techniques and dealt with the text phrase by phrase in quite a free manner.

Among the earliest exponents of the madrigal were several Franco-Flemish composers working in Italy, including Philippe Verdelot (c.1480–1545), who was active in Florence, and Adrian Willaert (c.1490–1562), one of the most influential musicians of his generation, who eventually settled in Venice. Jacob Arcadelt (c.1505–c.1568) was employed at the papal chapel in Rome but later became a member of the royal chapel in Paris. The Italian madrigal reached its peak of development in the second half of the 16th century and was favoured as a genre by such composers as Andrea Gabrieli, Orlando di Lasso and Giovanni da Palestrina. Two other notable Flemish composers were Cipriano de Rore (c.1516–65), who was much admired by Monteverdi, and Philippe de Monte (1521–1603), the most prolific of all madrigalists, who saw service with the Holy Roman emperor in Vienna and Prague.

The Franco-Flemish composers Adrian Willaert (top) and Philippe de Monte (above). Both were leading exponents of the madrigal in the 16th century, helping to shape the genre and take it to new heights of emotive expressiveness.

In the hands of these and other composers there was a widening of emotional expressiveness. Towards the end of the century came bold experiments in chromaticism, coupled with increased elaboration and a declamatory style, typified by the work of the Italian, Luca Marenzio (c.1553–99), who spent most of his life in Rome, but was briefly employed at the Polish court. He influenced the later English madrigalists in particular. Nicola Vicentino was a madrigalist and theorist. His book *L'antica musica ridotta alla moderna prattica* ('Ancient Music adapted to the Modern Practice', 1555) dealt with the current concerns of chromaticism, 'modulation' and their connection with ancient music. He invented a keyboard instrument known as the arcicembolo that was able to perform the different microtonal versions of various enharmonically spelt notes.

Carlo Gesualdo (1561–1613) was born probably in Naples, where he was to spend most of his life, although he did spend several years in Ferrara, which was a thriving musical centre. Altogether he published six books of madrigals and three collections of sacred songs. As a composer he was individualistic and unorthodox. Gesualdo's music is characterised by the use of unusual harmonies, dissonances and a bold chromaticism.

In 1588 the publication by Nicholas Yonge, a chorister at St Paul's cathedral, of *Musica Transalpina*, a collection of Italian madrigals with the texts translated into English, encouraged the composition of madrigals in England. These soon developed a unique form and the genre flourished until early in the 17th century. The English court was already familiar with Italian madrigals and both Henry VIII and Elizabeth I employed Italian musicians. One of them, Alfonso Ferrabosco (1543–88), was a source of inspiration to his English contemporaries, notably William Byrd.

The leader of the English school of madrigalists was Thomas Morley (c.1557–1602), who had been a pupil of Byrd. Morley was influential as a composer, theorist and music editor. His *Plaine and Easie Introduction to Practicall Musicke* (1597) and the collection of madrigals by English composers in praise of Elizabeth I, *The Triumphes of Oriana* (1601), demonstrate his familiarity with Italian music and its influence upon English madrigalists. Morley wrote over 100 madrigals on the subjects of love and nature. Among his lighter secular works are balletts, less elaborate than madrigals and noted for their dance-like rhythms and fa-la refrains, a fine example being 'Now is the month of Maying'. His canzonets (best described as madrigals in miniature) were, like the balletts, modelled on Italian originals. He also wrote sacred works including Latin motets, English anthems and psalms, and instrumental music.

One of the younger generation of madrigalists was Thomas Weelkes (c.1576–1623). Weelkes, who contributed to *The Triumphes of Oriana*, composed over 100 pieces noted for their imaginative word-painting and skilled use of counterpoint. They include 'Thule, the Period of Cosmographie' and the ballett 'O care, thou wilt despatch me'. However, he also excelled as a composer of church music and his work includes nearly 40 anthems and the sacred madrigal 'When David heard, As Vesta was, from Latmos Hill descending'.

John Wilbye (1574–1638), a contemporary of Weelkes, wrote two books of madrigals, published in 1597 and 1609 respectively, which display his musical inventiveness and his great craftmanship. Among his most outstanding madrigals are the gently melancholic 'Adew, sweet Amarillis' and 'Draw on sweet night'.

The chanson

In France the social and political climate at the beginning of the 16th century, notably the emergence of a prosperous middle class, encouraged the growth of secular vocal music. This music found its chief expression in the polyphonic chanson, a new form of the medieval chanson, which Josquin Desprez had done so much to revitalise. In the 1530s and 1540s composers near Paris developed the so-called 'Parisian chanson' as a suitable medium for the new-style lyric poetry then being written. These chansons were published in various collections by Pierre Attaignant (c.1494–1552), whose use of a movable music type, allowing him to print the staff and the notes together in a single impression, enabled him to issue music in much larger quantities than had hitherto been possible.

The early chansons were typically for four voices, with the chief melody in the highest voice, and closely followed the rhythms of the poetic text. The Parisian Claudin de Sermisy (c.1490–c.1562) wrote masses and motets but is best remembered for his chansons, nearly 200 of which survive. His chansons, of which a notable example is 'Tant que vivray', a setting of a poem by Clément Marot, are often concerned with love in its many aspects and are characterised by simplicity and lyricism. His contemporary, Clément Jannequin (c.1485–c.1560), was particularly famous for his long, descriptive chansons, in which the music vividly imitates the events depicted in the poems. Pieces like 'Le chant des oiseaux' ('The Songs of Birds'), 'La guerre' ('War') and 'La chasse' ('The Hunt') are full of onomatopoeic sounds.

e Concert', c.1550. The three men in the painting are playing m Claudin de Sermisy's chanson ore for 'Jouissance vous nneray', performed with lute, te and voice. Over 200 of rmisy's chansons survive.

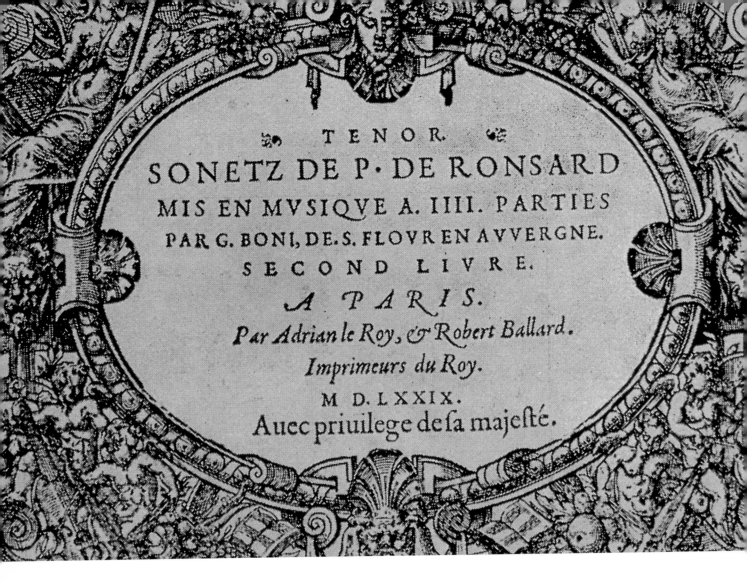

TENOR.
SONETZ DE P·DE RONSARD
MIS EN MVSIQVE A. IIII. PARTIES
PAR G. BONI, DE.S. FLOVR EN AVVERGNE.
SECOND LIVRE.
A PARIS.
Par Adrian le Roy, & Robert Ballard.
Imprimeurs du Roy.
M D. LXXIX.
Auec priuilege de fa majeflé.

The title page of a book of sonnets by Pierre de Ronsard put to music. It is from the second book in the four-part series printed in 1579. Ronsard, together with Clément Marot, was an exponent of the new-style lyric poetry for which the 'Parisian chanson' was developed.

The chanson continued to flourish in the second half of the century, although its development was increasingly influenced by the Italian madrigal. Composers of this period included Claude Le Jeune (1528–1600) and Guillaume Costeley (1531–1606). Le Jeune composed over 100 chansons as well as airs, madrigals, psalms and motets. Both Le Jeune and Costeley were exponents of the irregular metric structure known as 'musique mesurée', in which long and short syllables were set to correspondingly long and short notes, the long notes having twice the value of the short ones. This followed misguided attempts by French poets to introduce the rules of classical prosody into their verses.

Other composers who brought the same skills to writing chansons as they did to madrigals were Orlando di Lasso and Jacob Arcadelt. The Dutch composer, Jan Sweelinck, also wrote chansons which reflected the French Renaissance tradition. Towards the end of the century there appeared the 'chansons spirituelles', secular compositions sometimes accompanied by sacred texts, which reflected the Protestant view of the Wars of Religion which so troubled France at this period.

Music in Germany

It was Heinrich Isaac who brought the techniques of the Franco-Flemish school to Germany and, together with his pupil Ludwig Senfl (c.1492–1555), set in motion those forces that were to make the German tradition dominant in European music. The lied, which remained the most popular form of secular music, had first appeared in the 13th century as a monophonic melody sung by the courtly musicians known as the Minnesingers. It was subsequently taken up by the Meistersingers, middle-class citizens who formed themselves into musical guilds and whose lives were portrayed by Richard Wagner in his opera *Die Meistersinger von Nürnberg*. The Meistersingers performed monophonic, unaccompanied songs, which were composed according to a strict formula.

Musical tastes in the German lands were relatively conservative and it was not until the 15th century that there was a real flowering of polyphonic lieder. The *Lochamer Liederbuch*, which was put together in the 1450s, contains both monophonic and polyphonic songs. In the polyphonic lieder, which are in three-part settings, the tenor or middle part carries the melody. Heinrich Isaac was a master of the 15th-century lied, which was to reach its fullest development in the work of the Swiss-born Ludwig Senfl. His lieder cover a multitude of subjects from the satirical and the comic to courtly amorous adventures. Hans Leo Hassler (1564–1612), the leading German composer of the late 16th century, wrote some 60 lieder which combined a polished Italian style with a native lyricism. He was also noted for his sacred and instrumental music, canzonets and madrigals. Another composer worthy of mention was Orlando di Lasso, whose prolific output in all the musical genres included a fine collection of lieder. By the later years of the 16th century, however, German lieder began taking on strongly Italianate characteristics and the growing influence of the madrigal led to their decline.

woodcut from the title page of the st edition of a lyrical poem by ns Sachs, written in support of artin Luther in 1523. The eformation that Luther sparked s to have a profound effect on e development of music. Hans chs was immortalised in agner's comic opera 'Die eistersinger von Nürnberg'.

Music in Germany as elsewhere derived enormous benefits from the invention of printing from movable type by Johannes Gutenberg of Mainz in the 1440s. The printing of polyphonic music was begun in Venice in 1501 by Ottaviano Petrucci and soon spread to other countries in western Europe, reaching Germany in the 1540s. Previously music had circulated only in manuscript form – a time-consuming and expensive procedure. Now for the first time relatively cheap editions of sheet music were made available in their own language to a growing class of amateur music makers who were learning to read music, to sing in small groups and to play instruments. Music making was fast becoming an enjoyable pastime and leisure activity.

Another factor of enormous importance in the evolution of music in Germany was the Reformation. Although the origins of the movement can be traced back to a much earlier period, its generally recognised starting point was the attack launched in 1517 by the theologian Martin Luther on the doctrines and practices of the Roman Catholic Church. Luther was a

Music in Germany as elsewhere derived enormous benefits from the invention of printing from movable type by Johannes Gutenberg of Mainz in the 1440s. Now for the first time relatively cheap editions of sheet music were made available in their own language to a growing class of amateur music makers.

Right: Martin Luther was a fine musician as well as a theologian. He believed that the whole congregation should sing during religious services rather than only the priest and choir, and that this would help to strengthen the foundations of the new religion.

Below left: A 17th-century woodcut showing the interior of a German printing works. As well as helping to spread the ideas of Luther and others, the invention of printing from movable type in the 1440s meant that sheet music was more widely and more cheaply available than ever before.

man of considerable musical talents: he had a fine tenor voice, was a performer on both the lute and flute, and greatly admired the music of the Franco-Flemish school, in particular that of Josquin Desprez. He was, moreover, convinced that church music had a central role to play in strengthening the Protestant religion. He wanted the entire congregation to participate in divine service, singing in their own language, rather than listen to the chanting by priest and choir of prayers in Latin, which was incomprehensible to most people. Working in collaboration with Johann Walther, a pupil of Ludwig Senfl, in 1534 he produced the first Protestant hymn book. Some of the melodies were new, others adapted from secular music, including folk-songs with which the worshippers would already be familiar, or from plainchant. They include the famous 'Ein' feste Burg ist unser Gott' ('A safe stronghold our God is still'), the words of which were written by Luther and possibly the music as well. These congregational hymns, or chorales as they were called, formed a central part of the Lutheran service and the chorale came to occupy a special position in German music in the 17th and 18th centuries.

Polyphonic sacred music

The Catholic Church countered the growth of Protestantism by convening the Council of Trent, which met for the first time in 1545–47. Its aim was to put an end to abuses within the Church and to bring about much-needed reforms. Church music was not very prominent on the agenda, but it was nevertheless the object of serious criticism. Many deplored both the use of secular melodies in the mass and the complicated polyphony which obscured the words of the liturgy. There were also objections to the playing of inappropriate instruments and some churchmen urged a return to monophonic plainchant. The Council did not go so far as to prohibit polyphonic music but contented itself with stating, among other things, that: 'They shall also banish from church all music that contains, whether in the singing or in the organ playing, things that are lascivious or impure.'

Giovanni Pierluigi da Palestrina (c.1525–94) took his surname from the small town near Rome where he was born. In 1577 his reputation was such that he was asked to supervise the revision of the Church's plainchant books in accordance with the decisions of the Council of Trent, a task that he did not manage to complete before his death. Palestrina's vast output includes over 100 masses. Written in a variety of styles for from four to eight unaccompanied voices, they capture to perfection the essentially conservative spirit of the Counter-Reformation and are perhaps his finest achievement. Some of his masses are based on the cantus firmus technique using a pre-existing melody for one of the voice parts, generally the tenor. However, for the majority he employed the more modern parody technique, borrowing existing pieces by other composers (or his own) in their entirety, and transforming them through his genius. A few are the so-called freely invented masses in which no pre-existing music was used and they include the notable 'Missa brevis' for four voices of 1570.

His most famous mass was the six-voice 'Missa Papae Marcelli', dedicated to Pope Marcellus II, which, according to legend, satisfied the church authorities that the use of polyphony did not obscure the text of the liturgy, and thus saved polyphonic sacred music from condemnation. Palestrina's many motets also demonstrate the composer's extraordinary versatility and skill in word-painting, notably those based on the Song of Solomon. He avoided the more unorthodox chromaticism of many of his contemporaries and carefully controlled the use of dissonance, consistently creating suspensions on downbeats and resolving them stepwise on upbeats. In addition to the disciplined approach to the harmonic implications of his counterpoint, Palestrina's melodies are also smooth and controlled and look back to the plainchant of earlier times. Palestrina is generally considered the greatest Italian composer of music for unaccompanied voices and he was the first composer whose work was considered by later generations as a model of polyphonic style worthy of imitation.

Although justly famous for his madrigals and chansons Orlando di Lasso (c.1530–94) was also a leading composer of sacred music and the last of the great Franco-Flemish school. Born at Mons, now in Belgium, he later travelled extensively in Italy and lived for a short time in Antwerp before settling in Munich. Lasso was remarkably prolific, with over 2,000 compositions to his credit, having published his first book of motets and chansons at the age of 24. A true internationalist, he shows French, Italian, German and Flemish influences in his work.

An illuminated page showing 'Miserere mei ...' by Orlando di Lasso, the last of the great Franco-Flemish composers. Lasso travelled Europe extensively and wrote over 2,000 compositions, all of which bear witness to the universal genius of this most cosmopolitan of composers.

He is perhaps best remembered for his motets, of which he wrote more than 500. They are remarkable for the way in which Lasso's imaginative genius allowed him to create such a powerful emotional response to the text. His best-known motets include the collection of penitential psalms 'Psalmi Davidis Poenitentiales' and the secular 'Prophetiae Sibyllarum'. His villanellas, lieder, chansons and madrigals range from the light-hearted to the intensely spiritual, from coarse drinking songs to tender expressions of love.

At the end of the 15th century music in Spain as in the rest of western Europe was coming under the influence of the Franco-Flemish school, although some composers, while writing polyphonic music, remained faithful to the country's earlier musical heritage. Juan del Encina (1468–1529) was noted for his 'villancicos', songs with several verses linked by refrains and deriving from earlier popular traditions. Francisco de Peñalosa (c.1470–1528) is mainly remembered for his liturgical music. The leading Spanish composer of the early 16th century was Cristóbal de Morales (c.1500–53), who spent some time in Rome as a member of the papal chapel. He wrote mainly sacred music, including masses, motets and magnificats.

However, by far the greatest Spanish composer of the age was Tomás Luis de Victoria (1548–1611). He was born in Avila, but later lived in Rome for some 20 years, possibly studying under Palestrina, before returning to Spain in the 1580s when he settled in Madrid. In 16th-century Spain the spirit of the Counter-Reformation found expression in a zealous Catholicism

Giovanni Pierluigi da Palestrina is credited with saving polyphonic sacred music from being banned by the Catholic Church. In 1577 he began the task of supervising the revision of the Church's plainchant books in accordance with the decisions of the Council of Trent.

A 16th-century Italian painting of the Council of Trent, which was called to discuss measures to reform abuses within the Catholic Church. One of their concerns was that the new polyphonic music obscured the words of the liturgy.

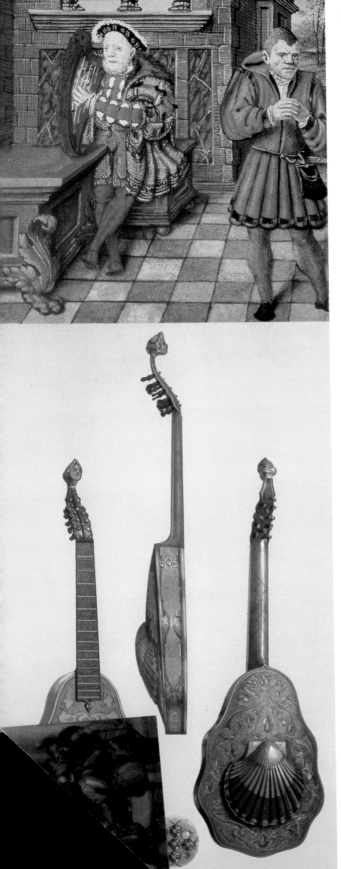

which penetrated almost every aspect of daily life. Victoria was a man of deeply felt beliefs and, unique among the great composers of the period, wrote only sacred music. He composed more than 20 masses for from 4 to 12 voices, most employing the parody technique, which are based on his own motets (numbering about 50 in all). Both masses and motets are among the finest of the period and include the well-known 'O magnum mysterium' and 'O quam gloriosum'. His last work was the great 'Officium defunctorum', the requiem for the Spanish empress Maria. Some of his masses are polychoral, in which the voices are divided into two and sometimes three choirs. Much of his music combines a relatively sophisticated, modern technique with the profound emotional intensity expressive of a strong religious faith.

Music in England

At the end of the 15th century, with the advent of the Tudor dynasty, there was a revival of music in England, which was undoubtedly helped by the enthusiasm of Henry VIII. William Cornysh (c.1465–1523) is known both for his secular songs and motets. Some of his sacred music, together with that of his contemporary, Robert Fayrfax (1464–1521), is found in the manuscript collection known as the Eton Choirbook, a remarkable work compiled between 1490 and 1502 for use at Eton College. Most of Fayrfax's music was written for the Church and includes masses for five voices and votive antiphons, but he was also the author of secular songs and instrumental music.

John Taverner (c.1490–1545) was undoubtedly the leading English composer of the early 16th century. His work, which is chiefly sacred music, includes masses, notably 'Western Wynde', using the cantus firmus and written in a highly ornamented style typical of English music of the period, three magnificats and 28 motets. His setting of the 'In nomine' section of his mass 'Gloria tibi trinitas' for instruments was later to become popular as a basis for a variety of instrumental compositions.

Thomas Tallis (c.1505–85), the foremost English composer of the mid 16th century, lived at a time of religious upheaval and during his long life served four different rulers, writing mainly sacred music. Early in his career he composed masses and votive antiphons, but after the accession of the Protestant Edward VI wrote anthems to English texts for the new Anglican liturgy. In the reign of Mary Tudor, which marked a brief return to Catholic orthodoxy, he composed Latin hymns, and the seven-voice mass 'Puer natus est nobis' probably dates from this period. Under Queen Elizabeth Tallis set music to both Latin and English texts. In 1575 Elizabeth granted Tallis and his pupil, William Byrd, a monopoly to print and publish music in English. Their first publication, which appeared later the same year, was a collection of Latin motets by both composers entitled 'Cantiones sacrae'. Among Tallis's most beautiful and eloquent works are two settings of the Lamentations of Jeremiah from the Hebrew Scriptures. His most beautiful composition, however, was the 'Spem in alium', a motet in 40 parts for eight five-voice choirs.

A contemporary of Tallis, Christopher Tye (c.1505–72), wrote a considerable amount of church music, including motets and masses, in Latin but also some English anthems, which may have been composed in the reign of Edward VI.

'The Outdoor Concert', a 16th-century Italian painting depicting the pleasures of music making. Although instruments had been used throughout the Middle Ages, they had generally performed a secondary role to the human voice.

Instrumental music

One of the most significant developments in the late 15th and early 16th centuries was the growth of music for instruments. This was accompanied by the appearance of publications giving instructions on how to play them. Instrument makers now began to deploy new skills in their manufacture and to deal successfully with problems of pitch and tuning. Whole families of instruments or 'consorts' came into being, with a range of sounds capable of matching that of the human voice. Composers began to write music especially for groups of instruments, notably recorders and viols, although the lute was the most popular solo instrument. There was a huge variety of wind instruments, including shawms, crumhorns, trombones and sackbuts. Most of these had a less strident tone than their present-day equivalents.

The process by which the human voice was replaced by instruments in many fields of musical creativity was inevitably a slow one. In Italy the canzona began its existence in the early 16th century as a popular version of the French chanson. Its brisk momentum and vigorous rhythms made it suitable for transcription, particularly for the lute and keyboard instruments. By the end of the century it was becoming a purely instrumental composition and, in the hands of Giovanni and Andrea Gabrieli, who wrote canzonas for ensembles as well as solo instruments, achieved great distinction. The introduction of two or more contrasting 'themes' into a composition led to the creation of the distinct sections which can be seen in 17th-century music.

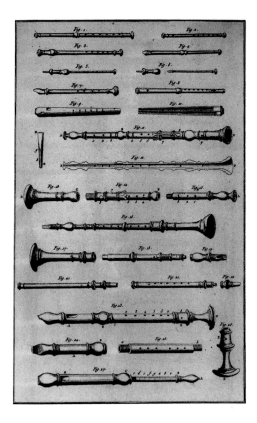

An illustration from an 18th-century book of arts and sciences showing a selection of wind instruments. Until the 16th century the chief function of instruments had been to act as a substitute for the voice parts in both secular and sacred polyphonic compositions.

The ricercare, like the canzona, was derived from vocal music, in this case the motet. It was generally slow and solemn, and consisted of a number of themes in succession, each in imitative style. Most ricercari were intended to be performed by an ensemble, but they could also be played by a single instrument such as the lute or harpsichord. Ricercari for organ written by Andrea Gabrieli were notable for their use of contrapuntal effects.

In the 16th century dancing became a firmly established activity in the royal courts of Europe and was considered a necessary social accomplishment. Its increasing popularity proved a stimulus to the creation of instrumental music. Moreover, although much dance music was improvised, printers such as Ottaviano Petrucci (1466–1539) brought out collections of pieces for dancing. Many of these were intended to be played by the lute, by harpsichord or clavichord, or by ensembles.

There was a gradual evolution from dance music written simply to accompany the movements of the dancers to music intended to be played or listened to. The strong rhythmic patterns essential to the act of dancing were discarded in favour of a characteristic instrumental style, in which the music itself became the focus of attention. Such music was at first written for a particular solo instrument, but later for whole ensembles. Dance medleys, grouped in pairs (or sometimes threes), a slow one such as the pavane, followed by the faster galliard, began to appear. In the later part of the century the allemande and the courante also became popular. The practice of improvisation by instrumentalists, either through embellishment of a theme or the adding of new contrapuntal lines, inspired written-down compositions for solo players with titles such as fantasia or toccata and a distinctive freedom of form and texture.

The Venetian school

Venice was a maritime republic which had reached the summit of its power and prosperity in the 15th century, having grown rich on trade with the East. The 16th century saw the beginning of a slow decline but the city's cultural life continued to flourish. Its centre was the 11th-century

An illustration from a Venetian pamphlet depicting a carnival procession. Such carnivals, known as Triumphs, were elaborate affairs which were held to celebrate important occasions, such as a visiting dignitary, and were the scene of much singing and dancing. By the end of the 16th century, the composers of Venice had become a major influence in European music.

cathedral of St Mark's, which was the scene of lavish civil and religious ceremonies, the splendour of which was the envy of the rest of the world. Its composers made a notable contribution to the city's fame and by the end of the 16th century were a dominant influence in European music.

Andrea Gabrieli (c.1510–86) was born in Venice but also travelled to Austria and Germany. Much of Gabrieli's sacred music was written for important ceremonial occasions and he showed particular skill in adapting his work to the unusual acoustics of St Mark's. He used several choirs and groups of instrumentalists scattered about in various parts of the church so that the listener would hear music coming from different directions, creating what would now be called a stereophonic effect. Andrea Gabrieli was a prolific composer: apart from his large-scale choral and instrumental work, including masses and motets, he also wrote madrigals based on poetic themes and settings of ricercari and canzonas for organ.

Andrea's nephew, Giovanni Gabrieli (c.1556–1612), published a collection entitled *Concerti* (incidentally, the first recorded use of the word 'concerto'), which contained a selection of works by Andrea and himself. Giovanni exploited the possibilities of contrasting groups of singers to an even greater extent than his uncle: his motet 'In ecclesiis', with its rich mixture of soloists, choir and a variety of instruments both combining and alternating, is a landmark in polychoral music. He wrote a considerable amount of music for instrumental ensembles, and his experimenting with large and small groups of musical instruments looked forward to the concerto grosso.

painting of St Mark's Basilica in
nice by Albert Goodwin. This
agnificent cathedral was at the
ntre of the explosion of musical
cellence that took place in
nice during the Renaissance
riod. Composers such as Andrea
d Giovanni Gabrieli, who were
th organists at St Mark's, were
the forefront of the Venetian
hool of music.

An elaborately framed miniature of Elizabeth I playing the lute, by Nicholas Hilliard. The lute was the most popular solo instrument during the Elizabethan period. The English composer John Dowland was a virtuoso lutenist who wrote over 80 ayres for voice and lute.

The reign of Elizabeth I was remarkable for its flowering of musical genius. The lute had become the most favoured solo instrument and John Dowland (c.1562–1623) was the foremost English lutenist. He was also a composer of great originality, particularly noted for his mastery of the distinctive English short song known as the ayre, writing over 80 of these for voice and lute. The melodies are delightful but the songs are frequently imbued with melancholy, such as 'In darkness let mee dwell' and 'Flow, my teares'. However, they demonstrate Dowland's remarkable ability for word painting, matching the mood of the music to that of the text. His instrumental work includes many pieces for solo lute, which make skilful use of dance forms. In 1604 he published his collection for viols and flute known as *Lachrimae, or Seaven Teares*, a set of variations on 'Flow, my teares' which became widely popular and won him international fame.

Keyboard instruments found particular favour with Elizabethan composers. Both those of the harpsichord type, such as the virginals and the spinet in which the strings were plucked, and the clavichord, in which the strings were struck, were coming into general use in the 16th century. William Byrd (1543–1623), undoubtedly the greatest English composer of the age, was as well known for his instrumental keyboard music as he was for his vocal works. In 1575 he was granted, together with Thomas Tallis, whose pupil he had probably been at one time, a monopoly for printing and publishing music. Byrd's vast output includes some 60 anthems written for Anglican church services, but his best vocal work was his motets and masses written to Latin texts for the Catholic Church and intended for performance in the private chapels of Catholic families. An outstanding example was the motet for four voices 'Ave verum corpus', which was published in the collection entitled *Gradualia* (1605). His three Latin masses, for three, four and five voices respectively, demonstrate conclusively his mastery of this genre of sacred music.

William Byrd, undoubtedly the greatest English composer of the age, was as well known for his instrumental keyboard music as he was for his vocal works. Byrd wrote more than 100 pieces for solo keyboard instruments.

Byrd wrote more than 100 pieces for solo keyboard instruments (notably the virginals and the organ), which often included dance movements such as pavans and galliards, and he showed particular inventiveness in the reworking of existing melodies as a set of variations. His *Psalmes, Songs and Sonnets* (1611), a medley of sacred and secular music consisting of solo songs accompanied by a consort (ensemble) of viols, were marked by skilful use of contrapuntal techniques. He also broke new ground with his consort music for viols alone, which anticipated the development of the improvisatory fantasia. Many of his keyboard works were published in *Parthenia* (1612), an anthology of keyboard music. Others were included in *My Ladye Nevells Booke*, a fine manuscript collection devoted exclusively to keyboard pieces by Byrd, transcribed by John Baldwin in 1591.

John Bull (1562–1626), like Dowland, was another English composer who spent much time abroad and exerted a considerable influence on the work of northern European composers. Among Bull's surviving work are

canons, anthems and, above all, keyboard music. His reputation rests on
his numerous compositions for the virginals and the organ, which display
both a remarkable virtuosity and outstanding technical skill. Much of his
output for the virginals is included in the Fitzwilliam Virginal Book, which
appeared about 1620. He also contributed to *Parthenia* (mentioned above).
As a composer Bull was not particularly innovative. His genius lies in his
ability to take a simple melody and, through a series of variations, to
produce a brilliant elaboration of the original.

Orlando Gibbons (1583–1625) was talented both as an organist and as
a virginalist, but was best known for his sacred music and his madrigals.
His psalms, full anthems (for chorus only) and verse anthems (for chorus
and solo voice parts) were all written in English for the Anglican Church,
including the dramatic 'This is the word of John'. In 1612 he published his
Madrigals and Motetts of 5 Parts, a collection serious in tone and tinged
with melancholy: among the madrigals are the famous 'The Silver Swan'
and 'What is Our Life?' Gibbons also wrote a fantasia for voices and viols
based on the street cries of London. His instrumental music includes
works for keyboard and for viol consort, and he also contributed pieces for
the virginals to *Parthenia*. His son, Christopher Gibbons (1615–76),
composed anthems, viol fantasias and keyboard music.

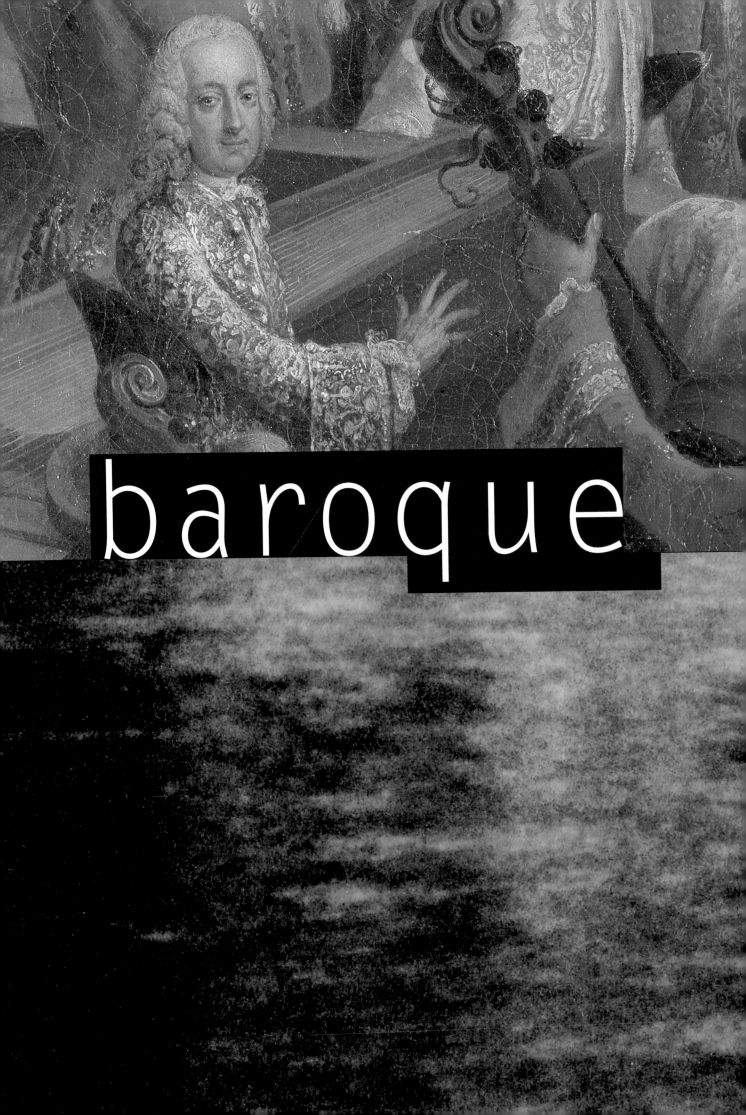

baroque

Europe entered the 17th century still deeply divided between two religious faiths. The Thirty Years War brought devastation to Germany and, under Louis XIV, France became the most powerful country in Europe. As Spain entered a period of decline, Holland grew in prosperity. In England Oliver Cromwell's victory in the Civil War paved the way for the supremacy of Parliament, and the colonisation of North America heralded a new era in world history. By the end of the century both Russia and Prussia had become forces to be reckoned with in international politics.

7th-18th
century

The term 'Baroque' was first applied, rather disparagingly, to the art and architecture from the end of the 16th century to the mid-18th century, supposedly characterised by extravagance and irregularity and lacking the harmonious proportions of the Renaissance style. Later, art critics emphasised its more positive aspects and, since the early 20th century, the term has been borrowed to cover approximately the same period in the history of music. In music, as in art and architecture, it is now generally used without any of the pejorative connotations it originally possessed.

The beginning of the 17th century undoubtedly marked an important turning point in the history of music and many composers were aware that they were making a definite break with the past. They were concerned with the idea of the 'doctrine of affections', in which a piece of music would express, in an objective manner, various feelings or states such as anger, wonder or nobility. Italy, and in particular Venice, dominated music in Europe. The rapid evolution of techniques led to the need for a distinction to be made between two very different musical styles, particularly as regards vocal music. Claudio Monteverdi defined these as *prima prattica* or *stile antico* and *seconda prattica* or *stile moderno*.

The *prima prattica* was the universal polyphonic style of the 16th century, with its origins in the music of the Franco-Flemish school, and was henceforth to be generally reserved for sacred music. The *seconda prattica* emphasised the importance of the text and the solo voice and was

ove: 'Lady seated at the
ginals', a 17th-century painting
Jan Vermeer. The virginal is a
aller version of a harpsichord,
ich quickly became a popular
usehold instrument. Its name is
rhaps derived from its use by
ung ladies, who strove to achieve
sical accomplishments.

t: The Chapel Royal at
rsailles, built during the reign
Louis XIV. Under Louis, an
thusiastic supporter of the arts,
ance became the most powerful
untry in Europe and at the same
e achieved cultural supremacy.

on the whole to be used for secular compositions, in which the complexity
of the music would no longer be permitted to spoil the clarity of the words.
Monteverdi was to be the first exponent of this 'modern style' which
opened the way for completely new forms of vocal music.

Instrumental music, too, was to undergo an important change, brought
about by the development of the 'basso continuo' or 'figured bass', in
essence a shorthand notational system. In the bass line accompaniment to
the main melody, usually a keyboard or plucked instrument (harpsichord,
organ or lute), figures written above or below the bass notes indicated the
harmonies. The accompanist was expected to improvise chords in order to
produce the required accompaniment. In polyphonic vocal music each
part had to be written down, since they were all of equal importance. Now
all the composer needed to do was to write out the melody and the bass
line with the necessary notation. This practice not only laid stress on a
new hierarchy in part-writing, with the bass and treble lines carrying most
importance, but highlighted the general trend in musical texture away
from polyphony towards homophony and harmonically defined
counterpoint. There was a new focus on the capabilities of the instruments
and of the players themselves, on so-called 'idiomatic writing' facilitated
by higher standards of playing, and on musicianship training and
instrument construction.

Until the 16th century the medieval church modes had provided the
basis for melody and harmony, but by the mid-17th century these had been

Opera was undoubtedly the most important musical development during the Baroque period. Its guiding principle was that music should be subordinate to the text and that its chief function was to increase the dramatic power of the words.

almost entirely replaced by the concept of tonality. Certain tendencies in
the music of the previous era such as the evolution of cadences and the
modulation to adjacent tonal centres gradually developed into the major
and minor key system. The rise of the basso continuo helped to emphasise
the importance of chords rather than lines. In tonal music the focus is on a
single 'key centre' rather than a scale. Harmonic movement is shaped
through the use of the root triad (chord I), the dominant (chord V), the
subdominant (chord IV) and various other secondary chords. The
emphatic V–I harmonic motion is especially characteristic of a perfect
cadence, the musical punctuation mark that defines the rest or resolution
of harmonic movement at the end of a phrase, section or piece. Harmonic
practice was eventually codified into theory. The use of dissonance and
chromaticism, instead of being the result of experimentation, became
subject to regulation and was itself an integral part of the systematic
tension and release that characterised tonal music.

The rise of Opera

Opera was undoubtedly the most important musical development during
the Baroque period. Its foundations as an art form were laid in Florence
in the 1570s when a group of poets, philosophers and musicians known
as the Camerata began meeting to debate various topics of intellectual
interest. In their discussions about musical forms their guiding principle

was that the music should be subordinate to the text and that its chief function was to increase the dramatic power of the words. Their ideas were reinforced by the work of the scholar Girolamo Mei (1519–94), who had made a special study of ancient Greek drama, in which he believed music had played an essential role. An attempt was made to revive this supposed Greek original by the invention of the recitative, a form of solo singing which imitates, but somewhat exaggerates, the patterns of normal speech and effectively conveys dramatic dialogue.

The earliest complete opera which has survived is *Euridice* by Jacobo Peri (1561–1633), commissioned in 1600 and notable for its use of recitative. Another member of the Camerata, Giulio Caccini (1551–1618), wrote an opera of the same name, but is chiefly remembered for his innovatory *Le nuove musiche*, a collection of monodic songs with a slow-moving continuo accompaniment. The first great masterpiece in the new genre and arguably the first true opera was Claudio Monteverdi's *La favola d'Orfeo*, produced in Mantua in 1607. Strongly influenced by the tradition of the intermedio, a popular court entertainment combining music and dialogue, *Orfeo* combined all the elements of the new style of music. The

Music for Act II of Monteverdi's opera 'La favola d'Orfeo'. Arguably the first true opera, Monteverdi employed about 40 instruments in his score, giving instructions about which ones were to play at particular points in order to match the mood of the text and to achieve the desired dramatic effects.

vocal music consisted mainly of recitative, arias (solo songs) and choruses, generally accompanied by a basso continuo. In his opera Peri had used only a few lutes, some other similar instruments and a harpsichord, all placed out of sight behind the scenery. Monteverdi, however, deployed about 40 very varied instruments that were to take part in no less than 26 orchestral numbers during the course of the opera, though not all the instruments were employed at one time. Orfeo's celebrated aria in Act III, 'Possente spirito' ('Powerful spirit'), is remarkable for the beauty of the highly ornamented vocal line.

The opening in Venice in 1637 of the San Cassiano theatre, the first public opera house, made the city a new focal point in the world of opera. Such theatres played an important role in bringing opera, previously a court entertainment, to a much wider audience, which was inevitably going to have an influence on the kind of music produced.

Opera proved extremely popular and in the 1620s Rome became the centre of the new art. One of the best-known librettists of the period was Giulio Rospigliosi, later Pope Clement IX. He wrote the libretto for the first comic opera, *Chi sofre, speri* (1639). Roman opera displayed several new features, including an overture in the style of a canzona, which became an established pattern for opera overtures during the rest of the century.

Above left: This engraving shows stage design for a scene from Antonio Cesti's opera 'Il pomo d'oro'. The opera was notable for spectacular scenery.

Above right: Etching of the interior of the theatre that was specially built for the production of 'Il pomo d'oro' in Vienna in 1667, performed to celebrate the marriage of the Emperor Leopold II.

The opening in Venice in 1637 of the San Cassiano theatre, the first public opera house, made the city a new focal point in the world of opera. Over a dozen more were to be built in Venice before the end of the century. They played an important role in bringing opera, previously a court entertainment, to a much wider audience, which was inevitably going to have an influence on the kind of music produced. Among notable changes were more spectacular settings, a distinctly less melodic recitative sharply distinguished from the aria and the emergence of the latter as a vocal form in its own right. Monteverdi composed his last two operas, *Il ritorno d'Ulisse in patria* (1640) and *L'incoronazione di Poppea* (1642), for performance in Venice.

Another important Venetian opera composer was Pier Francesco Cavalli (1602–76), a pupil of Monteverdi, who also wrote sacred music. His many operas include *Egisto* (1643), *Ormindo* (1644) and *Ercole amante* (1662). Cavalli's rival, Antonio Cesti (1623–69), wrote the opera *Orontea*, which was notable for the importance placed on the human voice. The tendency to concentrate on the solo singing was already present in the operas of Cavalli and thus the work of both composers foreshadows the 'bel canto' style which was to become the hallmark of Italian opera. Cesti's *Il pomo d'oro* was notable for its spectacular scenery and the major provision of *stile moderno*, that words were to be more important than music, seemed to be forgotten in many of the Venetian operas. Plots were convoluted and comic scenes were added in order to make the drama more entertaining.

Monteverdi was born in Cremona, northern Italy, the son of a chemist and part-time surgeon. He published his first book of madrigals in 1587. His fourth and fifth books of madrigals, published between 1603 and 1605, marked a move away from the polyphonic technique of the Renaissance. The increased use of choral recitative was intended to ensure that all the words were intelligible to the listener. In his fifth book, in which he introduced a basso continuo, the employment of dissonances to convey the full meaning of the verse provoked strong criticism from the musical

claudio monteverdi 1567–1

Major Works

Operas
Seven operas of which
three survive:
1607	*La favola d'Orfeo*
1641	*Il ritorno d'Ulisse in patria*
1642	*L'incoronazione di Poppea*

Ballets
1608	*Il ballo delle ingrate*
1616	*Tirsi e Clori*

Secular oratorio
1624	*Il combattimento di Tancredi e Clorinda*

Secular vocal music
Nine books of madrigals:
1587	Book I
1590	Book II
1592	Book III
1603	Book IV
1605	Book V
1614	Book VI
1619	Book VII
1638	Book VIII
1651	Book IX
	plus
1607 & 1632	Scherzi musicali

Sacred music
1583	*Madrigali spirituali*
1610	*Vespers*
1640	*Selva morale e spirituale* plus masses, magnificats, psalms, etc

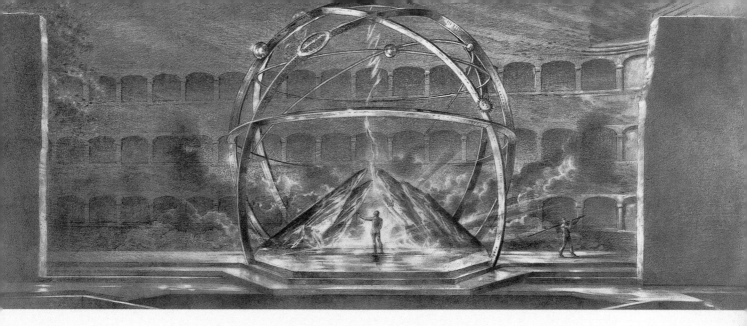

ft: Contemporary portrait of
audio Monteverdi, by Domenico
tti. Monteverdi imbued his
mpositions with a progressive
irit during a time of transition
m the Renaissance to the
roque, capturing the essence of
sical drama and creating music
great emotional depth.

ve: Sketch of the stage design,
Mauro Pagano, for the
duction of Monteverdi's 'Il
rno d'Ulisse in patria' at the
5 Salzburg Festival.

w: Title page of a poetry
hology commemorating
nteverdi's funeral in 1643.
e instruments decorating the
e represent those that he used
is orchestration.

establishment. Monteverdi's madrigals brought him recognition outside northern Italy, but it was his first opera, *La favola d'Orfeo* (1607), that established his position as a composer on the grand scale. In 1608 he completed a second opera, *Arianna*, shortly after the death of his wife. The score has been lost apart from the celebrated 'Lamento', a passionate outburst of grief which may well reflect the composer's own feelings.

In 1610 he turned his hand to sacred music, publishing the collection of *Vespers* dedicated to Pope Paul V, which successfully combined Renaissance polyphony and the expressive techniques of the Baroque era, including traditional psalms, recitative and aria, and the use of instrumental groups of various sizes. In 1612 Monteverdi was appointed maestro di cappella (director of music) at St Mark's, Venice, where his output included an impressive amount of sacred music. However, he did not completely neglect his secular work. He wrote the ballet *Tirsa e Clori* in 1616 and, in 1627, a comic opera, *La finta Pazza Licori* (now lost).

During the early years of his appointment in Venice Monteverdi returned to the composition of madrigals. The sixth book, published in 1614, contains an arrangement for five voices of the 'Lamento' from *Arianna*, and the seventh book (1619), a mixture of styles, including solo songs, duets, and songs for groups with instrumental support, among them the famous canzonetta 'Chiome d'oro'. The eighth book, entitled *Madrigali guerrieri et amorosi* ('Madrigals of love and war'), did not appear until 1638. It makes considerable use of the 'stile concitato' ('agitated style') which is characterised by the rapid repetition of notes in order to produce the effect of vigorous activity. It includes the *Combattimento di Tancredi e Clorinda*, first performed in 1624 as a theatrical entertainment.

In his last years Monteverdi composed the operas *Il ritorno d'Ulisse in patria* (1641) and *L'incoronazione di Poppea* (1642). These masterpieces of musical drama are remarkable for their depths of characterisation and their skill at depicting human passions. After Monteverdi's death his music suffered a period of neglect which lasted until the second half of the 19th century. Now that he has found his rightful place in the pantheon of great composers, he is seen as a key figure in the period of transition between the Renaissance and the Baroque. He was not only the first composer to reveal the full possibilities of opera as a genre, but also brought a greater emotional range to the madrigal and introduced a new, progressive spirit into music written for the Church.

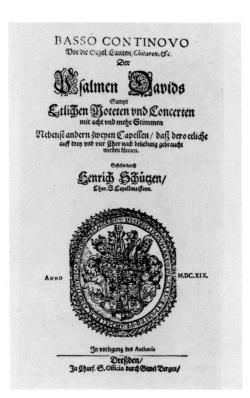

Title page of Heinrich Schütz's 'Psalmen Davids', published in 1619. Schütz was the first great German composer, managing to combine the new Italian style of the Baroque era with a strong, Protestant German tradition.

The development of the oratorio

Sacred music was to come under the influence of secular music, especia in the use of operatic forms, monody and basso continuo. Oratorio is a large-scale, dramatic composition, generally on a sacred theme, for soloists, chorus and orchestra. The *Rappresentazione di anima e di corpo* ('Representation of the Soul and Body') by Emilio de' Cavalieri (c.1550–1602), first produced in 1600, has claims to be considered the first oratorio but its reliance on actors, costumes, ballet and scenery places it rather in the category of sacred opera. In fact, although it share with opera the aria, the chorus and the use of recitative as a means of narrative, the true oratorio was to develop without scenery, costumes or action of any kind, achieving its first real distinction in the hands of Giacomo Carissimi (1605–74).

Carissimi's most famous oratorio, *Jephtha*, has a narrator and three other solo voices representing different characters, a chorus fully integrated into the story and an instrumental accompaniment. Carissimi other sacred music includes 13 oratorios, motets and masses, and some notable secular cantatas, among them *A piè d'un verde alloro*. His oratorios strongly operatic in their approach, were to have an important influence on the future development of the genre.

In Germany the oratorio was to achieve its first flowering in the music of Heinrich Schütz (1585–1672). In 1619 he published his first collectio of sacred music, the *Psalmen Davids*, and in 1623 his *Easter Oratorio*, followed in 1625 by the *Cantiones sacrae*, a collection of Latin motets. Hi *Dafne*, the first known German opera, the score of which has been lost, w performed in 1627. In 1629 there appeared his first collection of *Symphoniae Sacrae*, for combinations of voices and instruments. In 1635 he composed the magnificent funeral piece known as the *Musikalische Exequien* for soloists and choir with cello and harpsichord accompanimen His two sets of *Kleine Geistliche Konzerte* (1636 and 1639), motets for so voices with organ accompaniment, are notable for their powerful declamatory style. His *Christmas Oratorio* (published 1664) for soloists, choir and instruments was followed by his last works, settings of the Matthew, Luke and John Passions. Written for unaccompanied voices, these were markedly austere in their approach.

A lament from the fourth book of toccatas by Johann Froberger. Froberger, the leading German keyboard composer of the early 17th century, studied with the Italian keyboard composer Frescobaldi, and his toccatas contain prominent Italian elements.

A contemporary painting of the Danish composer Dietrich Buxtehude (with the sheet of music). Buxtehude, known mainly for his sacred music, gave public concerts on Sunday afternoons in the weeks leading up to Christmas. Such was the fame of the composer that these attracted the attention of musicians from all parts of Germany, including J.S. Bach.

Instrumental music

In the 17th century developments in instrumental music were just as important as those in vocal and choral music. The main categories of instrumental music included the canzona and the ricercare, which evolved into the fugue in the later Baroque period, various types of stylised dance music, which were usually integrated in a suite, music based on a repeated baseline such as the chaconne and passacaglia, and the toccatas, preludes and fantasias which were improvisatory. Two major influences on the evolution of instrumental music were Giovanni Gabrieli (see Chapter Four) and the Dutch composer Jan Sweelinck (1562–1621). The bulk of Sweelinck's output (over 250 pieces in all) consisted of vocal music, including motets and madrigals, but he is chiefly remembered for his keyboard works. These included fantasias, toccatas and sets of variations.

Belonging to the generation after Sweelinck was the Italian Girolamo Frescobaldi (1583–1643). His output of sacred and secular vocal music was small and he devoted his energies to keyboard compositions, mostly for the harpsichord. These included ricercares, canzonas, dances, toccatas and variations, and display his genius for improvisatory techniques. After his death interest in keyboard music in Italy declined for the next 50 years or so, but Frescobaldi was to have a far-reaching influence on composers of the German Baroque school.

In 17th-century Germany composers turned increasingly to instrumental and keyboard music. The organ now took pride of place, evolving its own forms of contrapuntal music: the choral prelude, fugue,

'Interior of the church of
St Stephen, Vienna', by David
Roberts. The organist-composer
Johann Pachelbel was appointed
assistant organist at St Stephen's
in 1673. Pachelbel's strength lay in
his organ music, which was to have
a strong influence on J.S. Bach.

toccata and suite. The leading German keyboard composer of his day wa
Johann Froberger (1616–67). He wrote toccatas, ricercares and fantasia
which contain prominent Italian elements. In his harpsichord suites in th
French style, which are generally considered his most important work, he
helped to standardise the allemande, courante, sarabande and gigue as
integral parts of the dance suite.

The Danish organist and composer Dietrich Buxtehude (1637–1707)
chiefly known for his sacred music. Much of Buxtehude's surviving vocal
music consists of church cantatas. His most important instrumental piece
are those for organ, many of which are freely composed, and include
toccatas, fugues, preludes and chaconnes.

Not least among the remarkable collection of German organist-
composers was Johann Pachelbel (1653–1706). Pachelbel is undoubted
best known as the composer of the famous Canon and Gigue in D for thre
violins and continuo, but his chief strength lies in his organ music, in
particular his chorale settings, fugues, toccatas and preludes. His
liturgical vocal music includes motets and magnificats.

Music in France

First attempts to introduce Italian opera to France in the mid-17th centu
were not very rewarding. To obtain any kind of success in France this new
musical art form needed to take account of the popularity of the *ballet de
cour* ('court ballet') – a lavish and colourful spectacle combining element

of poetry, music and dance – and of the pre-eminent position of the classical drama, typified by the plays of Molière. The man who managed to reconcile these various demands was Jean-Baptiste Lully (1632–87). In the 1660s he collaborated with Molière in the creation of the comedy-ballet, a stage work in which music and dancing enhanced the main dramatic action. The best known of these was *Le Bourgeois Gentilhomme* (1670). Lully now began composing his *tragédies lyriques*. Skilfully adapting Italian recitative to the demands of the French language in *Alceste* (1674), *Armide* (1686) and others, he succeeded in creating a distinctly French type of serious opera in which the action was interspersed with interludes of dancing and choral singing.

Lully was much admired for the attention he paid to the scoring of orchestral numbers. His instrumental ensemble contained what would be the basis of the string section of the symphony orchestra. Called the king's 24 violins, this section contained soprano, alto, tenor and bass violins in set proportions. He was also responsible for establishing the so-called French overture in his operas and ballets, in which a slow introduction using dotted rhythms is followed by a lively second section. The French overture was also used as an introductory movement in ballets, oratorios and instrumental pieces such as the suite and the sonata as well as being a genre in its own right. Among his other works are sacred music, including motets and a Miserere (1664), and some instrumental dance music.

Lully's contemporary, Marc-Antoine Charpentier (c.1645–1707), also collaborated with Molière, writing music for *Le Malade Imaginaire* (1673).

Charpentier is best known for his church music, in particular the oratorios which he established as a genre in France, skilfully superimposing the French declamatory style on Italian models. His other work includes motets, masses, notably the *Missa Assumpta est Maria*, a Te Deum, secular cantatas and an opera in the Lully style, *Médée*.

Lully and Charpentier were best known for their vocal music. Marin Marais (1656–1728) wrote four operas but is remembered chiefly for his instrumental music. His collection of pieces for the bass viol, over 500 in all, were published in five volumes between 1686 and 1725. His near contemporary, Michel-Richard de Lalande (1657–1726), was famous for his 'grands motets', but also wrote music for ballet and the instrumental 'Sinfonies pour les soupers du roi' to be played at the court at Versailles.

Music in England

There was some decline in musical life in England after the passing of the last of the great Elizabethan composers. However, music for consorts (ensembles) flourished in the hands of John Jenkins (1592–1678). He is best known for his music for viols, of which there are some 800 surviving pieces. His compositions include fantasias for viols and organ and for two violins and bass, the latter group reminiscent of the structure of the Italian trio sonata.

The masque, a courtly entertainment with poetry, music, dancing and lavish sets, reached its peak of development in England in the early 17th century. The most famous example was John Milton's *Comus*. The music was by Henry Lawes (1596–1662), who was also one of several composers to contribute to *The Siege of Rhodes* (1656). As a play set to music, it has strong claim to be considered the first English opera. Another contributor to *The Siege of Rhodes* was Matthew Locke (c.1630–77). In 1653, together with Christopher Gibbons (1615–76), he wrote the music for the masque *Cupid and Death* and in 1661 composed the music for the coronation procession of Charles II. Apart from his dramatic music for masques and *Psyche* (1675), Locke's main importance lies in his instrumental compositions, notably the *Consort of Fower Parts*, consisting of six suites for strings, and the famous music 'for His Majesty's Sagbutts and

Cornetts'. He also wrote incidental music for plays, composing the instrumental dances for a version of Shakespeare's *The Tempest* (1674).

John Blow (1649–1708), who is perhaps chiefly remembered as Henry Purcell's teacher, wrote a considerable amount of both church and secular music to be played on ceremonial or state occasions, but managed to impress his own individuality on his compositions. His sacred vocal music, the most important part of his output, includes about 100 mainly verse anthems (some with string parts), services (notably the Service in G Major) and Latin works. His other great claim to fame is *Venus and Adonis*, written during the early 1680s and described by him as a masque. The first work of its kind in which the whole text is set to music, it is an opera in all but name and combines both French and Italian influences. Among his secular vocal music are odes written for court occasions and his 'Ode on the Death of Mr Henry Purcell'. He also composed catches and songs for one or more voices, many of which were published in his collection *Amphion Anglicus* (1700).

The royal court attracted the talents of the English composers of the period, including the greatest of them all, Henry Purcell, and provided an environment in which they could flourish.

After the Restoration of 1660 the development of music in England was considerably encouraged by the enthusiasm of Charles II. The royal court attracted the talents of the English composers of the period, including the greatest of them all, Henry Purcell, and provided an environment in which they could flourish. However, an interest in music was to be found at all levels of society and in 1672 John Banister, a former director of the king's band, began organising in London some of the earliest public concerts, in which performances were given by professional musicians. In 1678 a merchant, Thomas Britton, converted a room above his shop into a concert hall, and by the end of the century a number of such venues existed both in London and elsewhere.

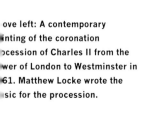

ove left: A contemporary
inting of the coronation
ocession of Charles II from the
wer of London to Westminster in
61. Matthew Locke wrote the
sic for the procession.

ght: Frontispiece to the 'Ode to
Cecilia' by Henry Purcell,
blished in 1684. Purcell wrote
ur odes for St Cecilia's Day, the
st composed in 1692, and all
splay the vitality of the
mposer's musical talent.

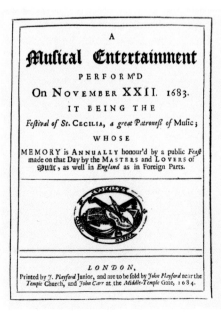

A

Musical Entertainment

PERFORM'D

On NOVEMBER XXII. 1683.

IT BEING THE

Festival of St. CECILIA, a great Patroness of Music;

WHOSE

MEMORY is ANNUALLY honour'd by a public *Feast* made on that Day by the MASTERS and LOVERS of Music, as well in *England* as in Foreign Parts.

LONDON,
Printed by *J. Playford* Junior, and are to be sold by *John Playford* near the *Temple* Church, and *John Carr* at the *Middle-Temple* Gate, 1684.

HENRI PURCELL
Né à Londres en 1658—Mort à Londres en 1735.

henry purcell
c.1659-1695

Major Works

Instrumental music

c.1680	13 Fantasias
c.1680	2 In nomines
1683	Chacony in G minor;
	12 sonatas in 3 parts
1696	8 suites for harpsichord
1697	10 sonatas in 4 parts

Vocal music

	c.70 full anthems and
	verse anthems, including:
c.1683	*Rejoice in the Lord alway*
1685	*My heart is inditing*
1694	*Te deum and Jubilate*
	plus 24 odes, including
	4 odes for St Cecilia's Day
	and 6 birthday odes; over
	160 songs; c.60 catches

Opera

1689	*Dido and Aeneas*

Semi-operas

1690	*Dioclesian*
1691	*King Arthur*
1692	*The Fairy Queen*
1695	*The Indian Queen*

The son of a court musician, Henry Purcell spent his life as a court musician himself, holding many prestigious royal appointments during h lifetime. He wrote the music for the coronations of both James II in 1685 and William III in 1689. His last official duty was to write the music for th funeral of Queen Mary, William's consort. Purcell left unfinished the mus for a semi-opera, *The Indian Queen*, when he died. He was buried in Westminster Abbey.

Purcell's earliest known works, composed about 1680, are a collectio of fantasias for viols. Written at a time when consort music of this kind w in decline, they show his mastery of contrapuntal skills. More in keeping with the fashion of the times are his trio sonatas for violins, bass viol and organ (or harpsichord), the first of which were published in 1683. They display strong Italian influences, but retain some of the traditional qualities of English chamber music. His other instrumental music includ the Chacony in G minor and pieces for organ and harpsichord. Despite th continuing popularity of his instrumental works Purcell's supreme geniu lies in his vocal music, both sacred and secular.

His sacred music consists of some 60 anthems, both for full choir an for soloists and choir. Among the best known of these are *Rejoice in the Lord alway* (the 'Bell Anthem'), *My heart is inditing*, written for the coronation of James II, and the *Te Deum and Jubilate*, composed for St Cecilia's Day celebrations in 1694. In his official capacity he wrote a number of odes and welcome songs for various court occasions. His various odes, including *Come ye sons of art away* (1694), with the famous

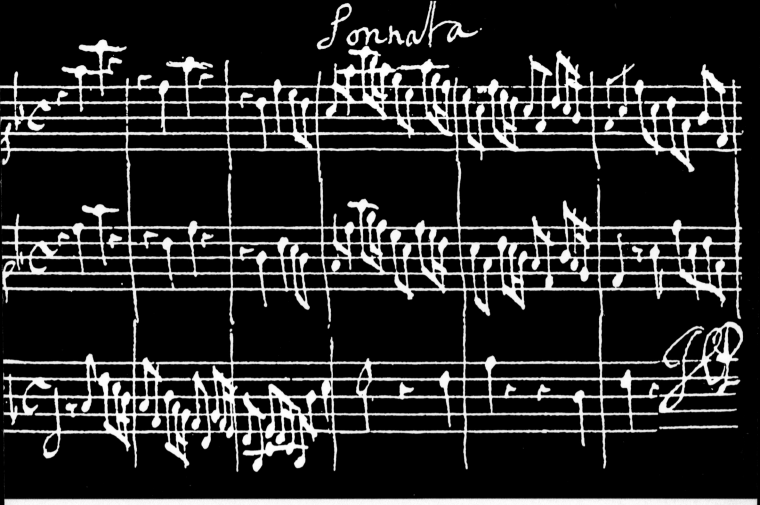

Sonnata

Above left: A 19th-century copy of a contemporary drawing of Henry Purcell, the greatest English composer of the Baroque era. England had to wait another 200 years for a musician of comparable stature.

Above right: Autograph score of Purcell's 'Golden Sonata', 1683. Purcell's compositional skills were diverse, ranging from songs and incidental music for theatre to ceremonial and religious music.

aria 'Sound the Trumpet', and the four odes for St Cecilia's Day, display the diversity of his musical talent. He also wrote over 150 songs for one to three voices and some 60 catches. These were rounds or canons to be sung by unaccompanied (generally male) voices, and frequently had humorous and bawdy themes.

Purcell was also much in demand as a writer of songs and incidental music for theatre productions and composed music for over 40 plays. Since much of what he wrote accompanied spoken drama it did not allow him much scope. Only during the last few years of his life did he begin to display the qualities which might have allowed him to create a tradition of English opera. *Dido and Aeneas* had its first performance in 1689. Despite its brevity (less than an hour) it is a masterpiece and the first true English opera. Its climax, the famous Lament 'When I am laid in earth', is one of the most deeply moving arias in all opera, the emotion intensified by the repetition of a ground bass. Purcell went on to collaborate on several semi-operas, in which the music had an extensive role. They included *King Arthur* (1691), *The Fairy Queen* (1692) and *The Indian Queen* (1695), which was completed after his death by his brother Daniel.

Like Mozart and Schubert Purcell had a brief but immensely productive career. His great talents enabled him to cover a wide field from chamber and keyboard compositions to ceremonial court odes, music for church and theatre and music for private entertainment. He successfully blended what was best in Italian and French styles with the traditions of his own country, while endowing everything he wrote with his own unique genius.

The sonata and the concerto

The evolution of instrumental music in the 17th century was assisted in no
small measure by the growing importance of the violin. Derived from the
fiddle and the lira da braccio, it first appeared in Italy about the middle of
the 16th century. Unlike the members of the viol family which were held
between the knees, it was played on the arm, with obvious advantages in
mobility. The first successful maker of a violin was apparently a certain
Gasparo da Salò at Brescia. Andrea Amati at Cremona refined Salò's
original design and later generations of Amatis continued to make
improvements to the instrument. Nicolò Amati (1596–1684), the most
illustrious of the family, passed on his skills to Antonio Stradivari
(1644–1737) and Giuseppe Guarneri (1698–1744), whose superb
craftsmanship ushered in the golden age of violin making. By the end of
the 18th century, apart from some minor changes, the violin had reached
its present form.

In its early years the violin had a distinctly popular image and was use
chiefly as an accompaniment to dancing. However, the richness and
beauty of its tone led to a rapid rise in the hierarchy of musical
instruments and during the 17th century it replaced the treble viol in
chamber music, eventually ousting the viols altogether. Among the earlies
composers to realise the potential of the violin were Giovanni Battista
Vitali (c.1632–92), who wrote mainly music for strings and played an
important part in the development of the trio sonata, and Giuseppe Torell
(c.1653–1708), a virtuoso violinist, who also made a notable contribution

to the evolution of the concerto. However, the foremost exponent of the new instrument was Arcangelo Corelli (1653–1713).

During the middle to late Baroque the Italians were to dominate in the area of ensemble writing. At the end of the 16th century the term 'sonata' began to come into general use as instrumental music assumed increasing importance. Derived from the Italian word *sonare*, it implied something sounded as opposed to 'cantata' (something sung). Applied very loosely to a variety of instrumental pieces, it was at first virtually interchangeable with the term 'canzona' but ultimately assimilated it. During the 17th century the sonata gradually acquired a more precise definition, becoming generally associated with small groups of instruments. Sonatas began to be divided into a number of contrasting sections or movements and were written for different combinations of instruments. A distinction was made between the *sonata da chiesa* ('church sonata') and the *sonata da camera* ('chamber sonata'), since many of the pieces were apparently intended for use in church. The *sonata da chiesa* was commonly split into four sections in a slow-fast-slow-fast pattern. The arrangement of the *sonata da camera* was generally more flexible. It frequently took the form of a suite of three or more stylised dances. The dominant form in the later 17th century was the trio sonata, usually arranged for two violins and a basso continuo – a cello or other bass instrument, with harpsichord accompaniment. Notable exponents of the trio sonata included Corelli and Purcell.

Sonatas for solo instruments began to achieve popularity during the early 18th century. Corelli quickly established a reputation as a violinist

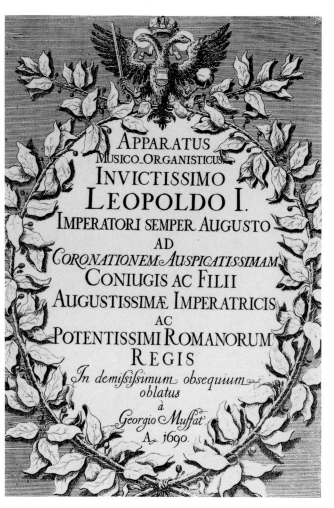

and conductor. His compositions include the Opus 1 collection of trio sonatas (1681) and the Opus 2 chamber works (1685). In many ways Corelli's trio sonatas were quite conservative. The harmonic language is simple, involving diatonic and modulating sequence, little chromaticism and only the most straightforward key relationships, with each sonata usually containing only one or two related tonal areas. The string writing i essentially idiomatic, yet non-virtuosic except in the solo sonatas where multiple stops and fast figuration are employed.

Towards the end of the 17th century genres of composition became more specific as to the number of players required for each part. Instead of the size of the ensemble being determined by circumstances and resources, it was reliant on the type of piece being performed. The concerto at this time generally implied the use of an 'orchestra'. The word 'concerto' first came into use at the end of the 16th century. It originally meant any kind of harmonious blending of musical elements, including choral music, but came increasingly to be applied to instrumental compositions in particular. The gradual development of the idea of contrast between two groups of players led to the concerto grosso in which a small group of soloists, the 'concertino', were set against a full string orchestra, the 'ripieno' (also known as the 'tutti' or, somewhat confusingly, the 'concerto grosso').

In the early Baroque period the combination of solo instruments in the concertino followed the pattern of the trio sonato – two violins and a bass continuo – although wind instruments were sometimes used in addition to or as a substitute for the violins. The number of movements varied, although the three-section fast-slow-fast order became the one generally adopted. Compositions of the concerti grossi type did not really distinguish between the solo and tutti group through the kind of materials given to each. Instead the larger group reinforced and echoed the soloists at key points in the piece such as the cadence. The 'contrast' was one of texture and dynamics rather than of theme.

Exponents of the concerto grosso include Archangelo Corelli, the German composer Georg Muffat (1653–1704) and Giuseppe Torelli. Torel was himself responsible for the development of the solo concerto. In the first outer movements of the solo concerto Torelli exploited the so-called 'ritornello' form, similar in many ways to the rondeau, except that the recurring ritornello theme was stated in several different keys. In the hands of Torelli the solo concerto was to begin to mark a new dramatic relationship between soloist and orchestra. The two were now contrasted through through the use of new material and modulations. Tomaso Albinoni (1671–1751) also composed solo concertos, but the genre was t achieve most distinction in the compositions of Antonio Vivaldi.

The title page of Georg Muffat's 'Apparatus Musico-Organisticus', published in Vienna and dedicated to Leopold I. It contains 12 toccatas and other pieces for organ. Muffat was one of the foremost exponents of the concerto grosso.

A portrait of Alessandro Scarlatti. Scarlatti, who spent most of his working life in Naples, was a prolific composer of operas, of which 70 survive. His work displays all the elements of the new Neapolitan style.

Neapolitan opera

Towards the end of the 17th century it was the turn of Naples to become a important new centre of opera and to establish a standardised form of the genre that was to be dominant in Europe for the next 100 years. The so-called *opera seria* ('serious opera') took its subject matter, usually a topic suitable for heroic or tragic treatment, from history or classical mythology The opera now consisted of a series of recitatives and arias, the recitatives being at first divided between the *recitativo seco* ('dry recitative'), which wa

View of the palace near Naples', painted by Angelo Maria Coasta in 696. Naples was a leading centre f opera by the end of the 17th entury and it was here that the tandardised form of the genre, hich was to be dominant for the ext 100 years, was established.

accompanied by the basso continuo, and the *recitativo accompagnato*, which was accompanied by the full orchestra. The aria, almost invariably a da capo aria in which the third section was a repeat of the first, gave great scope for the 'bel canto' type of singing, with its concentration on smoothness and beauty of tone. This led to a kind of opera in which the mellifluous qualities of the voice took precedence over dramatic expression. Comic scenes with ordinary people had often featured in serious opera in the past, but were now rigorously excluded. Consequently, in the early 18th century a special kind of purely comic opera, known as *opera buffa*, began to evolve. Another important innovation was the establishment of the introduction to the opera, known as the sinfonia or Italian overture, which consisted of three short movements in a fast-slow-fast sequence and was a direct ancestor of the symphony of the Classical period.

The most influential exponent of the new kind of Neapolitan opera was Alessandro Scarlatti (1660–1725). Scarlatti achieved early success with his operas, of which he composed over 100. *Il Mitridate Eupatore* (1707) and *La Griselda* (1721) are among his best and demonstrate his awareness of the dramatic potential of the aria and his gift for characterisation. He also wrote about 600 chamber cantatas, mostly for soprano voice and continuo. They display a more or less fixed pattern in which recitative and aria alternate, sometimes including a section in arioso style (a type of singing between recitative and aria). Scarlatti's other work includes compositions for keyboard and a considerable amount of sacred music – masses, oratorios, motets and magnificats.

Scarlatti wrote only a few comic operas. The first real master of the genre was Giovanni Pergolesi (1710–36), who was a notable violinist. His *La serva padrona* ('The Maid as Mistress'), originally an intermezzo or comic interlude forming part of a serious opera, proved extremely popular. Pergolesi also wrote serious operas and sacred music.

The cantata

The cantata, literally 'to be sung', as opposed to sonata, 'to be played', was first used in Italy in the early 17th century. Its meaning was at first more specific than it has since become: a collection of strophic arias. By the middle of the century the term was being applied to a shortish composition for solo voice with continuo, divided into several contrasting sections. The subject matter was usually the expression of personal feelings, a favourite subject being love betrayed. Early cantata composers were Alessandro Grandi (c.1575–1630), Luigi Rossi (c.1597–1653), Antonio Cesti (1623–69) and Giacomo Carissimi. These secular or chamber cantatas now began to acquire a standardised structure consisting of several da capo arias alternating with recitatives and reached a high point in the work of Alessandro Scarlatti.

The cantata, literally 'to be sung', as opposed to sonata, 'to be played', was first used in Italy in the early 17th century. By the middle of the century the term was being applied to a shortish composition for solo voice with continuo. The subject matter was usually the expression of personal feelings, a favourite subject being love betrayed.

The chamber cantata began to find favour in other European countries In France Marc-Antoine Charpentier wrote secular cantatas in the Italian style and Louis-Nicolas Clérambault (1676–1749), also influenced by Italian models, wrote some of the finest French cantatas. Johann Hasse (1699–1783), a German pupil of Alessandro Scarlatti, and best known for his operas, was largely responsible for introducing the secular cantata to Germany. Here, however, it underwent a transformation and the church cantata was born. A Lutheran minister and poet, Erdmann Neumeister (1671–1756), encouraged the use of sacred poetical texts as suitable subjects for musical setting in cantata form. The church cantata, with arias, recitatives and chorales, reached its most perfect form in the work of J.S. Bach, but Johann Kuhnau (1660–1722), Friedrich Wilhelm Zachow (1663–1712) and, especially, Georg Philipp Telemann (1681–1767) were worthy exponents of the genre.

Telemann was a remarkably prolific composer and the speed at which he could write music was the envy of his contemporaries. He was fluent in wide range of styles, absorbing influences even from the folk music of eastern Europe. His most famous collection, the three sets of *Musique de table* (1733), which include orchestral suites, concertos and chamber pieces, show his mastery of both the Italian and French idiom. During his lifetime it was his sacred music which was most admired: he wrote over 1,700 church cantatas, numerous settings of the Passion and, in his old age, began composing oratorios. His secular work was no less varied: mor than 100 overtures in the Italian style and nearly 50 concertos for solo instruments. Of his operas the comic ones were most successful, notably *Pimpinone* (1725). After his death Telemann was overshadowed by the great composers of the Classical period. His reputation went into a decline in the 19th century and only within the last 50 years or so has he been restored to his rightful position as a major composer of the Baroque era.

The late Baroque in France

The tradition of French instrumental music was carried into the 18th century by François Couperin (1668–1733). Couperin is best known for his works for harpsichord, which he published in four books, grouped in *ordres* or suites. Each *ordre* consists of over 20 miniature descriptive pieces, usually in a dance rhythm and in binary form, and they have whimsical titles such as *Papillons* ('Butterflies'), *La Visionnaire* ('The Dreamer') and *Les Ombres errantes* ('The Wandering Shadows'), which suggests that some of them may be intended as portraits of individual people. The pieces are technically varied and highly ornamented and demonstrate Couperin's success in adapting Italian styles to the expressive qualities of French music. This blending of traditions is also to be found in his trio sonatas, which show the influence of Archangelo Corelli.

Among Couperin's other chamber music is the collection known as the *Concerts royaux*, composed about 1715 and intended for performance before Louis XIV. His sacred vocal music includes the impressive *Leçons de ténèbres* for soprano voices. Not the least of his accomplishments was

low left: A contemporary portrait :he French composer, .psichordist and organist .nçois Couperin. Couperin is st known for his harpsichord .npositions, of which he wrote re than 230.

low right: A contemporary graving of the German composer d organist Georg Philipp iemann. Telemann, a leading .oonent of the church cantata, was astonishingly prolific composer a wide range of styles.

his treatise on playing the harpsichord, *L'Art de toucher le clavecin* (1716), in which Couperin attempts to codify the practice of ornamentation, describing all the various 'agréments' and how they were to be performed. The types of melodic ornaments found in Couperin's work, such as trills, turns and mordents, form an integral part of the delicate texture of the music and often create small, passing dissonances. Ornamentation was widely practised during the Baroque era and was indicated either by symbols above the stave or improvised by the musician. A certain type of elaboration, known as 'division', consisted of the embellishment of a slow melody, often in operatic arias but also in instrumental writing.

In successfully pursuing the two traditions of opera and keyboard music Jean-Philippe Rameau (1683–1764), the greatest French composer of the 18th century, was the natural heir of both Lully and Couperin. In his *Traité de l'harmonie* ('Treatise on Harmony'), a work which was to bring him great fame as a theorist and an original thinker, Rameau sets down the importance of the triad as the building block of tonality and justifies this by showing the simple harmonic ratios that produce it. He also theorised upon the more adventurous aspects of the tonal system, expansion of chords by the addition of thirds, inversions and modulations. Examples of daring harmonic sequences can be found in his compositions such as in Act II of *Hippolyte et Aricie*. He also wrote collections of pieces for the harpsichord, which show originality of approach and boldness in their use of harmony.

In addition, Rameau was fired with the ambition to write an opera and, with the writer and librettist Abbé Simon-Joseph, he composed his first, *Hippolyte et Aricie*. Described as 'a tragedy in music', it was based on the play *Phèdre* by Jean Racine and was performed publicly for the first time at the Paris Opéra at the end of 1733. It was followed by the opera-ballet *Les Indes galantes* (1735), and the serious opera *Castor et Pollux* (1737). All three were successful and Rameau's fame as a composer was now assured, although there was much criticism in some quarters at his supposed departure from the standards of French opera established by

Above left: A drawing of Jean-Philippe Rameau by Louis Carrogi Carmontelle, 1760. Although Rameau did not compose his first opera until the age of 50, he went on to write around 25 in all and it his theatrical music upon which hi main fame rests.

Left: A drawing of the leading French soprano Madeleine Sophie Arnould, singing the role of Thelaïre in Rameau's 'Castor et Pollux'. Rameau's theatrical musi looked forward to the great innovations of the Classical era.

Lully. There were, indeed, notable differences: Rameau's orchestration
was rich, complex and varied, and his recitative more declamatory and
expressive. He also experimented with the French overture by expanding
its second part or even substituting it for an Italian-style overture.

Rameau devoted the rest of his life to writing music for the theatre.
Among his more notable works were the serious operas *Dardanus* (1739)
and *Zoroastre* (1749), and a very successful comic opera *Platée* (1745). His
later operas were generally in a much lighter vein and rarely achieved any
great distinction. Moreover, he had the misfortune to be caught up in a
quarrel between those who championed traditional French opera (of which
he was regarded the chief exponent) and the partisans of the new Italian
comic opera, which was rapidly finding favour with the Parisian public.

The late Baroque in Italy

The tradition of instrumental music in Italy was continued in the late
Baroque period by composers such as Antonio Vivaldi (1678–1741). In 1703
he was appointed to the position of violin master at the Ospedale della
Pietà, an institution in Venice which looked after orphaned or abandoned
girls and gave them a musical education. As a teaching aid, Vivaldi wrote
concertos for a variety of solo instruments and combinations of
instruments, which demonstrated the wide-ranging abilities of his young
pupils. In 1711 his *L'estro armonico*, a collection of concertos for violin and
string orchestra, was published in Amsterdam and soon brought the

composer to the attention of a much larger public. Vivaldi's achievements in vocal music, both secular and sacred, were also considerable. In 1713 his opera *Ottone in villa* was produced (the first of nearly 50) and around the same time he wrote the nine-part Gloria in D, a tribute to his skill in arranging choral music. His other sacred works included oratorios, notably *Juditha triumphans* (1716), motets and psalms.

About 1725 Vivaldi published the collection entitled *Il cimento dell'armonia e dell'inventione* ('The Contest between Harmony and Invention'), which includes the popular violin concertos known as 'The Four Seasons'. He subsequently ceased having his music published, since it proved more profitable to sell manuscripts directly to interested customers. His last years were spent in comparative poverty and for a long time he was remembered only as a virtuoso violinist. It was not until the 19th century that there was a reawakening of interest in his music, which paved the way for the enormous popularity he enjoys today.

Vivaldi was undoubtedly one of the most influential composers of the Baroque period and his reputation is based solidly on his concertos. He wrote over 500 of these, of which about 230 were for solo violin and over 100 for other solo instruments, including cello, flute and bassoon. Even when there are several solo instruments, prominence is given to one or two of them. It was Vivaldi who did much to establish the form of the concerto in three movements, with its fast-slow-fast pattern and the use of the ritornello in the outer allegro (fast) movements. In between is a melodious slow movement in which the solo instrument plays a dominant part.

Below left: A contemporary portrait of Antonio Vivaldi. The son of a professional violinist who was employed at St Mark's cathedral, Vivaldi became a virtuoso violinist himself. His concertos, upon which his reputation as a composer is based, were much admired and used as models by such composers as J.S. Bach, who transcribed some of them for keyboard instruments.

Below right: A contemporary portrait of the gifted Italian keyboard composer Domenico Scarlatti. Born in the same year as Bach and Handel, Scarlatti began his musical education at an early age, closely supervised by his father, Alessandro. His creative powers reached their peak during his time in Spain.

Vivaldi's concerto music is marked by strong rhythms, vigour and passion and shows great skill in the use of instrumental colour. He was also a pioneer in the development of programme music in which the music has a descriptive or narrative function. For example, in 'The Four Seasons' each concerto depicts a different season of the year and the activities and sounds of nature associated with it, although this was never permitted to upset the basic form of the concerto. Vivaldi was to have a particular influence on the instrumental music of J.S. Bach and others, although in some ways his simpler, homophonic style, the dramatic role of the soloist and his use of genres such as the sinfonia and orchestral concerto could be seen to point even further into the future towards the Classical era.

The tradition of Italian keyboard music, which had declined after the death of Girolamo Frescobaldi, received a fresh impetus at the hands of Domenico Scarlatti (1685–1757). His early sacred music includes a Stabat Mater and he also wrote operas, though he did not achieve any great success with them. In 1729 he moved to Spain where he was to spend the rest of his life. His years in Spain were to be the most productive in his career. Although he continued to write some vocal music, his remarkable creative powers found their expression in a series of one-movement harpsichord sonatas, of which the first collection was published in 1738. In all he wrote more than 550 sonatas.

It seems that Scarlatti's move to Spain had an extraordinarily liberating effect on his talent. Not only was he now free of the restrictive traditions of Neapolitan keyboard music, but his imagination was greatly stimulated by the folk tunes and the sights and sounds of his adopted country, and the influence of Spanish dance rhythms and guitar music is apparent in many of the sonatas. These last scarcely more than three minutes, yet they display an astonishing virtuosity as the music shifts dramatically across the whole keyboard, using such brilliant effects as rapidly repeated notes and arpeggios, and the crossing of hands. Scarlatti's greatest achievement was, while creating a form that was uniquely his, to advance both the technique and the musical potential of keyboard composition.

The late Baroque in Germany

In Germany the Thirty Years' War had a disastrous impact on the country's cultural life, not least its musical output. However, in the late 17th century there was a great resurgence in German music, which was to reach its climax in the work of Bach and Handel. Born within four weeks of each other, both men came from similar backgrounds and both were brought up in the Lutheran Protestant tradition. Their careers, however, took very different paths. Bach spent all his life in Germany, enjoyed a modest income and was best known to his contemporaries as a church organist. Handel travelled widely, had wealthy patrons and was a prominent figure on the international music scene. Both men composed very different kinds of music. Handel's, intended for a wide public, was the more readily appealing and remained constantly popular. Bach's music, written mainly for the church, was more complex, demanded much more on the part of the listener and was neglected for many years after his death. Yet both men, in their very contrasting ways, raised the music of the Baroque era to new sublime heights.

johann sebastian bach

1685-1750

Major Works

Sacred vocal music

1724	St John Passion
1727	St Matthew Passion
1725	Easter Oratorio
1734	Christmas Oratorio
1723	Magnificat in D major
1749	Mass in B minor
	plus over 200 church cantatas; 6 motets

Secular vocal music

	Over 20 cantatas, including:
1732	'Coffee Cantata'
1742	'Peasant Cantata'

Orchestral music

1721	Brandenburg Concertos Nos 1–6
1717 –1723	2 concertos for violin and orchestra
1738 –1739	1 concerto for 2 violins and orchestra; 14 concertos for one, two, three or four harpsichords
1725 –1731	4 orchestral suites

Chamber music

c.1720	6 partitas (sonatas) for unaccompanied violin
c.1720	6 suites for unaccompanied cello
1747	6 sonatas for violin and harpsichord; 7 flute sonatas; 3 sonatas for viola da gamba and harpsichord; trio sonatas; *Musical Offering*

Organ music

Over 150 chorale preludes; preludes and fugues; toccatas and fugues; fantasies and fugues; sonatas; concertos; passacaglia

Keyboard music

c.1720	*Chromatic Fantasy and Fugue*
1722 & 1742	*The Well-Tempered Klavier*, 2 volumes.
c.1722	*6 English Suites*
c.1722	*6 French Suites*
1735	*French Overture*
1735	*Italian Concerto*
1741	*Goldberg Variations*
1745–	*The Art of Fugue*
	plus toccatas; inventions; suites; fantasies; preludes; fugues; capriccios

Bach was born in Eisenach, Thuringia, in 1685. In 1708 his musical talents won him the position of court organist at Weimar, where he wrote some of his best known works for that instrument. He also began transcribing some of Vivaldi's concertos for organ and harpsichord. In 1717 Bach accepted the post of director of music to Prinz Leopold of Köthen. There followed a particularly fruitful period in which he composed much of his finest instrumental and keyboard music, including the *Brandenburg Concertos* (1721), and the first book of *The Well-Tempered Clavier*. In 1722 he was appointed Kantor (director of music) at Leipzig. The *St John Passion* (1724) and the *St Matthew Passion* (1729) represent the peak of his achievement during this period, but he also wrote numerous church cantatas, the *Easter Oratorio* (1725) and the *Christmas Oratorio* (1734). In 1741 he published the *Goldberg Variations*, followed by Book II of the *Well-Tempered Clavier* (1742), *The Art of Fugue* (1745–, left incomplete at his death) and the *Musical Offering* (1747). The *Mass in B Minor* was completed in 1749.

During his lifetime Bach was best known for his skills as an organist and harpsichord player. As a composer he was thought conservative and old-fashioned by his contemporaries, who considered his music complex and his melodies not readily accessible. His work suffered a period of neglect and the full extent of his genius was not recognised until the 19th century. A performance of the *St Matthew Passion* in 1829 directed by Felix Mendelssohn greatly helped this revival of interest.

Although Bach never left German soil he familiarised himself with the methods of the leading Italian and French composers by making his own arrangements of what they had written. His vast output covered every musical genre with the exception of opera and to each one he brought his own creative insight and the ability to develop new potential in already existing forms. Many of his organ works were written during his Weimar period and include chorale preludes, preludes and fugues, toccatas and fantasias. He produced a prodigious quantity of fine music while at Köthen, including the six *Brandenburg Concertos*, which follow the Italian fast-slow-fast pattern with a ritornello in the fast movements. They are scored for remarkable combinations of instruments and demonstrate a skilled blending of Italian and German styles.

Teaching played an important part in Bach's career and the 24 preludes and fugues of *The Well-Tempered Clavier*, one in each of the 24 major and minor keys, were intended for instructional purposes. Collections of pieces in every available key had appeared before for instruments such as the lute, but it was not until the equal division of the octave into 12 parts (equal temperament) that a prelude and fugue in all 24 keys could be attempted for the keyboard. Among other keyboard compositions from the early 1720s are the six *English Suites* and the six *French Suites*, each with the usual four dance movements (allemande, courante, sarabande and gigue), although the *English Suites* begin with a prelude. From this period also date the unaccompanied partitas for violin, suites for unaccompanied cello and three violin concertos, including the *Double Violin Concerto in D minor*.

During his years in Leipzig Bach composed numerous cantatas, of which about 200 survive. He created the so-called chorale sonata, of which *Wachet auf, ruft uns die Stimme* ('Sleepers, wake, the voice is calling') is probably the most famous example. It interweaves verses of a well-known advent hymn, with recitatives and arias, using a mixed chorus and orchestra and vocal soloists to marvellous effect. The greatest achievements of Bach's sacred music are his two settings of the Passion for soloists, choir and orchestra as narrated in the Gospels of St John and St Matthew respectively. The *St Matthew Passion* in particular contains many beautiful passages, among them the alto aria *Erbarme dich, mein Gott* ('Have pity, my God') and the final chorus *Wir setzen uns mit Tränen wieder* ('We sit down with tears'). The *Mass in B minor* (1749) is a work of imposing grandeur. His six surviving motets, for chorus only, were among the few vocal works that continued to be heard after Bach's death. They include the well-known *Singet dem Herrn* ('Sing to the Lord'). His two notable Christmas compositions were the exuberant *Magnificat* (1723, revised 1730) for five-part chorus, soloists and orchestra, and the *Christmas Oratorio*, a group of six cantatas. Although underappreciated during his lifetime, Bach is now regarded as the most important of the Baroque composers.

Below left: A 19th-century portrait of J.S. Bach, by Gustav Zerner. Bach came from a family whose origins could be traced back to the middle of the 16th century and which produced a remarkable number of fine musicians. He was described by Wagner as 'the most stupendous miracle in all music'.

Below right: Autograph score of Bach's cantata No 180, 'Schmücke dich, o liebe Seele'. Many of Bach's contemporaries thought his compositions old-fashioned, over-complex and inaccessible, and his genius was not fully recognised until the 19th century.

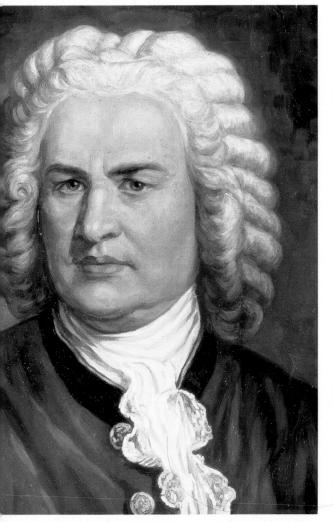

Handel was born in Halle, Saxony. His first opera, *Almira*, was performed to considerable public approval at the Hamburg opera house in 1705 and he was sufficiently encouraged to write three more in quick succession. In 1706 he travelled to Italy, where he met Corelli, Alessandro and Domenico Scarlatti, and Vivaldi. It was a productive period in Handel's life: operas such as *Rodrigo* (1707) and *Agrippina* (1709) enjoyed immediate success, and he also wrote cantatas and an oratorio.

In 1710 he was appointed director of music to the Elector in Hanover. In 1711 he travelled to London, where his opera *Rinaldo* was performed. This was such a triumph that Handel paid a return visit, composing two operas, an ode for the birthday of Queen Anne and a Te Deum to celebrate the signing of the Peace of Utrecht. Frequently away in London, Handel had somewhat neglected his duties at the court of Hanover. When Queen Anne died in 1714 the Elector George became king of England and Handel, who had incurred the royal displeasure through his long absences, had to make amends as best he could. The story goes that his *Water Music* (1717), written to accompany a royal procession by barge along the Thames, effected a reconciliation between monarch and composer.

About 1718 Handel became director of music to the Duke of Chandos for whom he composed sacred music, including the 11 'Chandos' anthems, and two dramatic works – the masques *Acis and Galatea* (1718–20) and *Haman and Mordecai* (1720). The latter, based on a biblical story, was later reworked as *Esther* (1732) and became, in effect, the first English oratorio. In 1719 the Royal Academy of Music was founded with the aim of promoting Italian opera in London. Handel, one of its directors, set off on a continental tour to listen to opera singers and engage those whom he thought suitable to perform in England. On his return he began composing a series of Italian operas. They included *Julius Caesar* (1724) and *Rodelinda* (1725), which proved very popular. During this period Handel was appointed composer of the Chapel Royal. It was in this official capacity that he wrote four anthems for the coronation of George II in 1727, including the famous *Zadok the Priest*, which is still played at coronations.

The success in 1728 of John Gay's *The Beggar's Opera*, a political and social satire, proved a real threat to Italian-style opera in London. Handel persevered with Italian opera, however, and in 1729 undertook another journey to the continent in search of fresh talent. Over the next ten years or so his output included *Orlando* (1733), *Alcina* (1735) and *Berenice* (1737), but the English public proved fickle in its tastes and his operas had a mixed reception. He proceeded to turn increasingly away from opera and towards oratorio, although in 1739 he produced the delightful *Xerxes*, which includes the famous aria 'Ombra mai fu'. His first important works in the

george frideric

handel
1685-1759

A contemporary portrait of Handel. Best known for his oratorios, Handel was also a gifted organist and composed many operas.

Left: A poster for a performance of John Gay's 'The Beggar's Opera' in 1920. The original production of this work was a great success and signalled the decline in popularity of Italian-style opera, of which Handel was a leading exponent. He eventually turned to writing the oratorios upon which his fame rests.

Below: 'Handel playing the organ', in the interior of Covent Garden Theatre, from Ackermann's 'Microcosm of London', 1808. Handel settled in London in 1712, and when he died his funeral was attended by some 3,000 people.

new genre were *Saul* and *Israel in Egypt* (both 1739). In 1740 he published the concerti grossi for woodwind and strings and a set of organ concerto His most famous oratorio, *Messiah*, was written in the space of three week in 1741. During the next few years he composed the oratorios *Samson*, *Semele*, *Joseph* and *Belshazzar*, and *Judas Maccabaeus* in 1747. In 1749 wrote the *Music for the Royal Fireworks* to celebrate the Peace of Aix-la-Chapelle. He was working on the manuscript of his last oratorio, *Jephtha* in 1751 when his eyes began to cause him trouble. Although he went completely blind in his left eye and almost sightless in the right one, he continued to compose, to direct performances and to play the organ.

Handel has always been best known for his oratorios, yet he spent more than 30 years writing operas and they contain some fine music.

A print of the fireworks display that was held on the Thames on May 15, 1749, as part of the celebrations for the Peace of Aix-la-Chapelle. Handel wrote the accompanying 'Music for the Royal Fireworks'.

When he first arrived in London he found a public already acquiring a taste for Italian 'serious opera' and Handel duly obliged, producing some 36 in all, among them such masterpieces as *Rodelinda* and *Julius Caesar*. In Handel's operas the recitatives are used to carry forward the dramatic action, while the melodious arias (usually da capo arias in three sections, in which the third section is a repeat of the first), often written to suit the talents of a particular singer, are vehicles for the expression of strong emotions. His six concertos for woodwind and strings and his twelve concerti grossi for strings and harpsichord are undoubtedly among the best of his instrumental music, together with the two suites, the *Water Music* and the *Music for the Royal Fireworks*. His set of solo sonatas and trio sonatas are also worthy of mention. His composition of music for state occasions, in particular, endeared him to the English public, who felt that his music expressed their patriotic feelings.

Although Handel enjoyed the patronage of royalty and the aristocracy he knew how to shape his music to suit the tastes of ordinary English people to such an extent that it became part of the national heritage.

However, it is his oratorios, usually based on Old Testament biblical stories, that have given Handel his enduring fame. They were composed for a public which had begun to tire of serious opera and their use of English rather than Italian made a favourable impression on the audience. The most popular of Handel's oratorios, *Messiah*, made particularly famous by the aria 'I know that my Redeemer liveth' and the 'Hallelujah Chorus', remains one of the most frequently performed, and in Britain at Christmas time has become a national institution. Handel's oratorios were three-act dramatic works intended for performance in theatres and concert halls. Two of them, *Semele* (1744) and *Hercules* (1745), which take their subjects from classical mythology, have been staged as operas with considerable success. Handel created a uniquely English form of oratorio, most clearly seen in the prominent role given to the chorus in the development of the story. He employed great contrasts in texture between fugal and homophonic passages, superimposed melodic lines of different speed and fully exploited the possibilities of the vocal range of the choir in the voicing of harmonies.

Unlike many other composers Handel continued to enjoy undiminished prestige after his death. His music has always had an immediate appeal to the listener. Although he enjoyed the patronage of royalty and the aristocracy he knew how to shape his music to suit the tastes of ordinary English people to such an extent that it became part of the national heritage of the country which he had adopted as his own.

classical
style

France entered the 18th century as the most powerful country in Europe but the French Revolution of 1789 brought about the collapse of the old order and ushered in the era of Napoleon I. Britain was fast becoming an important colonial and maritime power. During the 18th century the philosophical movement known as the Enlightenment asserted the supremacy of reason in human affairs and advocated the rights of the individual. Its adherents attacked established institutions such as the Church and the monarchy. The arts were also entering an era of change, with artists looking to the ancient civilisations of Greece and Rome for inspiration. This was also the time of the Industrial Revolution, which was to transform the Western world from a rural to an urban society.

8th-19th
century

e: 'Rain, steam and speed – Great Western Railway', by am Turner, 1844. The lopment of steam power led to ndustrial Revolution, bringing it a period of social upheaval, n had inevitable repercussions e development of music.

'A dance in the Barroco-co palace', by Francesco glioli, 18th century. In tecture graceful rococo motifs used to soften the severity of que grandeur, a development was echoed in music by the duction of flowing melodies.

In the early years of the 18th century a new style of art and architecture was emerging in France. Known as 'rococo', it was derived from the word *rocaille* meaning 'fancy shell-work', and was originally used to described the decorative scrolls and arabesques used in architecture. It was characterised by lightness, grace and a certain elegant frivolity. In music, emphasis was laid on similar qualities of gracefulness and elegance and flowing, 'natural' melodies in contrast to the complex profundities of the Baroque. Counterpoint was replaced by a simpler combination of melody and harmony, and musical discourse was articulated by periodic phrase structure and regular, clear cadence points. The works of composers such as Sammartini, Stamitz, J.C. and C.P.E. Bach and others were considered to exemplify many aspects of this style of music, which marked an intermediate stage between Baroque and Classical.

The description 'Classical' is here applied to the music which flourished from the middle of the 18th century to the 1820s. The greatest composers of this period were Haydn, Mozart, Beethoven and Schubert. Vienna, where they all lived and worked, now became the focal point of musical development in Europe. The outstanding qualities of Classical music were emotional restraint, simplicity and clarity of formal structure. It was also the era in which instrumental music assumed greater significance than vocal music and in which musical genres such as the symphony, sonata, concerto and chamber music assumed their most concrete form.

The evolution of opera

During the first half of the 18th century Italian opera, both serious and comic, remained dominant in Europe. Serious opera in particular underw important changes, largely through the influence of Pietro Metastasio (1698–1782). The author of more than 70 librettos, he made considerabl effort to introduce greater dramatic realism to opera. The most famous exponent of Metastasio's new version of Italian opera seria was Johann Hasse. Hasse's output, which comprised some 70 or 80 operas, genera consisted of recitatives, in which the action takes place, alternating wit arias, in which characters express their emotions. The arias were gener in da capo form and provided considerable scope for vocal virtuosity. Orchestral support was generally confined to moments of high drama.

By the mid-18th century comic opera was beginning to rival serious opera in popularity. The libretto dealt with topical events and familiar situations in a light-hearted manner and the music, stripped of excessi ornamentation, was tuneful and easy to understand. In Italy, where it w known as opera buffa, comic opera also began to lose some of its more farcical elements. Typical of Italian light opera of this period was *La bu figliola* ('The Virtuous Maid') by Nicolò Piccinni (1728–1800). Giovanni Paisiello (1714–1816), with over 80 other operas to his credit, wrote *Il barbiere di Siviglia* ('The Barber of Seville'), which was first performed a Petersburg in 1782. *Il matrimonio secreto* ('The Secret Marriage') by Domenico Cimarosa (1749–1801), another significant contribution to Italian comic opera, received its premiere in Vienna in 1792.

In France a lighter style of opera, known as opéra comique, began to appear in the 1720s. French opéra comique showed increasing sophistication and awareness of social issues in the work of such composers as François Philidor (1726–95) and Ernest Grétry (1741–1813). Philidor's *Tom Jones* (1765) was based on the novel by Henry Fielding and Grétry's *Richard Coeur de Lion* (1784) established a fashion for 'rescue operas' in which the hero is eventually saved from an unpleasant fate by the actions of a brave friend. The opéra comique which, like its English and German counterparts, used spoken dialogue, remained a firm favourite with audiences until well into the 19th century.

t: This contemporary print
ows riots breaking out at Covent
rden Theatre in London in 1763
en the management refused to
nit people at half-price to
taxerxes'. The opera, by Thomas
e, is an Italian-style opera seria
d was the only one of its kind to
ieve success in England.

ht: A portrait of the soprano
stina Bordoni. The wife of
ann Hasse, she was also one of
ndel's singers, creating the role
Rosanne in 'Alessandro'. An
ident where Bordoni fought on
ge with a rival singer was
rised in 'The Beggar's Opera'.

In England the ballad opera was launched with John Gay's *The Beggar's Opera* in 1728. The mixture of popular tunes with spoken dialogue had instant public appeal. Thomas Arne (1710–78), who is perhaps best known as the composer of 'Rule Britannia', wrote the ballad opera *Love in a Village* (1762). His *Artaxerxes* (1762), an opera seria in the Italian style with recitative, was the only one of its kind to achieve any success.

In Germany light opera appeared in the form of the singspiel, modelled on the English ballad opera and the French opéra comique. Johann Hiller (1728–1804) began by adapting English comic opera but went on to compose a series of his own, including *Die Jagd* ('The Hunt', 1770). They

Left: 'Christoph Willibald Gluck at the spinet', Paris, 1775. Gluck spearheaded the reform of opera seria. He was much admired by Mozart but his true heirs lay ahead in the next century.

Below: Title page of the French edition of Gluck's 'Orfeo ed Euridice', produced in Paris in 1774. Gluck's greatest importance was his ability to achieve a balance between music and drama and to produce work of a noble and Classical simplicity.

were written in a simpler style than opera seria and used popular melodies. The Viennese composer Karl Ditters von Dittersdorf (1739–99) made an important contribution to the establishment of the singspiel, combining, as in his *Doktor und Apotheker* (1786), the style of Italian comic opera with the traditions of native folk music. The singspiel, however, was to find its greatest artistic expression in the comic operas of Mozart.

The growing popularity of comic opera seriously undermined the status of opera seria, resulting in a strong desire to introduce greater naturalism to the genre. The guiding spirit in this was to be Christoph Willibald Gluck (1714–87). Gluck's early operas are written in the conventional style of t day and it was not until 1762 that the first of his 'reform operas', *Orfeo ed Euridice*, was performed, followed by *Alceste* (1767). In both works Gluck put into practice his ideas: that the function of the music should be at the service of the text and the requirements of the plot. He dropped the unaccompanied recitative in favour of recitative with orchestral support and gave a more important role to the chorus, which he believed should be an integral part of the action. Gluck avoided complex plots and in *Orfeo* in particular shows how a familiar mythological tale can form the basis for a simple and moving story of human emotions. In 1774 his *Iphigénie en Aulide* was performed in Paris to great acclaim.

ne of the most important developments in instrumental music during the Classical eriod was the establishment of the so-called sonata form.

The sonata form

One of the most important developments in instrumental music during the Classical period was the establishment of the so-called sonata form. By the latter half of the 18th century sonatas, concertos, symphonies, opera overtures and string quartets were being written in three or four movements, each movement characterised by contrasting mood and tempo. The term 'sonata form', 'first-movement form' or 'sonata-allegro form' was applied to the structural pattern of the first movement of all of these musical genres, which is divided into three main sections. First, there is the exposition, in which two themes or two groups of themes, a primary and a secondary, linked by bridge passages, are contrasted, the first group being in the tonic key of the work, the second in the dominant or relative major key. This is followed by the development, which uses thematic material from the exposition and elaborates it in various ways, often treating it contrapuntally. The third section, the recapitulation, restates the primary and secondary themes, now entirely in the tonic key, and reconciles the musical themes which were contrasted in the exposition. The recapitulation is sometimes followed by a coda.

However, this 'blueprint' for sonata form does not describe the structure of all Classical period first movements. Haydn especially deviated from the standardised pattern and his first movements often reveal an absence of the second subject, thematic development in all parts of the movement and the addition of a slow introductory section. Perhaps the most important characteristics of sonata form and similar structures are the elements of drama and contrast that can be seen in both the use of tonal areas and thematic material. Harmonic movement was significantly slowed down during the Classical period and might be seen to have polarised into the opposition of tonic and dominant which characterises so much of the music of this time.

The symphony

From the period of the late Renaissance the Italian term 'sinfonia' had been employed to designate various kinds of instrumental music but by the beginning of the 18th century its use was being restricted to the 'Italian' opera overture with its three-movement, fast-slow-fast pattern.

Above left: Portrait of the Viennese composer Karl Ditters von Dittersdorf, 1816. Dittersdorf was an early exponent of the singspiel, combining Italian comic opera with native folk music, as well as a prominent symphonist.

Above right: Contemporary portrait of J.C. Bach, by Thomas Gainsborough. Bach's large output included several operas, keyboard music, songs and chamber works. In 1764–5, during Mozart's visit to London, Bach befriended the young composer and was to have a lasting influence on him.

Towards the middle of the century these opera overtures had acquired a separate existence and were being played as independent pieces in concerts. Early symphonies retained the three movements but the addition of a minuet and trio before the last movement soon became standard practice among the more adventurous composers, thus establishing the familiar outlines of the Classical symphony – an instrumental composition in four movements structured like a sonata but played by a full orchestra.

One of the first known composers of the symphony was Giovanni Sammartini (c.1700–75), who wrote more than 70. Although his earlier works are Baroque in style, his later symphonies, with their extended use of wind instruments, anticipate the shape of the Classical symphony. Another variation on this genre was to be found in Paris in the latter half of the 18th century. The 'symphonie concertante' was a work for orchestra and several soloists, whose main exponents include Joseph Boulogne Saint-Georges (1739–99) and Giuseppe Cambini (1746–1825).

By the 1740s the focus of symphonic composition had shifted to Germany and Austria. An important figure was Johann Stamitz (1717–57), who wrote more than 50 symphonies. Stamitz helped to lay the foundations of the modern symphony orchestra – four sections comprising strings, woodwind, brass and percussion. Significantly, the basso continuo ceased to be the harmonic foundation of the orchestra and Stamitz indulged in such innovative practices as giving the melody to the contrabasses or using the wind instruments to sustain harmonies.

In Vienna Matthias Monn (1717–50) and Georg Wagenseil (1715–77) both made a notable contribution to the evolution of the four-movement symphony and to the still tentative use of the sonata form. J.S. Bach's youngest son, Johann Christian Bach (1735–82), was a notable exponent of the symphony. He was equally at home in both instrumental and vocal music but it is his symphonies (about 50 in all) which have remained his most outstanding contribution. Written in the three-movement Italian pattern, they are both elegant and stylish and were an important formative influence on the early Classical symphony.

Other major figures in the transitional period were C.P.E. Bach and Luigi Boccherini, who each wrote about 20 symphonies. Karl Ditters von Dittersdorf was also a prominent symphonist. Both Haydn and Mozart experimented with the symphonic form during their early years but their mature works show the establishment of the four-movement pattern which typified the Classical symphony: a lively first movement (allegro) in sonata form; a lyrical slow movement; a minuet and trio; and a brisk finale in rondo form or combined with the sonata form as a rondo-sonata form.

The Classical concerto

The internal structure of the first movement of a concerto was usually based on ritornello form or a composite of ritornello and sonata form. Another feature of the solo concerto was the cadenza, an unaccompanied passage near the end of a movement which allowed the soloist to display his or her virtuosic skills and technical ability. C.P.E. Bach wrote about 50 harpsichord concertos, many of them displaying the intensity and dramatic power of his symphonies. J.C. Bach's keyboard concertos are more conventional, yet they too provide a foretaste of the perfection to be found in the concertos of Mozart. Another important figure in the evolution of the solo concerto was Luigi Boccherini, whose virtuoso cello concertos brought added lustre to that instrument.

ht: A 19th-century portrait of P.E. Bach, by Alfred Lemoine. rl Philipp Emanuel Bach was the st gifted and famous of J.S. ch's sons, writing about 50 rpsichord concertos as well as nerous symphonies.

right: Title page of a music blication by C.P.E. Bach, issued ring his time as musical director Hamburg in 1770. Bach had a utation as a teacher and a orist as well as a composer.

Chamber music

Music for small ensembles had been in existence for nearly 200 years. Chamber music in the modern sense of the term, that is, music for two or more players suitable for performance in a room or a small concert hall and with only one player to a part, really dates from the end of the 18th century. At this time a group consisting of two violins, a viola and a cello established itself as the most popular ensemble and was to remain the principal form of chamber music. Keyboard instruments, usually the harpsichord, had previously been confined to a subordinate role in the now defunct trio sonata, but the supremely versatile piano was rapidly becoming the dominant partner in certain kinds of chamber music, notably the piano trio and the piano quartet. The redundancy of the continuo part led to a new equality among the instruments of an ensemble, which in turn introduced new and unusual textures.

The string quartet was to find its supreme exponent in Joseph Haydn, but Luigi Boccherini (1743–1805) also made an important contribution. Boccherini wrote music in a variety of genres, but he displays the elegance and grace of his music most strongly in his chamber music, which included more than 100 string quintets and 90 some string quartets.

Chamber music in the modern sense of the term, that is, music for two or more players suitable for performance in a room or a small concert hall and with only one player to a part, really dates from the end of the 18th century.

Contemporary portrait of Luigi Boccherini, by an unknown Italian artist. Boccherini showed great ability as a cellist from an early age. His compositions include string quartets, string trios, string quintets, cello concertos and sonatas for keyboard and violin.

lute concert at Sanssouci, with
Frederick II playing the flute and
C.P.E. Bach at the piano. Bach's
life in Frederick's service was not
a happy one, due to the restrictive
nature of his duties, coupled with a
meagre salary. On leaving his royal
patron's service in 1767, however,
Bach took up the post of musical
director in Hamburg and entered
the most prolific and adventurous
stage of his career.

The importance of Domenico Scarlatti in the evolution of the sonata
was seen in Chapter Five. Scarlatti's vast output of one-movement
keyboard sonatas did much to enhance the importance of the sonata for
solo harpsichord. In Spain Antonio Soler (1729–83), a student of Scarlatti,
was best known for his harpsichord sonatas. His keyboard sonatas, in one
to three or four movements, are vigorous and lively, demanding
considerable virtuosity on the part of the performer.

In the latter half of the 18th century the harpsichord and the clavichord
began to be ousted by the much more versatile piano. One of its leading
exponents was Carl Philipp Emanuel Bach (1714–88), J.S. Bach's third
son. Bach was an outstanding keyboard player and his *Essay on the True
Art of Playing Keyboard Instruments* (1753–62) added to his reputation as a
teacher and theorist. In 1767 he was appointed musical director in
Hamburg, where he composed symphonies, keyboard music and concertos
as well as sacred works (notably the *Magnificat* of 1749) and chamber
music. Bach was an important figure in the development of the so-called
empfindsamer Stil ('sensitive style'), in which the music is the vehicle for
subjective emotional qualities. This music found its most characteristic
expression in the 150 or so sonatas Bach wrote for the keyboard. His
favoured instrument was the clavichord, which was more responsive to
sudden modulations, abrupt pauses and other effects than the harpsichord.

By the late 18th century the sonata was generally a piece in three
contrasted movements in a fast-slow-fast pattern, with the occasional
addition of a fourth one, usually a minuet and trio, in between the second
and third movements.

Major Works

Symphonies

c.1761	No 6 in D major
1761	No 7 in C major
c.1761	No 8 in G major
1764	No 22 in E flat major
c.1770	No 26 in D minor
c.1770	No 39 in G minor
c.1772	No 44 in E minor
1772	No 45 in F sharp minor
c.1769	No 48 in C major
1768	No 49 in F minor
1774	No 56 in C major
c.1782	No 73 in D major
1786	No 82 in C major
1785	No 83 in G minor
c.1785	No 85 in B flat major
1785	No 87 in A major
1789	No 92 in G major
1791	No 93 in D major
1791	No 94 in G major
c.1793	No 100 in G major
c.1793	No 101 in D major
1795	No 103 in E flat major
1795	No 104 in D major

Other orchestral music

c.1765	Cello concerto in C major
1783	Cello concerto in D major
1796	Trumpet concerto in E flat major plus 3 violin and 3 harpsichord concertos

String quartets

1772	Opus 20, Nos 1–6
c.1781	Opus 33, Nos 1–6
1787	Opus 50, Nos 1–6
1788	Opus 54, Nos 1–6
1788	Opus 55, Nos 1–6
1790	Opus 64, Nos 1–6
1793	Opus 71, Nos 1–3
1793	Opus 74, Nos 1–3
1797	Opus 76, Nos 1–6
1799	Opus 77, Nos 1–2
1803	Opus 103, unfinished

Other chamber work

Over 120 baryton trios; trio sonatas; notturnos; divertimentos

Keyboard music

Approximately 50 sonatas; variations; capriccios

Operas

1777	*Il Mondo della Luna*
1781	*La Fedeltà premiata*
1784	*Armida*

Oratorios

1767	*Stabat Mater*
c.1796	*The Seven Last Words*
1798	*The Creation*
1801	*The Seasons*

Sacred vocal music

1796 – 1802	Six masses for Prince Nikolaus
1796	'Missa in tempore belli'
1798	'Nelson Mass'
1799	'Theresienmesse'
1802	'Harmoniemesse'

Other vocal music

Cantatas; arias; arrangements of English and Scottish folk songs

franz joseph haydn 1732–1809

Haydn was born in Rohrau, a village near the Austrian border with Hungary, the son of a wheelwright. He began composing in the 1750s and his earliest efforts include chamber works, keyboard pieces, music for the theatre and probably his first symphony. In 1761 he entered the service of the aristocratic Esterházy family, where he spent most of his working life, though he also travelled throughout Europe. Haydn composed music in a variety of genres, including sacred works, operas, pieces for the baryton and divertimentos, but his creative genius lay in his symphonies and string quartets. By the 1770s Haydn's fame was spreading rapidly and commissions for new works came from all over Europe. Among these were the six 'Paris' symphonies, an orchestral work for Cádiz Cathedral, and concertos and notturnos for a hurdy-gurdy at the request of the king of Naples. In 1791–2 and 1794–5 he visited London, where he conducted concerts and wrote the 12 London symphonies. During his last years he wrote his two oratorios and his six masses.

Haydn was undoubtedly the most prolific of symphony composers of the Classical period, with more than 100 to his credit. The earliest were conventional in character and followed the three-movement fast-slow-fast pattern of the Italian overture, but Haydn soon adopted what was to become the standard Classical form: a first-movement allegro, a second-movement andante moderato, followed by a minuet and trio and, finally, an allegro. The works of his middle period, notably the symphonies Nos 26, 39, 45, and 49, all in a minor key, were no longer intended as pure entertainment, but embodied greater intensity of feeling.

It was, however, the 'Paris' and 'London' symphonies which were the crowning achievement of Haydn's orchestral work and showed the composer at his most inventive. The first movements were considerably expanded, variations were introduced into the slow movements and the finales displayed brilliant use of an increasingly complex rondo form (a recurrent theme alternating with new themes – ABACADA). By adding solo flute, clarinet parts and occasionally 'exotic' percussion instruments such as the triangle and cymbal, and by treating the woodwind and brass instruments more independently than before, he also succeeded in giving greater colour and depth to the sound of the orchestra. The London symphonies also exhibit signs of a maturing of the Classical style with the inclusion of contrapuntal passages (such as in Nos 95 and 101) as well as pointing towards the Romantic period and its concern with folk music. The andante of Symphony No 103 employs Croatian melodies and in general the minuet and trios of these last symphonies can be seen to adopt a more folk-like character.

Haydn proved equally innovative in the realm of chamber music. His earliest string quartets (he wrote more than 70) reflect the light-hearted rococo spirit of the age, but those composed from the late 1760s onwards show increasing originality in a genre which had previously been regarded as suitable for amateur musicians. Haydn established the four-movement pattern, with a fast opening movement in sonata form, followed by a slow movement, a minuet and trio, and lively finale. The first violin had the virtuosic role, but the other instruments, in particular the cello, were assuming greater importance. In his later quartets he displayed increasing range and depth and, like the later symphonies, they illustrate his growing interest in fusing the counterpoint of the Baroque with the Classical style. His final quartets, which contain some of his best work, are characterised by a skilful use of chromatic progressions to create emotional depth. These works are extraordinarily varied, ranging from the serious to the whimsical, yet they all testify to Haydn's confident mastery of the genre.

The best of Haydn's piano music is to be found in the sonatas and piano trios which he composed in his mature years. His output of concertos lagged far behind his other work. His Cello Concerto in D (1783) and his Trumpet Concerto in E flat (1796) are among his best in this genre. He wrote a number of operas during his stay at the Esterházy court, but his most accomplished vocal music belongs to the last period of his life. *The Seven Last Words of our Saviour on the Cross* (1785), originally commissioned as an orchestral piece, was later arranged for voices. His great oratorio *The Creation* (1798) gave marvellous expression to his own devout religious faith. This was followed in 1801 by *The Seasons*, a lesser work but delightful for its depiction of events in nature. His six masses, including the 'Nelson Mass' (1798), owe much to his knowledge of opera and his command of the symphonic style.

Major Works

Note: The 'K' followed by a number which accompanies all the entries listed here refers to their place in the chronological catalogue of Mozart's works compiled by Ludwig von Köchel

Symphonies
1773	No 25 in G minor, K183
1774	No 29 in A major, K201
1778	No 31 in D major, 'Paris', K297
1782	No 35 in D major, 'Haffner', K385
1783	No 36 in C major, 'Linz', K425
1786	No 38 in D major, 'Prague', K504
1788	No 39 in E flat major, K543
1788	No 40 in G minor, K550
1788	No 41 in C major, 'Jupiter', K551

Piano concertos
1784	No 15 in B flat major, K450
1784	No 17 in G major, K453
1784	No 18 in B flat major, K456
1784	No 19 in F major, K459
1785	No 20 in D minor, K466
1785	No 21 in C major, K467
1785	No 22 in E flat major, K482
1786	No 23 in A major, K488
1786	No 24 in C minor, K491
1786	No 25 in C major, K503
1788	No 26 in D major, 'Coronation', K537
1791	No 27 in B minor, K595

Other concertos
For violin:
c.1773	B flat, K207
1775	D major, K211
1775	G major, K216
1775	D major, K218
1775	A major, K219

For other instruments:
1774	B flat major, for bassoon, K191
1778	C major, for flute and harp, K299
1778	C major, for oboe, K314
1779	Sinfonia concertante for violin and viola, K364
c.1782 –1787	3 for horn in E flat major, K417, K447, K495
1791	A major, for clarinet, K622

Chamber music
String quartets:
1782	G major, K387
1783	D minor, K421
1783	E flat major, K428
1784	B flat major, K458
1785	A major, K464
1785	C major, K465
1786	D major, K499
1789	D major, K575
1790	B flat major, K589
1790	F major, K590

String quintets:
1787	C major, K515
1787	G minor, K516
1790	D major, K593
1791	E flat, K614
1789	Clarinet quintet in A major, K581

Keyboard music
Violin sonatas:
1778	E minor, K304
1778	D major, K306
1782	F major, K376
1781	F major, K377
1781	G major, K379
1781	E flat major, K380
1784	B flat, K454
1785	E flat, K481
1787	A major, K526

Piano sonatas:
1775	D major, K284
1778	A minor, K310
1781	D major, for two pianos, K448
1783	A major, K331
1784	C minor, K457
1785	Fantasia in C minor, K475
1786	F major, for two pianos, K497
1788	F major, K533
1789	B flat major, K570
1789	D major, K576

Piano trios:
1786	G major, K496
1786	B flat major, K502
1788	E major, K542
1788	C major, K548

Other piano music:
1784	Piano and wind quintet in E flat major, K452
1786	Rondo in D major, K485
1786	Rondo in F major, K494
1786	Trio for piano, clarinet and viola in E flat major, K498
1787	Rondo in A minor, K511
1788	Adagio in B minor, K540

Other orchestral music
1776	Serenata notturna, K239
1776	Serenade in D major, 'Haffner', K250
1779	Serenade in D major, 'Posthorn', K320
1787	Eine kleine Nachtmusik, K525
c.1781	Serenade for 13 Wind Instruments, K361
1781	Serenade in E flat major, K375
c.1782	Serenade in C minor, K388

Sacred music
1779	'Coronation' Mass in C major, K317
1780	Missa solemnis in C major, K337
1773	'Exsultate, jubilate', motet, K165
1791	'Ave verum corpus', motet, K618
1785	'Davidde penitente', oratorio, K469
1791	Requiem in D minor, K626

Operas
1769	*La finta semplice*, K51
1770	*Mitridate, re di Ponto*, K87
1775	*La finta giardinera*, K196
1775	*Il re pastore*, K208
1781	*Idomeneo*, K366
1782	*Die Entführung aus dem Serail*, K384
1786	*The Marriage of Figaro*, K492
1787	*Don Giovanni*, K527
1790	*Così fan tutte*, K588
1791	*The Magic Flute*, K620
1791	*La Clemenza di Tito*, K621

wolfgang amadeus mozart 1756–179

Mozárt was born in Salzburg, Austria, and received his early musical education from his father, Leopold, a notable violinist. Leopold devoted a his energies to furthering his son's career and in 1763 the family set off c a grand tour of western Europe. In Paris Mozart published his first sonata and in London he wrote his first symphonies. In 1768 the 12-year-old Mozart composed a one-act German singspiel, followed in 1769 by *La fint semplice*, his first attempt at opera buffa. In 1769 he also wrote an opera seria, *Mitridate, re di Ponto*.

During the early 1770s Mozart was prolific, composing symphonies, divertimentos, sacred pieces and string quartets. While staying in Vienna he came into contact with the music of Haydn, which inspired a further burst of creativity in the form of symphonies and string quartets. In 1774 he was given a court appointment in Salzburg, where he produced more symphonies, piano sonatas, violin concertos and piano concertos and wrote an opera buffa, *La finta gardiniera*. Further travels took him to Paris

...zart seated at the clavichord ...ing a concert at Versailles. By ...e age of five Mozart was already ...owing remarkable gifts both as a ...sician and a composer. Touring ...rope with his family, the young ...zart displayed his prodigious ...ents as a performer and ...proviser to audiences in musical ...ntres everywhere.

where his 'Paris' symphony was performed to some acclaim, and to Munich, where his new opera seria, *Idomeneo*, was enthusiastically received.

Mozart now took up residence in Vienna where he made a living by teaching, playing in concerts and publishing his music. At first he was quite successful and in 1782 his singspiel *Die Entführung aus dem Serail* proved popular with the Viennese public. The Vienna years were the most creative in Mozart's career. He produced some of his finest piano music, and some notable chamber works. His collaboration with the librettist Lorenzo da Ponte (1749–1838) led to the first of his three comic operas, *The Marriage of Figaro* (1786). After returning from a visit to Prague in 1787, where his latest opera, *Don Giovanni*, was enthusiastically received, Mozart was given a court appointment.

Despite a precarious financial situation, Mozart remained at the height of his creative powers, producing in 1788 his last three great symphonies in the space of seven weeks. *Così fan tutte* was given its first performance in 1790.

In 1791 he was asked to compose the score for *La Clemenza di Tito* and *The Magic Flute*, and in September he finished his Clarinet Concerto. He had earlier received a commission to write a Requiem, but had been unable to start until h had finished his other work. Mozart now drove himself into a state of exhaustio in an effort to complete the commission. He died at the age of 35, leaving the Requiem unfinished. (It was completed by his pupil, Franz Süssmayr.)

For all its apparent simplicity his music is inimitable and beneath its polished, elegant surface hides great depths of passion. Of the great composers he is the one who stands highest in the affections of music lovers the world over.

As a composer of symphonies Mozart was in many ways not as origina or innovative as Haydn. His use of the sonata form is less adventurous, always including the contrasting lyrical second subject and occasionally lacking developmental passages altogether. He absorbed the influences c other composers and his early symphonies are fairly conventional. Yet in th end he added great lustre to the Classical symphony. The Symphony No 2 in G minor, K183 (1773), and the Symphony No 29 in A major, K201 (1774 are memorable. It was, however, his last six symphonies, written during hi years in Vienna, which show his true mastery. He succeeded in investing the symphonic form with a greater intensity and a keener sense of drama than had ever been achieved before. The opening bars of the Symphony No 40 in G minor, K550, for example, have a distinctive, haunting quality of pathos. This work stands in marked contrast to the majestic grandeur the first movement of the Symphony No 41 in C major, K551.

In perfection of form and execution the Classical concerto reached its peak in the work of Mozart. Piano concertos constituted an important par of his output during his Vienna years. In his later piano concertos the mus

Left: 'Auditorium of the Old Burgtheater in Vienna', by Gustav Klimt, 1888 (the year in which it was demolished). Mozart's opera 'Così fan tutte' was first performe there in January 1790 but was relatively unsuccessful.

Right: Stage design for act I, scene i of 'The Magic Flute', for i production at the Berlin opera house on January 18, 1816. This opera contains some of Mozart's finest music.

for the solo part became increasingly a demonstration of the impressive range of sounds of which the instrument was capable. Those he composed last are among his finest works in any genre. They include No 20 in D minor, K466 (for Mozart the minor key is charged with strong emotion), No 21 in C major, K467, famous for the lyricism of its slow movement, and No 24 in C minor, K491, a work of intense pathos and tragic beauty. Among concertos for other instruments are an early masterpiece, the Sinfonia Concertante in E flat major for violin and viola, K364, violin concertos and horn concertos. The Clarinet Concerto in A major, K622, one of the last pieces of music he ever wrote, is famous for its sparkling opening allegro.

Mozart wrote more than 20 string quartets, of which the last ten are among his most accomplished. They include the Hunt Quartet in B flat, K464, with an imitation of a hunting horn used as a motif in its opening movement, and the Dissonance Quartet in C major, K465, with its tonally ambiguous introduction. No less important are his string quintets, notably the highly dramatic K515 in C major and the profoundly emotional K516 in G minor. The beauty of the Clarinet Quintet in A major was enhanced by brilliant use of the woodwind instrument.

In his early violin sonatas the piano plays a preponderant role, but in the later ones there is a balanced duet between the two instruments: K526 in A major is a fine example. His piano sonatas include the intense K310 in A minor (the first in a minor key) and K331 in A major, with its celebrated 'rondo alla turca' imitating Turkish military music. Of his seven piano trios K498 in E major, K502 in B flat major and K542 in E major are memorable. His serenades, written for a variety of combinations of instruments, embraced elements of both the symphony and the concerto. They include the Haffner Serenade, K250, the Serenade for 13 Wind Instruments, K361, and the famous *Eine kleine Nachtmusik*, K525, which was originally a string quartet. The music that Mozart wrote for the church is perhaps less memorable than his other work but it does include the

'Coronation' Mass, K317, the *Missa solemnis*, K337, the motets 'Exsultate, jubilate' and 'Ave verum corpus', K165 and K618 respectively, and of course the unfinished Requiem in D minor, K626.

Despite his ability to excel in every musical genre it is in Mozart's operas that we find the fullest flowering of his genius. He was successful in all forms of opera, including opera seria such as *Idomeneo*, his first important dramatic work, and *La Clemenza di Tito*, hurriedly composed during the last few months of his life. *Die Entführung aus dem Serail* ('The Abduction from the Seraglio'), a singspiel in the German tradition about the rescue of the heroine from the court of a Turkish pasha, found great favour with the Viennese public. In 1786 his four-act opera buffa *The Marriage of Figaro* had its first production. The first of Mozart's operatic masterpieces, it is notable for its psychological insight. Mozart's score makes effective use of duets and ensembles both to advance the action and to delineate the characters. The success of *The Marriage of Figaro* led to a commission to write *Don Giovanni*. The opera, in two acts, is described as a 'dramma giocoso' and the intensely dramatic music depicting Don Giovanni's final downfall is followed by a light-hearted sextet in the opera buffa tradition.

The plot of *Così fan tutte* ('Thus do all women'), a two-act opera buffa, is rather contrived but the melodious quality of Mozart's music is unsurpassed.

The Magic Flute can be classed as a singspiel – the libretto is in German, the recitative is spoken and the opera contains some comic scenes – but in reality it includes elements of both opera seria and opera buffa. The opera blends fairy-tale, masonic symbolism and mysticism, and this rich tapestry provides the composer with the opportunity to write music of a remarkably wide range and depth, including marches, coloratura arias, folk tunes and choral music. Yet Mozart succeeds in fusing these contrasting styles into one harmonious whole.

Mozart's music was always popular during his lifetime and, although he never suffered the decline in esteem that afflicted J.S. Bach, he was during the 19th and much of the 20th century overshadowed by Beethoven. It is only in comparatively recent times that the universality of his musical genius has been fully recognised. For all its apparent simplicity his music is inimitable and beneath its polished, elegant surface hides great depths of passion. Of the great composers he is the one who stands highest in the affections of music lovers the world over.

From Classical to Romantic

Towards the end of the 18th century a group of German writers began to use the word 'Romantic' to describe a new movement in literature, which they wished to distinguish from the prevailing Classicism. Their opposition to Classicism was based on a belief in the superiority of emotion over reason as the source of all truth and the supreme importance of the imagination. The concept rapidly spread to the other arts. In music it came to mean a preference for the expression of personal feelings and a loosening of the restraints imposed by the established forms. The first stirrings of Romanticism in music can be seen in Beethoven's broadening of the traditional structures of the Classical era to enable him to express his own emotional exuberance, in the lyricism of Schubert's songs and in the operas of Carl Maria von Weber. In what was to become a characteristic trait of the Romantic era, both Schubert and Weber drew upon themes from folklore and the world of fantasy for their music.

Among the important composers of this transitional period was the Italian pianist and composer Muzio Clementi (1752–1832). Clementi's sonatas (he wrote over 70) and other keyboard music were much admired by Beethoven. He was also the author of *Gradus ad Parnassum* (1817), a famous collection of keyboard studies. Another piano virtuoso was the Austrian Johann Nepomuk Hummel (1778–1837), a pupil of Mozart. He is best known for his piano sonatas, piano concertos and chamber music. His work, notable for its elegance and clarity of texture, looks forward to that of Romantic composers such as Chopin and Mendelssohn.

Below left: Portrait of Luigi Cherubini, by Jean-Auguste Ingres, 1842. Cherubini, like a number of Italian composers, achieved success abroad. His operas, though Classical in style, looked forward to the development of French grand opera in the Romantic period.

Below right: Portrait of Carl Maria von Weber by Ferdinand Schimon. Weber took up the post of conductor of opera at Prague in 1813 and it was there that he began to formulate his ideas for a true German opera imbued with the ideals of the Romantic movement.

The illustrations above show set designs for the dramatic Wolf's Glen scene in Weber's opera 'Der Freischütz'. A supreme example of the macabre in music, its first performance, in Berlin in 1821, was a triumph for Weber, helped not only by its sensational setting but also by the beauty of the music.

Luigi Cherubini (1760–1842) began his career by writing sacred music but went on to compose operas, two of which, *Médée* (1797) and *Les Deux Journées* (1800), were notably successful and the latter, with its 'rescue' theme, influenced Beethoven's *Fidelio*. In his later years Cherubini turned to church music once again. His Requiem in C minor, in particular, was admired by Beethoven. Cherubini's operas remained eminently Classical in style, but their remarkable dramatic power paved the way for the French grand opera of the later 19th century.

Another opera composer whose work stands on the threshold of Romanticism was the German Carl Maria von Weber (1786–1826). He achieved his first real success with his one-act opera, *Abu Hassan* (1811). Six years later he began work on *Der Freischütz*. Taking its subject from German folklore and partly set in a mysterious and menacing forest, the opera features both ordinary village people and elements of the supernatural. Its first performance, in Berlin in 1821, was a triumph for Weber. It marked the beginning of a German national opera freed from Italian and French influences. Weber's notable contribution to keyboard music includes the famous *Invitation to the Dance*, the *Konzertstück* for piano and orchestra and four piano sonatas.

John Field (1782–1837) was born in Dublin and published his first piano sonatas in 1801. He eventually settled in St Petersburg, where he was to enjoy considerable popularity as a virtuoso performer. His compositions from this period include seven piano concertos, but he is best remembered for his nocturnes which display a remarkable originality. The mood of melancholy and the feeling of intimacy which pervade these shorter pieces in some ways anticipate the work of Chopin.

Major Works

Symphonies

1800	No 1 in C major, op. 21
1802	No 2 in D major, op. 36
1803	No 3 in E flat major, 'Eroica', op. 55
1806	No 4 in B flat major, op. 60
1808	No 5 in C minor, op. 67
1808	No 6 in F major, 'Pastoral', op. 68
1812	No 7 in A major, op.92
1824	No 8 in F major, op. 93; No 9 in D minor, 'Choral', op. 125

Piano concertos

1795	No 1 in C major, op. 15
1798	No 2 in B flat major, op. 19
1800	No 3 in C minor, op. 37
1806	No 4 in G major, op. 58
1809	No 5 in E flat major, 'Emperor', op. 73

Violin concertos

1806	Violin Concerto in D major, op. 61
1804	Triple Concerto in C major for violin, piano and cello, op. 56

Other orchestral music

Romances for violin and orchestra:

1807	*Coriolan*, overture, op. 62

Leonora overtures:

1807	No 1, op. 138
1805	No 2, op. 72A
1806	No 3, op. 72B
1822	*Consecration of the House*, overture, op. 124

Piano sonatas

1799	No 8 in C minor, 'Pathétique', op. 13
1801	No 14 in C sharp minor, 'Moonlight', op. 27 no 2
1804	No 21 in C major, 'Waldstein', op. 53
1805	No 23 in F minor, 'Appassionata', op. 57
1810	No 26 in E flat major, 'Les Adieux', op. 81A
1818	No 29 in B flat major, 'Hammerklavier', op. 106
1822	No 32 in C minor, op. 111

Other piano music

Bagatelles:

1802	Op. 33
1822	Op. 119
1824	Op. 126

Variations:

1802	Op. 34
1802	Op. 35
1809	Opus 76
1823	'Diabelli Variations', op. 120

Chamber music

String quartets:

1800	G major and C minor, op. 18, nos 2 and 4
1806	F major, E minor, C major, 'Razumovsky', op. 59, nos 1, 2 and 3
1825	E flat major, op. 127
1825	A minor, op. 132
1826	B flat major, op. 130
1826	C sharp minor, op. 131
1826	F major, op.135
1826	Grosse Fuge in B flat major, op. 133

Violin sonatas:

1801	No 5 in F major, 'Spring', op. 24
1803	No 9 in A minor, 'Kreutzer', op. 47

Piano trios:

1808	D major, 'Ghost', op. 70 no 1
1811	B flat major, 'Archduke', op. 97

Dramatic music

1801	*The Creatures of Prometheus*, op. 43, ballet
1805	*Fidelio*, opera (rev. 1806 and 1814)

Incidental music

1810	*Egmont*, op. 84
1811	*The Ruins of Athens*, op. 113
1811	*King Stephen*, op.117

Vocal music

1803	*Christus am Ohlberge*, oratorio, op. 85
1823	*Missa solemnis* (Mass in D major), op. 123
1816	*An die ferne Geliebte*, song cycle, op. 98

Engraving of Ludwig van Beethoven. Despite his notorious abruptness of manner and refusal to behave with deference to those of higher birth, Beethoven successfully established himself a freelance musician and a composer of the first order.

Beethoven was born in Bonn, Germany, and received his earliest musical education from his father who, aware of his son's promise as a pianist, tried unsuccesssfully to turn him into a child prodigy. In 1787 Beethoven moved to Vienna to study with Mozart, but returned to Bonn when he heard that his mother was dying. In 1792 he went back to Vienna, where he was to spend the rest of his life, and began composition lessons with Haydn. However, the two men proved temperamentally incompatible and Beethoven preferred to pursue his studies with the composer and theorist Johann Albrechtsberger (1736–1809) and with Antonio Salieri (1750–1825). In 1795 he made his public debut, playing his Piano Concerto No 2 in B flat, and rapidly acquired a reputation as a piano virtuoso. By the end of 1802, which is usually referred to as his early period, Beethoven had composed his first two symphonies, his first three piano concertos and a considerable amount of piano music, including the 'Pathéthique' and 'Moonlight' sonatas, and his first group of string trios and quartets.

In 1798 he experienced the first symptoms of approaching deafness and by 1802 he realised that his impaired hearing was a permanent condition which would inevitably become worse. Facing his affliction with fortitude, he embarked upon his remarkably creative second period. His Symphony No 3, the 'Eroica', was completed in 1804 and the 'Waldstein' sonata appeared the same year, followed by the 'Appassionata' in 1805. In 1805–6 he wrote his only opera, *Fidelio*, and his three 'Razumovsky' quartets. In 1806 there appeared his violin concerto, his fourth piano concerto and his Symphony No 4. To 1808 belong the Symphony No 5 and the Symphony No 6, the 'Pastoral'. The Symphonies Nos 7 and 8 were completed in 1812 and the triumph of the 7th in particular firmly established Beethoven's reputation as the greatest composer of the age.

From about 1815 Beethoven entered the third period of his creative life. He was plagued by ill health but nevertheless continued to compose. His output was now much smaller, yet the music of these later years is undoubtedly some of his finest. It includes the 'Hammerklavier' Sonata (1818), the *Missa solemnis* and the Diabelli Variations (both 1823), the Symphony No 9, the 'Choral' (1824), and his final quartets (1825–6).

Beethoven's First Symphony has the traditional four-movement structure of the Classical work and is reminiscent of Haydn. It is notable for its use of woodwind and the minuet in the third movement is a scherzo in all but name. The Second Symphony, conceived on a much larger scale, is characterised by the long coda in the first movement and the third movement is now called a scherzo. The revolutionary Third Symphony, the 'Eroica', is twice the length of most previous symphonies. The first part is remarkable for the use of a relatively simple theme constructed from the notes of the E flat major triad and its subsequent continuous development that expands the movement to a monumental 20 minutes in length. His Fourth Symphony is comparatively light-hearted and cheerful, standing in complete contrast to the Fifth, with its relentless four-note motif and final

Facsimile of a page of music from a 19th-century biography of Beethoven by Anton Schindler. Beethoven always strove for perfection in whatever he composed and for many he epitomises the Romantic artist.

triumphant change of key to C major. The Sixth Symphony, the quasi-programmatic 'Pastoral', which, unusually, is in five movements, celebrates the composer's love of nature. The Seventh Symphony is an exuberant work, distinguished by the insistent, march-like rhythm of its second movement and the inspired, headlong rush of the finale. The Eighth Symphony is nearer to the traditional symphonic form but has a particularly stirring last movement. The Symphony No 9, the 'Choral', o of the composer's finest achievements, marked a turning-point in the history of the symphony not simply because it introduced a chorus and soloists into the last movement, a setting of the poet Schiller's 'Ode to Joy', but because of the vast scope of the whole work.

Beethoven's first two piano concertos were composed during his ear Vienna years. They were Classical in style and the No 1 in C major shows signs of future promise. However, it is not until the No 3 in C minor, with its long, beautiful slow movement, that the composer begins to display maturity in both technique and emotional depth. The supremely lyrical Piano Concerto No 4 in G and the magnificent No 5 In E flat, the 'Emperor', retain the Classical form while enlarging the expressive range Both are notable for the introduction of the solo instrument before the exposition of the main theme by the orchestra. The 'Emperor' was not a first received with great enthusiasm and took some time to establish its A similar fate befell the Violin Concerto – it had to wait until the mid-19t century to achieve the recognition it deserved.

In Beethoven's 32 piano sonatas we can trace the development of his creative genius, since he often used the piano as a vehicle for new ideas which later found their fullest expression in another genre. The first were written in the 1790s and the majority had been composed by the end of 1802. A number of his early sonatas are in four movements, the minuet being sometimes replaced by the scherzo. The sonatas of this period include the No 8 in C minor, the 'Pathétique', with its dramatic repeated slow-movement introduction, and the No 14 in C sharp minor, the 'Moonlight', imbued with a restrained romantic introspection. Later sonatas include the No 21 in C major, the 'Waldstein', the No 23 in F minor, the 'Appassionata', the No 26 in E flat major, 'Les Adieux', and th vast 'Hammerklavier' (No 29 in B flat major).

Although Beethoven remained faithful to the general structure of the sonata, he increased both its length and scope to almost symphonic proportions. The No 32 in C minor, his last, has only two movements and ends with a long set of variations which show the composer at the height his powers. His last piece for the piano alone was the 'Diabelli Variations in which he completely transformed a rather uninteresting waltz into a work of wonderful complexity.

Beethoven's string quartets are as important in the development of chamber music as his symphonies are in the evolution of orchestral music. The earliest ones of Opus 18 show the influence of Haydn's later works, yet already bear the individual stamp of the composer. Of

particular interest are the No 2 in G major and the No 4 in C minor. The three composed in 1806 (Opus 59) demonstrate both Beethoven's breadth of vision and his skilful use of the technical resources of the piano. In his last five quartets, composed during 1825–6, he added immeasurably to the range of ideas that could be expressed in music, introducing intense chromatic and dissonant passages not found in his earlier quartets, and in so doing created works of sublime beauty.

His chamber works for violin and piano include the Violin Sonata No 5 in F major, the 'Spring', a graceful and melodious early work, the No 9 in A major, the 'Kreutzer', which anticipates the expansiveness of the late piano sonatas, and the magnificent Piano Trio in B flat major, the 'Archduke'. In the last period of his life Beethoven developed an interest in fugal techniques. His late piano sonatas and string quartets include a number which are fugal in texture, for example, the finale of the 'Hammerklavier' sonata. The 'Grosse Fuge', Opus 133, a long and elaborate masterpiece, was originally the finale of the String Quartet in B flat, Opus 130.

Beethoven's first venture into the theatre was his suite of ballet music, *The Creatures of Prometheus* (1801). His only opera, *Fidelio*, was not well received at first. In his vocal music Beethoven never achieved the success that attended his instrumental work and the writing of *Fidelio* proved an onerous task. It was extensively revised before a final version was staged in 1814. His best known overtures include *Coriolan* (1807), the three *Leonora* overtures (1805–7) and *Consecration of the House* (1822). He also wrote a song cycle, *An die ferne Geliebte*, and many delightful individual songs, all of which are overshadowed, however, by the *Missa Solemnis* (1823), which demonstrates his mastery of choral music.

Beethoven's influence on the music of the 19th century was to be immense. For many he epitomised the Romantic artist: a free spirit burdened with personal affliction who used the forms of Classical music to convey his intensely personal vision. Beethoven's great achievement was that, although he worked within the restraints of the musical genres as they had been developed by his predecessors, he pushed them to their limits in order to give expression to his deepest emotions and in doing so transformed them into something entirely new.

A portrait of Schubert at the piano painted by Gustav Klimt in 1899. The work was destroyed in World War II. Schubert showed an extraordinary aptitude for music from an early age and produced a remarkable number of compositio during his short life, the best remembered being his songs.

franz schubert
1797–1828

Born in Liechtenthal, near Vienna, the young Schubert won a choral scholarship which secured him a place in the imperial court chapel in Vienna and a musical education at the Konvikt College under such tutors as Antonio Salieri. Among his early works are 'Gretchen am Spinnrade', two symphonies (including the ever-popular fifth), a Mass in C major and some rather less successful operas. In 1816 he went to live with a friend, Franz von Schober, through whom he met the baritone singer J.M. Vogl, wh introduced Schubert's songs to a wider public. His songs at this time includ 'Der Tod und Das Mädchen' and he also wrote his first piano sonatas.

In 1818 he began composing the operetta *Die Zwillingsbrüder*. In 1819 h wrote the famous 'Trout' Quintet and the Piano Sonata in A major. The composer's reputation was now steadily growing and wealthy admirers gav private concert parties devoted to his music. Nevertheless, he never managed to appear on the public concert platform, failed to achieve any success with his operas and consequently remained permanently short of money. In 1822 he began work on his Symphony No 8 in B minor ('the Unfinished'), completed an opera, *Alfonso und Estrella*, which was rejected, and wrote the 'Wanderer' Fantasy for piano. At the end of that year he contracted syphilis, an event which inevitably cast a blight over the rest of his short life. His output, however, remained steady and in 1823 he produced the song cycle *Die schöne Müllerin* and the incidental music for th play *Rosamunde*. The following year saw the composition of two fine string quartets, in A minor and D minor respectively, and the Octet in F major. His last and finest orchestral work, the Symphony No 9 in C major, was probab

composed in 1825. During the last two years of his life, with his physical
condition rapidly declining, Schubert wrote some of his greatest music.

Schubert was a remarkably prolific composer who excelled in almost
every genre but he is best remembered for his songs in which he revealed
his outstanding ability to create beautiful melodies. In his hands the
traditional German lied was transformed into an art form in which the
human voice and the piano accompaniment played an equal role. At ages
17–19 he wrote 'Gretchen am Spinnrade', 'Erlkönig', 'Heidenröslein' and
'Der Wanderer'. Basing his songs on lyric poems, Schubert matched words
and music perfectly, using the piano to marvellous effect. His total output
of songs was vast – over 600 – and 1817 was a particularly fruitful year,
with the dark-toned 'Der Tod und das Mädchen' ('Death and the Maiden'),
'Die Forelle' ('The Trout') and 'An die Musik' – all supremely lyrical pieces.
The great song cycles of his mature years include *Die schöne Müllerin*, its
sequel *Die Winterreise*, in which the hero mourns his lost love in a bleak
winter landscape, and the posthumously published *Schwanengesang*.

Schubert wrote a total of nine symphonies in his short career as a
composer. All are regularly Classical in form, with some innovative
features, and the No 5 in B flat major (1816) is the best of his youthful
works. The No 8 in B minor, 'The Unfinished', stands in sharp contrast to
the previous ones. The music has a strong emotional appeal and the two
movements which Schubert completed display an impressive command of
orchestration. 'The Great' C major Symphony, his orchestral masterpiece,
was conceived on a vast scale and is the most profound of the composer's

symphonic works. The manuscript lay undiscovered for some years and the symphony received its first public performance in 1839, with Felix Mendelssohn conducting.

Schubert's early chamber music is reminiscent of Haydn and Mozart but his own individual style soon becomes apparent. The 'Trout' Quintet o 1819, which incorporates a set of variations based on his song 'Die Forelle', has a particularly beautiful slow movement. The so-called Quartettsatz in C minor (1820), an unfinished quartet, marks the beginnings of the more mature style which was apparent in the String Quartet in A minor and the String Quartet in D minor (also known as 'Death and the Maiden' because it contained variations on the song of tha

Schubert is best remembered for his songs in which he revealed his outstanding ability to create beautiful melodies. In his hands the traditional German lied was transformed into an art form in which the human voice and the piano accompaniment played an equal role.

name) of 1824. In this year he also wrote the lyrical Octet in F major for strings and wind instruments. In 1826 appeared the important Quartet in G major and in 1828, shortly before his death, he completed the sublime Quintet in C major, generally considered his greatest chamber work.

A German woodcut, c.1840,
depicting the theme of Schubert's
song 'Erlkönig'. The song is based
on the story of a child whose soul is
snatched away during a ride
through a stormy night. It is on
songs such as this that Schubert's
main fame rests.

Among Schubert's most important piano music is the Fantasy in C
major (1822), a four-movement work, with variations based on his song
'Der Wanderer', and notable for its recurring theme. Schubert's most
memorable piano music is, however, his sonatas, of which he wrote more
than 20. They include the magnificent 'Grand Duo' in C major for two
pianos (1824) and the Piano Sonata in G major (1826). The three sonatas
of 1828, in C minor, A major and B flat major respectively, which are on a
larger scale than his previous ones, stand comparison with those of
Beethoven. Other piano music, all belonging to his late period, includes
the six short 'Moments musicaux', various impromptus and the Fantasie in
F minor for two pianos (1828).

Schubert and Beethoven both lived and worked in Vienna and Schubert
died just over a year after the older composer. Yet their careers ran on
entirely different paths. Beethoven was lionised by his contemporaries and
has always retained his high position in the musical hierarchy. Schubert
was known to only a small circle of people during his lifetime and very
little of his work was either played or published: the Quintet in C major, for
example, had to wait more than 20 years for its first performance.
Schubert, like Beethoven, stands on the threshold of the Romantic era, his
art still deeply rooted in the traditions of the Classical era, yet his long,
lyrical melodies indicating his affinity with the latter period. His music, in
particular his songs, chamber works and piano music, was to have a
strong influence upon succeeding composers and when he died at the age
of 31 he had in his last years produced work of astonishing maturity.

romanticism

e cross in the mountains', by the ling German Romantic artist par David Friedrich. The artists his period ranked imagination ve reason. The term 'romantic' erived from the word 'romance', ory or poem of the Middle Ages, a trend towards all things dieval manifested itself in all as of art, including music.

After the defeat of Napoleon in 1815, Europe managed to achieve a period of stability which lasted until 1848, when a wave of unrest swept across the continent. The revolts were put down, but the tide of nationalism remained a force to be reckoned with. By the early 1870s both Germany and Italy had achieved unification. Russia's autocratic rulers resisted any attempts at social and political reform. The newly industrialised European states sought to increase their wealth by founding colonies in Africa and Asia, and in the New World the United States was fast becoming one of the largest and richest nations on earth.

9th – 20th century

The transition between Classicism and Romanticism was marked not so much by a drastic change in musical style but by the growing importance of content over form. The emphasis in the Romantic period was on expression, individuality and the fantastic in music rather than on clarity of structure. Artists in all fields looked to the strange, nightmarish and mystical for inspiration. The medieval period held a particular attraction.

One of the most important results of these new artistic interests was that music was not often seen as being an autonomous creative medium. The extra-musical in the guise of programmes and sung texts dominates Romantic music and it is during this period that the relationship between words and music reached its most potent and mutually reflective form. Works that are programmatic in nature, that is descriptive, narrative or simply just suggestive of something outside the music, abound in the 19th century. Mendelssohn's overtures, Berlioz's *Symphonie fantastique* and especially the newest genre, that of the symphonic poem, exemplified in the work of Liszt, Richard Strauss and Saint-Säens, are examples of the Romantic tendency towards the programmatic. Programmaticism is also evident in the piano music of the Romantic age, although on a much smaller scale. Titles such as 'nocturne', 'intermezzo' and 'interlude' convey a Romantic flavour.

The forms of the Classical period were still widely used during the 19th century, but it soon became evident that such forms could not remain

Right: Engraving of Mephistopheles in flight, one of a series of 17 illustrations by Eugène Delacroix for Berlioz's 'The Damnation of Faust'. The Faust legend, about a 16th-century German who sold his soul to the devil, was ideal source material for Romantic composers.

Below: Portrait of Johann Wolfgang von Goethe, painted c.1790 by Johann Tischbein. Goethe's play 'Faust' formed the basis for many musical compositions, including an opera by Charles Gounod and a symphony by Liszt, and Hugo Wolf used many of Goethe's poems as the texts to his songs.

intact under the increasing pressure of the Romantic expressive content The types of music composed became polarised towards either the very largest forms (symphony and opera) or the smallest and most intimate (works for solo piano). Symphonies were becoming longer, demanded greater instrumental forces and often included a programme or sung tex Mendelssohn's Violin Concerto and Schumann's 'Scottish' Symphony allow movements to run on into one another and also show evidence of t use of recurring material across an entire work.

Melody had become one of the most important features of Romantic music and so it is not surprising that themes rather than key schemes we now used to hold together a piece of often considerable length. Berlioz called the recurring theme or motif an 'idée fixe' while Wagner referred t it as a 'leitmotiv'. The idée fixe in Berlioz's *Symphonie fantastique* is usec to represent the heroine of the piece and is used in an aria-like fashion. Tchaikovsky exploited the recurring 'cyclical' theme in his last symphoni while Mahler used this technique less frequently, including instead large amounts of sung text or relying on the programmatic nature of his musi to hold these huge symphonic structures together. Wagner broke down t traditional 'number' structure of opera in order to accommodate his nev style of endless, arioso-type melody. The music is a complex of leitmotif representing the different character and events in the story and often constitutes the greater part of the musical material of the opera.

Finally, tonality, the very foundation of serious music of the previous 200 years, began to break down as a result of the increasing chromatic harmonies and the delaying of cadence points. On a larger scale, entire works no longer started and ended in the same key, a tendency that can seen in most of Mahler's symphonies. Chromatic harmonies abound in the piano music of Chopin and especially in the later works of Liszt. His *Nuages gris* makes abundant use of the augmented triad which occurs in strange progressions. Wagner dealt a fatal blow to tonality in *Tristan und Isolde*. Constant modulation, chromaticism and a certain ambiguity as to the nature of harmonic progression and key effectively dissolve the function of tonality. Similarly, in Richard Strauss's *Salome* and *Elektra* the abundance of dissonance, modulation and even polytonality point to the end of an era and the shape of things to come.

Public concerts

The very first public concerts took place in London in the late 17th century. The idea soon spread to France. Paris acquired its first proper concert hall in 1811 and in 1828 saw the formation of the Société des Concerts du Conservatoire which promoted a series of successful concerts. The Philharmonic Society of London (later the Royal Philharmonic Society) was established in 1813. Previously most music had been performed in church, in theatres or in the houses of the nobility. However, aristocratic patronage was now in sharp decline, and the popularity of concert-going among the newly prosperous middle classes together with the increasing size of orchestras led to a demand for larger concert halls. Inevitably the taste of the new audiences was to be to some extent reflected in the kind of music composed.

Illustration of the Vauxhall sure gardens from ermann's 'Microcosm of don', published in 1809. The khall gardens provided concerts opular music and other forms of oor entertainment.

Right: Portrait of Franz Liszt by Henri von Heinrich, 1839. Liszt was the supreme exponent of the new genre of the symphonic poem. They were not intended as musical descriptions of their subject matter, rather the subject is a jumping-off point for an exploration of different ideas and emotions.

Below: Silhouette of the virtuoso violinist Nicolò Paganini, playing the instrument with characteristic exuberance. Paganini played in many European cities, and was idolised by audiences in the increasingly popular concert halls. His influence on the Romantic composers, especially Franz Liszt, was considerable.

Composer and virtuoso

Another consequence of the increasing importance of the middle classes in the world of music was that the composer was becoming a free agent. Until the end of the 18th century any musician who wanted to succeed would have found it necessary to seek a place with either a royal court or an aristocratic family. Haydn was perhaps the last great composer whose career followed the traditional pattern, but in later life he was able to earn a substantial income from his freelance activities. Mozart tried in vain to secure a court appointment and was forced to rely on the proceeds of subscription concerts. Beethoven was the first composer to be more or less independent of patronage and derived his income from a variety of sources, including public concerts and sales of his music.

If Beethoven in many ways typified the Romantic concept of the artist as hero, the career of the violinist and composer Nicolò Paganini (1782–1840) illustrated another phenomenon of the era – the cult of the virtuoso. The term had originally referred to musicians who pursued a solo career, but by the beginning of the 19th century it was being applied to performers who displayed outstanding technical skill. Paganini, who was born in Genoa, Italy, made his first appearance on the concert platform 1793. After touring in his native country he later achieved remarkable success in Vienna, Paris and London. Paganini's remarkable dexterity as violinist (notably his use of harmonics and pizzicato), his wild appearance, extravagant gestures and the emotional resonance of the music he played led to beliefs that he was endowed with satanic powers.

Opera in France

By the early years of the 19th century Paris had established itself as the main centre of opera in Europe. It was also to be the setting for the appearance of a peculiarly French institution, the so-called 'grand opera', a large-scale work in which the dramatic effects were as important as the music. It was designed to appeal to a new class of opera-goers who delighted in the lavish entertainment offered. Opera orchestras were enlarged and given a more prominent part in the development of the action.

The German-Jewish composer Giacomo Meyerbeer (1791–1864) began to enjoy success after moving to Italy, notably with *Il crociato in Egitto* (1824). His first French opera, *Robert le Diable* (1831), blending medievalism and the supernatural, was very popular. His second, *Les Huguenots* (1836), proved a triumph and firmly established his position as the leading exponent of grand opera. Three further operas, *Le Prophète* (1849), *L'Etoile du Nord* (1854) and *L'Africaine*, first performed in 1865 after the composer's death and the most spectacular of Meyerbeer's works, were also great successes, demonstrating his rich orchestration and his skill in the deployment of vast ensembles.

Contemporaries of Meyerbeer included Daniel Auber (1782–1871) and Fromental Halévy (1799–1862). In 1828 Auber composed *La Muette de Portici* ('The Dumb Girl of Portici'), whose revolutionary theme, striking effects and impressive crowd scenes were an important contribution to the development of grand opera. However, Auber was also the leading comic opera composer of his day. His *Fra Diavolo* (1830) and *Le Cheval de bronze* (1835) combined humour with tuneful melodies. Halévy's greatest work is the dramatic *La Juive* (1835).

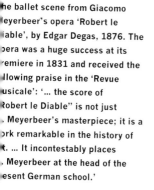

The ballet scene from Giacomo Meyerbeer's opera 'Robert le Diable', by Edgar Degas, 1876. The opera was a huge success at its premiere in 1831 and received the following praise in the 'Revue musicale': '... the score of "Robert le Diable" is not just Meyerbeer's masterpiece; it is a work remarkable in the history of art. ... It incontestably places Meyerbeer at the head of the present German school.'

Italian opera

In the early 19th century opera continued to be Italy's most important contribution to music, although even here the country's musical genius had been to some extent eclipsed by the remarkable achievements of the Viennese school. A notable figure in the evolution of Italian serious opera was a German, Johann Simon Mayr (1763–1845), who spent most of his life in Italy. He composed more than 70 operas and was to have a particular influence on the work of Gaetano Donizetti. The tradition of Italian comic opera, opera buffa, was, however, to be completely transformed by the genius of Gioacchino Rossini (1792–1868).

Rossini's first comic opera, *La Cambiale di matrimonio* ('The Marriage Contract', 1810), was performed in Venice, which was also the venue for his first serious work, *Tancredi* (1813), an immediate success. This was followed in the same year by the equally popular comedy, *The Italian Girl in Algiers*. *The Barber of Seville* (1816), which featured the same characters as Mozart's *The Marriage of Figaro*, was not at first well received, but eventually established itself as one of the greatest comic operas. In 1817 appeared *La Cenerentola* and *The Thieving Magpie*. In *Moses in Egypt* (1818) and *Semiramide* (1823) Rossini turned to more serious subjects. He moved to Paris in 1824, where he wrote his comic opera *Le Comte Ory* (1828) and the epic *William Tell* (1829). A large-scale work and Rossini's supreme achievement, it marked the beginning of grand opera in France. The enthusiasm and excitement of Rossini's music, his sparkling humour and his gift for melody have ensured his place as a master of comic opera.

Gaetano Donizetti (1797–1848) was born in Bergamo, Italy. Beginning in 1818, he wrote a series of operas which showed the influence of Rossini. In 1830 he achieved his first real international success with *Anna Bolena*. Subsequent operas included serious works such as *Lucrezia Borgia* (1833) and *Lucia di Lammermoor* (1835), the latter probably Donizetti's finest opera. The choice of subject matter showed the Romantic enthusiasm for historical themes treated in a melodramatic fashion. In 1838 Donizetti settled in Paris. He had already shown a talent for comic opera with *L'Elisir d'amore* (1832). *La Fille du Régiment* (1840) won the acclaim of French audiences and *Don Pasquale* (1843) stands comparison with Rossini's best work in this lighter vein. A prolific composer, Donizetti had the ability, like Rossini, to create melody and in his dramatic powers foreshadowed the work of Verdi.

Vincenzo Bellini (1801–35) was born at Catania, Sicily, into a musical family. He began composing operas at an early age, achieving international recognition with *Il Pirata*, which had its premiere at La Scala, Milan, in 1827. Further success came with *I Capuletti ed i Montecchi* (1830), based on Shakespeare's *Romeo and Juliet*, and *La Sonnambula* and *Norma* (both 1831), helped in no small measure by the efforts of Bellini's librettist, the dramatist Felice Romani (1788–1865). In 1834 Bellini settled in Paris where he wrote *I Puritani*, another triumph. Bellini's operas have a basically serious plot, often lightened by a sentimental Romanticism and an occasional happy ending. He is remembered for the lyricism of his music and the simplicity of his vocal line.

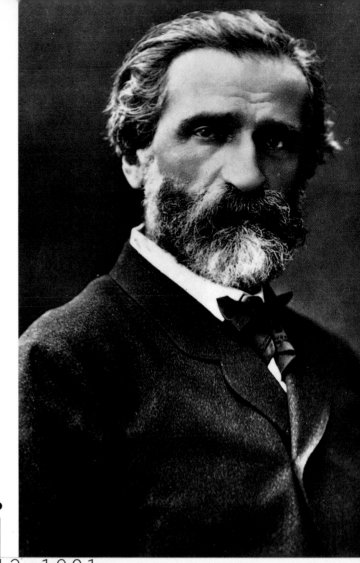

giuseppe **verdi**
1813-1901

Major Works

Operas

1839	*Oberto, Conte di San Bonifacio*
1840	*Un Giorno di regno*
1842	*Nabucco*
1842	*I Lombardi alla prima crociata*
1844	*Ernani*
1847	*Macbeth*
1849	*Luisa Miller*
1851	*Rigoletto*
1853	*Il Trovatore*
1853	*La Traviata*
1855	*Les Vêpres siciliennes*
1857	*Simon Boccanegra*
1859	*Un Ballo in maschera*
1862	*La Forza del Destino*
1857	*Don Carlos*
1871	*Aida*
1887	*Otello*
1893	*Falstaff*

Choral music

1874	*Requiem Mass*
1889	*Ave Maria*
1896	*Stabat Mater*

Verdi was born in the village of Le Roncole, near Parma, the son of an innkeeper. His first opera, *Oberto*, was produced at the La Scala opera house in Milan in 1839. Its modest success led to a commission to write three more operas. The first of these was a failure, but *Nabucco* (1842), whose story of Hebrew captivity in Babylon mirrored Italy's struggle for independence against Austria, established the composer's reputation in his own country. Further operas, including *I Lombardi* ('The Lombards', 1843) and *Giovanna d'Arco* ('Joan of Arc', 1845), were thinly disguised appeals to patriotic feelings. *Macbeth* (1847), with a dominant role for Lady Macbeth, was a more mature work than its predecessors. *Rigoletto* (1851), Verdi's first real masterpiece, includes the well-known aria 'La donna è mobile'. This was followed in 1853 by the notably melodious *Il Trovatore* and also *La Traviata*, in which Violetta, a courtesan dying of consumption, sacrifices true love at the request of her lover's father. Treating a subject considered inappropriate for opera, it was not first successful.

Les Vêpres siciliennes (1855), which had its premiere in Paris, marke the composer's debut in grand opera. *Simon Boccanegra* (1857) and *Un Ballo in maschera* (1859) show Verdi's increasing skill in conveying depth of characterisation. *La Forza del destino* (1862) mixed comedy and tragedy. *Don Carlos* (1867), another essay in grand opera, displayed both Verdi's gift for creating scenes of great dramatic power and his skill in orchestrating music for the theatre. *Aida* (1871), which was commission

ove left: Portrait of Giuseppe
rdi, c.1874. Verdi transformed
lian opera, successfully
egrating the dramatic and
sical elements into a single
rk of art. From humble origins,
rdi became the leading Italian
mposer of the 19th century.

ove right: The interior of
 Scala opera house in Milan, by
ancesco Durelli, 1819. Many of
rdi's operas were premiered
ere to great success, from his
st, 'Oberto', to his last, 'Falstaff'.

to mark the opening of the Suez Canal, is the story of the warrior
Radames, who is loved by both an Egyptian princess and an Ethiopian
slave. With its setting in ancient Egypt and its theme the conflict between
love and duty to one's country, it combined elaborate spectacle with fine
character delineation and richly melodious music.

Verdi remains the leading figure of 19th-century Italian opera: his genius lies in his fusion of the elements of music and drama into a single unified whole.

In his last two operas, *Otello* (1887) and *Falstaff* (1893), Verdi once
more found inspiration in the plays of Shakespeare. In *Otello* Verdi deals
with the themes of evil and jealousy and his musical score skilfully
reflects the development of both character and action. *Otello* is
generally considered the composer's tragic masterpiece. His last opera,
Falstaff, was a triumphant return to comedy after his failure with
Un Giorno di regno over 50 years earlier. In his later years Verdi also wrote
some sacred music, including a *Requiem Mass* (1874) and a *Stabat Mater*
(1897). Verdi remains the leading figure of 19th-century Italian opera:
his genius lies in his fusion of the elements of music and drama into a
single unified whole.

Wagner was born in Leipzig, Germany, and began composing at the age of 16. His first symphony was performed in 1832. His first opera, *Die Feen* ('The Fairies'), was not staged, but a second one, *Das Liebesverbot*, was given a single, disastrous performance in 1836. However, *Rienzi*, completed in 1840 received a triumphant premiere at Dresden in 1842. *Der fliegende Holländer* ('The Flying Dutchman') had its first performance in 1843. It marked a departure from the tradition of grand opera as exemplified in *Rienzi* and was less successful. Two more operas followed: *Tannhäuser* (1845) and *Lohengrin* (first performance, 1850), which includes the famous bridal chorus used in weddings. The setting of both operas was medieval Germany, with Wagner, as always, writing the librettos as well as the music. He was now moving toward a style of opera in which recitative and aria were no longer rigorously separated but formed part of a continuous melodic texture.

Implicated in the revolutionary activities of 1848, he was forced to flee Germany. He spent most of his exile in Switzerland and published his far-reaching theories on opera. He also began work on his great opera cycle *Der Ring des Nibelungen*, which occupied him for more than 20 years. A love affair with the wife of a rich benefactor was the inspiration for *Tristan und Isolde*. This massive work, which explored the Romantic concept of a man redeemed by the love of a woman, was the first opera to which he applied the term 'music drama'. The music in *Tristan* is intensely chromatic, and foreshadows the complete rejection of harmonic principles of a later age.

richard wagner 1813–1883

Major Works

Operas

1842	*Rienzi*
1843	*Der fliegende Holländer*
1845	*Tannhäuser*
1850	*Lohengrin*
1865	*Tristan und Isolde*
1868	*Die Meistersinger von Nürnberg*
1869	*Das Rheingold*
1870	*Die Walküre*
1876	*Siegfried*
1876	*Götterdämerung*
1882	*Parsifal*

Orchestral music

1870	*Siegfried Idyll*
1871	*Kaisermarsch*

Songs

1857–8	*Wesendonk Lieder*

Richard Wagner, c.1871. Wagner introduction of leitmotivs and the concept of music dramas, with words and music welded together into an integrated work of great emotional intensity, make him the chief exponent of German Romantic music and one of the most important innovators in the art of opera, on a par with Mozart and his contemporary, Verdi.

In 1861 Wagner was permitted to return to Germany, where he began work on *Die Meistersinger von Nürnberg*, his only comic opera. The music is more conventional than in his other operas. The story concerns a young nobleman who eventually wins a musical contest with a song which breaks all the hitherto accepted rules of composition. There is an obvious analogy with Wagner's own struggle for recognition in the face of hostile criticism.

The first two operas in *The Ring* cycle, *Das Rheingold* and *Die Walküre*, were performed in Munich in 1869 and 1870 respectively. However, Wagner felt strongly that the as yet unfinished tetralogy needed its own special opera house, and one was built at Bayreuth in southern Germany. The first Bayreuth Festival, in 1876, was inaugurated with a complete performance of the entire cycle – *Das Rheingold*, *Die Walküre*, *Siegfried* and *Götterdämmerung*. Based loosely on Norse legends, the complete *Ring* is a masterpiece of epic proportions, the continuity of action and music being held together by the use of the leitmotiv, a musical theme identified throughout the opera with a particular character, object or idea. In *The Ring* operas as well as in *Tristan und Isolde* Wagner made considerable additions to the size of the orchestra, notably in the brass section, his chief aim being to provide a greater variety of tonal colour. Wagner composed his last work, *Parsifal*, in 1882.

Wagner's conception of opera as a completely new art form was to have an enormous effect on the subsequent history of Western music. His music and his theories about music antagonised later composers as much as it inspired them, but his influence is undeniable.

ove: Brunnhilde, the soprano
e in Wagner's 'Ring' cycle, in a
oduction at Bayreuth between the
o world wars. The Norse legend
bject matter and his own
clared anti-Semitism resulted in
agner and his works being
alted above all other music in
azi Germany.

ght: A production of Wagner's
st opera 'Parsifal' in 1988.
arsifal', which Wagner described
a sacred festival drama,
plores the concepts of love,
demption and renunciation
thin the context of the legend of
e Holy Grail.

Salome" v.R. Strauss
Salome bittet um das Haupt des Jochanaan.

Emil Se

ELEKTRA
RICHARD STRAUSS
ERLIN. ADOLPH FÜRSTNER

The operas of Richard Strauss

Richard Strauss had already composed two operas when *Salome* was giv
its first performance in 1905. Based on the play by Oscar Wilde, it
scandalised many with its macabre and erotic subject but was
nevertheless an instant success. *Elektra* (1909) is, like *Salome*, a story of
vengeance, with an equally gruesome ending. Strauss's music is dissona
but stops short of atonality. Strauss's next opera, *Der Rosenkavalier*
('The Knight of the Rose', 1911), was a comedy of love and intrigue in
18th-century Vienna. It evoked an atmosphere of delightful nostalgia,
greatly assisted by charming (if anachronistic) Viennese waltzes. It
provided superb opportunities for the female voice and remains Strauss'
most popular opera. It was followed in 1913 by *Ariadne auf Naxos*. Anoth
opera, *Die Frau ohne Schatten* ('The Woman without a Shadow'), received
its first performance in Vienna in 1919. His last opera was *Capriccio*
(1942), a 'conversation piece' in one act.

Later opera in France and Italy

The emergence of the so-called lyric opera in France, a blending of
elements of grand opera with those of comic opera, began in the 1850s.
Its first notable exponent was Charles Gounod (1818–93). His early oper
were not very well received and it was not until the production in 1859 of
Faust that he achieved real success. Charming and melodious, it marked
new departure for French opera. His other dramatic works included *Rom
et Juliette* (1867).

Left: Spanish baritone Mariano Padilla y Ramos in the role of Escamillo in Bizet's 'Carmen'. Although not at first successful, the opera is now one of the most popular in the repertoire.

Below: French mezzo Celestine Galli-Marié as the first ever Carmen. Tchaikovsky said of her performance in that role: '[Galli-Marié] managed to combine with the display of unbridled passion an element of mystical fatalism.'

ve left: A scene from Richard auss's opera 'Salome' during its miere in Dresden on December .905. Its seething sexuality and ody climax brought acclaim and sure in equal measure. On its ning night, Strauss took a ggering 38 curtain calls.

:: Score for 'Elektra' by Richard auss. Derived from a play by hocles, 'Elektra', like 'Salome', a shocking tale of vengeance passion, which again had iences flocking to the theatres.

One of Gounod's pupils was Georges Bizet (1838–75), a gifted pianist. His precociously brilliant Symphony in C, composed in 1855, was subsequently lost and not performed until 1935. His operas *Les Pêcheurs de perles* ('The Pearl Fishers', 1863) and *La Jolie Fille de Perth* ('The Fair Maid of Perth', 1867) were not particularly well liked, although his incidental music for Alphonse Daudet's play *L'Arlésienne* (1872) eventually fared better. At its first performance in 1875 his opera *Carmen* had a poor reception (audiences were scandalised by its subject matter) and Bizet died a few months later an embittered man. Yet within a short while this starkly realistic story of jealousy and sexual passion, which completely transcends the genre of lyric opera, had gained great popularity. Its extraordinary rhythmic vitality, brilliant local colour and great richness of melody combined to produce a strong emotional impact, and Carmen was to have a considerable influence on the development of Italian *verismo* opera.

Among contemporary French opera composers was Ambroise Thomas (1811–96). His lyric opera *Mignon* (1866) enjoyed an extraordinary popular success, but his other works are now largely forgotten. Camille Saint-Saëns (1835–1921) was a child prodigy and a gifted piano player, but of his many operas only *Samson and Delilah* (1877) is still performed. He is also remembered for his symphonic poems and his zoological fantasy *Carnival of the Animals* (1886). Another popular opera composer was Jules Massenet (1842–1912), whose best known works – *Manon* (1884), *Werther* (1892) and *Thaïs* (1894) – have an enduring sensuous charm.

A new arrival on the French musical scene during the period of the Second Empire was the operetta, a form of light, satirical comic opera. I creator was Jacques Offenbach (1819–81). Of German-Jewish origin, he became a conductor at the Théâtre Français before opening his own theatre. Here he presented comic operas including a number of his own, among them *Orphée aux enfers* ('Orpheus in the Underworld', 1859), *La Belle Hélène* (1864), *La Vie Parisienne* (1866) and *La Périchole* (1868). H one grand opera, *Les Contes d'Hoffmann* ('The Tales of Hoffmann'), remained unfinished at his death. His tuneful music ensured the lasting popularity of his operettas and also inspired the 'waltz king' Johann Strauss the Younger (1825–99) to write two comic operas, *Die Flederma* (1874) and *Der Zigeunerbaron* ('The Gipsy Baron', 1885).

In Italy the name *verismo* (literally, 'realism') was applied to a kind o opera which dealt with the lives of ordinary people in a realistic manner, depicting in graphic detail the raw emotions unleashed by passion and jealousy. It was also in part a reaction against the operas of Wagner and the exalted themes of Italian grand opera as exemplified in the work of Verdi. The two leading figures in this new approach to opera were Pietro Mascagni (1863–1945) and Ruggiero Leoncavallo (1858–1919). Mascagni's one-act opera *Cavalleria Rusticana* ('Rustic Chivalry', 1890) i story of unfaithfulness and revenge in a Sicilian village. It is frequently

The gifted American soprano Geraldine Farrar in the tragic role of Madame Butterfly. Puccini excelled in creating female roles. On learning that her American husband has rejected her, Butterfly commits suicide.

performed together with Leoncavallo's short two-act opera *I Pagliacci* ('The Clowns', 1892), a similar tale of infidelity and murderous retribution.

The most outstanding of the later Italian opera composers was Giacomo Puccini (1858–1924), who was born into a family with a musical tradition extending back several generations. In 1876, after seeing a performance of Verdi's *Aida*, he determined to devote himself to writing opera. His early efforts enjoyed only limited appeal but the first performance of *Manon Lescaut* in 1893 was a triumph and established Puccini's reputation both in Italy and abroad. It was followed in 1896 by *La Bohème*, the first of his mature works, which deals with the life and loves of artists in mid-19th century Paris. Puccini now wrote two more highly successful operas – *Tosca* (1900) and *Madame Butterfly* (1904) – both of which illustrate his skill in creating tragic parts for women in love. Puccini's later operas include *La Rondine* ('The Swallow', 1917) and *Gianni Schicci* (1918), a comic one-act opera forming part of a trio. *Turandot*, which he left unfinished, again has a dominant role for a woman. When Puccini died in 1924 the great tradition of Italian opera died with him. There is an element of *verismo* in all his operas and they all shared an intense emotional appeal. The melodic inventiveness of his music and his capacity for rich orchestration have ensured that his works continue to occupy a prominent place in the opera repertoire.

ove: Signed photograph of
acomo Puccini. Puccini brought a
markable combination of
alities to his work as a
mposer, blending drama, sexual
ssion, pathos and, where
cessary, exoticism with an
ment of 'verismo'.

ght: Title page for the score of
ccini's opera 'Tosca', 1900.
e 'Madame Butterfly', 'Tosca' is
ragic tale of a woman in love,
th the heroine once again
mmiting suicide, this time after
e execution of her lover.

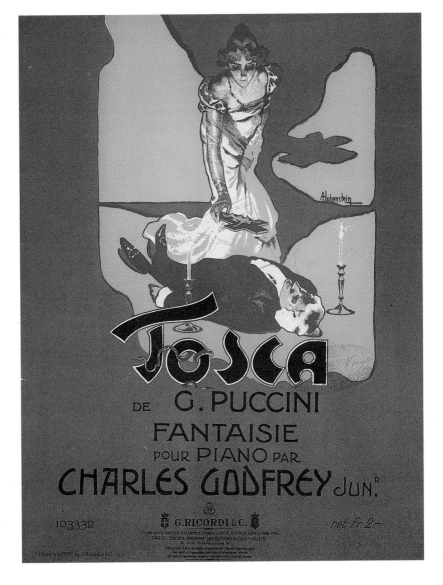

Vocal music <in the late 19th century>

In the early 19th century the German lied had been transformed by Schubert into a musical genre of the highest order. Further contributions were made by Mendelssohn, Schumann and Brahms, but the songs of Hugo Wolf (1860–1903) were particularly memorable. He was a fervent advocate of the operas of Wagner, whose musical style was to influence his own compositions. His string quartet, the *Italienische Serenade*, was published in 1887 and soon after he began a highly productive period of song writing. His *Spanisches Liederbuch* ('Spanish Song-Book') appeared 1891 and the *Italienisches Liederbuch* ('Italian Song-Book') in two parts, in 1892 and 1896 respectively. Wolf's songs were greatly appreciated by audiences in Vienna but his only completed opera, *Der Corregidor*, first performed in 1896, proved unsuccessful. His uniqueness as a song writer (he wrote nearly 300) lies in his ability to compose music which, with great subtlety and psychological insight, expresses the full meaning of the text.

In the later 19th century a distinctive kind of lyric song for solo voice and piano, known as the *mélodie*, became popular in France. The poetry of Verlaine and Baudelaire inspired composers such as Henri Duparc (1848–1933), whose collection of just a handful of songs, including 'Chanson triste' (1868) and 'L'Invitation au voyage' (1870), display a remarkable sensitivity. Gabriel Fauré (1845–1924) is chiefly remembered for his songs, notably 'Après un rêve' (1865), and his song cycles, among them *La Bonne Chanson* (1892), although he wrote much other music besides. His sacred pieces include the 'Cantique de Jean Racine' (1865)

Above left: Gabriel Fauré is best known for the famous 'Requiem' and for his songs, although he wrote many other compositions, all possessing the luminous beauty that is characteristic of his work.

Left: A photograph of Hugo Wolf taken in 1889. Wolf was a prolific songwriter, using as his text the poems of Möricke and Goethe, and German translations of Italian and Spanish poems.

and the famous *Requiem* (1877). He also wrote the incidental music to
Maurice Maeterlinck's *Pélleas et Mélisande* (1898) and Fauchois' *Masques
et Bergamasques* (1919). Among his chamber works are the *Elégie* for
piano and cello, and his orchestral music includes the *Pavane* (1887). His
music for piano is varied – nocturnes, barcarolles, preludes and
impromptus – and is as individual in style as his songs.

Orchestral music

The basic structure of the symphony orchestra had been established in the
18th century by Johann Stamitz. During the 19th century further changes
were introduced. In the woodwind section the numbers were increased
from two to three or even four. Trombones became a permanent feature of
the brass section, and extra horns and trumpets were included, the
chromaticism of these instruments being considerably improved by the
addition of valves. Other early 19th-century arrivals in the orchestra were
the tuba, the contrabassoon and the bass clarinet.

All the great symphonists of the 19th century were to some degree in
the shadow of Beethoven and each had to find his own way forward. Some,
including Schumann, Mendelssohn and Brahms, adhered more or less to
Classical forms, and wrote music which remained generally free of
programmatic elements. Others, such as Liszt and Berlioz, used music to
convey impressions of events, people and ideas. Their more radical
Romantic concept was carried on by Gustav Mahler and Richard Strauss.

Felix Mendelssohn (1809–47) became a prolific composer while still a
boy. His Octet in E flat major, written at the age of 16, and the overture to

A clarinet and bass clarinet made in William Heckel's wind instrument factory, founded in Germany in 1831. During the 19th century the woodwind section of the symphony orchestra was increased in number and the bass clarinet was first introduced.

Another early 19th-century arrival in the orchestra was the tuba. This tenor tuba was made by the Viennese instrument maker Florian Slack. The new instrument featured in Wagner's 'Ring' cycle and in Bruckner's symphonies.

A Midsummer Night's Dream, composed at the age of 17, are works of astonishing maturity. An enthusiast for the music of J.S. Bach, in 1829 he conducted the first performance of the *St Matthew Passion* since the composer's death. That year he undertook the first of a series of visits to England. A holiday in Scotland provided the inspiration for his *Hebrides* Overture. In 1830 he composed his Symphony No 5 in D major, 'the Reformation', and during a subsequent visit to Rome he began work on the Symphony No 4 in A major, 'the Italian', which received its first performance in 1833. He began work on his violin concerto in 1838, but this most melodious of works, with its graceful andante movement, was not completed until 1844. His Symphony No 3 in A minor, 'the Scottish' dedicated to Queen Victoria, was first performed in 1842. The oratorio *Elijah*, which received its premiere in Birmingham in 1846, greatly enhanced Mendelssohn's popularity with English audiences. His other works include the *Songs without Words* (1832–45) for piano, chamber music and a number of organ sonatas. In his symphonies as in his overtures Mendelssohn's essentially poetic nature was inspired by the landscapes he saw and the sounds of the countries he visited, yet his music is not programmatic and remains true to Classical models.

The symphonies of the Austrian composer Anton Bruckner (1824–96) stand somewhat apart from the mainstream. In the early 1860s he encountered for the first time the music of Wagner, whose innovations encouraged him to follow his own original path. His slowly maturing ability found expression in sacred vocal music (he wrote three masses between 1864 and 1868) and in the Symphony No 1 in C minor. The Symphony No 2 in C minor appeared in 1872, followed by three more during the same decade. They attracted much adverse criticism and many musicians considered them unplayable. Reluctantly, Bruckner considerably revised his scores in order to win public acceptance. Only in the 1880s did he gain the recognition he deserved, the Symphony No 7 in E major (1883), with its memorable second-movement adagio, winning widespread acclaim. In 1884 he composed the beautiful *Te Deum*, a work whose beauty testified to the emotions of a deeply pious man. Three years later he completed his Symphony No 8 in C minor, which he subsequently revised. The Symphony No 9 in D minor was a masterpiece which remained unfinished at his death. Bruckner's symphonies adhere to the four-movement Classical tradition, but they are constructed on a massive scale, taking Beethoven's Ninth Symphony as their departure point, and infused with the composer's strong religious feelings.

The contribution of Berlioz and Liszt

Hector Berlioz (1803–69) was greatly attracted to the music of Beethoven and profoundly influenced by Shakespeare and Goethe. He completed the *Symphonie fantastique*, a programmatic work in five movements, depicting episodes in the life of an artist, in 1830. His *Harold in Italy*, a symphony for viola and orchestra, was composed in 1833. His opera *Benvenuto Cellini* (1834–8) was not a success. From 1842 he spent much time touring Germany, England and Russia, where his gifts as a composer found a more appreciative audience than in his home country. Other masterpieces followed: a dramatic work, *The Damnation of Faust* (1846), an oratorio, *The Childhood of Christ* (1854), and his great five-act opera, *The Trojans* (1855–8), conceived on a truly heroic scale. Another opera, *Beatrice and Benedict* (1862), was based on Shakespeare's *Much Ado about Nothing*. Berlioz was also a notable music critic but his reputation must rest on the innovations he introduced into symphonic music, not least his genius for creating new orchestral colours and harmonies. His treatise on orchestration still remains a standard work on the subject.

Franz Liszt was responsible for the creation of a profoundly Romantic musical genre, the symphonic poem, a large-scale orchestral work in which the theme is a nonmusical one (usually pictorial or literary). His contribution to programmatic music of this kind included *Mazeppa* (1851), *Les Préludes* (1854) and the *Faust Symphony* (1854–7).

ve: A 19th-century silhouette of
on Bruckner conducting. The
sic of Wagner proved a rich
rce of inspiration for Bruckner,
Wagner in turn praised
ckner's work, stating that he
the 'only composer who
asures up to Beethoven'.

ht: Portrait of Hector Berlioz by
rles Baugniet, 1851. Berlioz
de notable contributions to the
elopment of the orchestra,
anding his views in his treatise
and Traité d'instrumentation et
rchestration moderne',
lished in 1843.

johannes brahms
1833–1897

Born in Hamburg, Brahms received his first music lessons from his father and later studied the piano under a distinguished teacher, Eduard Marksen. As a contribution towards his family's income, he played the piano in the taverns around the Hamburg docks, but also began composing. In 1853, accompanied by the violinist Eduard Reményi, he embarked upon a series of concerts. In Hanover he met the brilliant young violin player Joseph Joachim, who arranged an introduction to Liszt, who was impressed by the music of the young Brahms. The composer now moved to Düsseldorf where he met Robert Schumann, who responded enthusiastically to his music. In 1857 Brahms secured a position as a piano teacher at the court at Detmold, and was for a time conductor of a women's choir in Hamburg. In 1863 he moved to Vienna, where he began writing some of his most important music

Right: A photograph of Johannes Brahms, signed on the back and dated November 1874. Brahms avoided programmatic music, instead writing orchestral pieces in the Classical tradition with strong Romantic overtones.

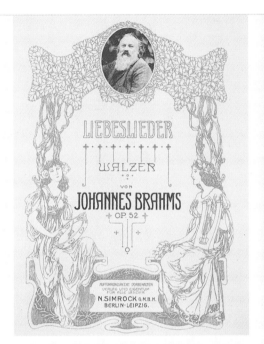

ft and above: Brahms wrote many ngs, which display his strongly mantic sensibilities. The title ge above is from the score of a ok of love songs, op. 52, printed 905. On the left is the title page 'Ausgewählte Lieder', 1889.

This included *A German Requiem* (1868), a magnificent choral work set to biblical texts which at once established his position as a leading figure on the musical scene, followed in 1869 by the lighter but phenomenally successful *Hungarian Dances* for piano duet. The *Variations on a Theme by Haydn* (the 'St Anthony', 1873), for orchestra and also for piano, were equally well received. His Symphony No 1 in C minor, which had been some years in gestation, appeared in 1876, and the Symphony No 2 in D major a year later. These two masterpieces were followed by a string of others, including the Violin Concerto in D major (1878), the Academic Festival Overture (1880), the Piano Concerto No 2 in B flat major (1882), and the third and fourth symphonies (1883 and 1885, respectively).

As a composer of chamber music Brahms had no equal after Beethoven. The best of his work in this field includes the String Sextets in B flat major (1860) and in G major (1865), the Piano Quintet in F minor (1864), the Piano Quartet in C minor (1875) and the Clarinet Quintet in B minor (1891). In 1896 he completed his last works, the *Four Serious Songs* and the *Eleven Choral Preludes for Organ*.

Brahms wrote in all the musical genres except opera. As a symphonist he is a true heir of the Classical tradition, skilled in his use of contrapuntal harmony and essentially conservative in his approach, retaining the four-movement format and avoiding any suggestion of programmatic music. There are, however, strongly Romantic elements, which are also to be found in the lyrical violin concerto and in his many songs.

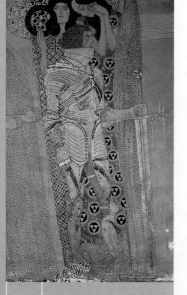

Above left: Gustav Mahler, 1898. At his death Mahler was best known as a conductor. He was a perfectionist, seeking ever-higher standards from his players and inaugurating one of the most illustrious periods in the history of the Vienna Opera House, of which he became director in 1897.

Left: 'The knight', a detail from the Beethoven frieze by the Austrian painter and designer Gustav Klimt that is said to be a portrait of Mahler.

Born in Bohemia of Jewish parentage, Mahler gave his first public piano recital at the age of ten. The most important of his early compositions, *D klagende Lied* (1878), a cantata for voices, chorus and orchestra, failed t win him any recognition. He composed the song cycle *Lieder eines fahrenden Gesellen* ('Songs of a Wayfarer') in 1883 and also started working on his first symphony. He now held a succession of increasingly important positions at Leipzig (1886–88), Budapest (1888–91) and Hamburg (1891–7), and began to make his name as a conductor of the operas of Wagner and Mozart. However, his own Symphony No 1 in D major was not well received at its first performance in Budapest in 1889. Described by Mahler as a 'symphonic poem', it seems to have rather mystified the audience. In 1894 he finished work on his gigantic, five-movement second symphony, which had a successful first performance in Berlin the following year. It included vocal parts for solo singers and choir and settings from his song cycle *Des Knaben Wunderhorn* ('The Boy's Magi Horn', 1892–8), which were also to appear in the third and fourth symphonies. In 1897 he secured the position of director of the Vienna Court Opera, inaugurating one of the most illustrious periods in its history

His fifth, sixth and seventh symphonies, composed between 1900 and 1905, are purely orchestral and much less programmatic than their predecessors. The song cycle *Kindertotenlieder* was completed in 1904. In 1907 Mahler was forced, in the face of a ferocious and strongly

Major Works

Symphonies

1888	Symphony No 1 in D major
1894	Symphony No 2 in C minor
1896	Symphony No 3 in D major
1900	Symphony No 4, G major – E major
1902	Symphony No 5, C sharp minor – D major
1904	Symphony No 6 in A minor
1905	Symphony No 7, B minor – C major
1906	Symphony No 8 in E flat major
1909	Symphony No 9, D major – D flat major
1910	Symphony No 10 in F sharp major (incomplete)

Songs

1880	*Das klagende Lied*
1885	*Lieder eines fahrenden Gesellen*
1892–8	*Des Knaben Wunderhorn*
1904	*Kindertotenlieder*
1909	*Das Lied von der Erde*

The poster for Mahler's 8th symphony, which he conducted a its premiere in Munich in 1910. I this composition Mahler employe two choral movements, the first a setting of a Latin hymn and the second a setting of the final scen of Goethe's 'Faust'. It was a massive undertaking, requiring over a thousand people, hence its quickly acquired nickname 'The Symphony of a Thousand'.

'The orchestra', by Max Oppenheimer, 1935. The painting depicts Gustav Mahler conducting the Vienna Philharmonic, a post he obtained in 1898. His ruthless pursuit of the best in music both inspired and antagonised, however, and in 1901 he was obliged to relinquish the post, because of the resentment that his dictatorial methods aroused.

anti-Semitic press campaign against him, to resign his position with the Vienna Opera. He accepted an appointment in New York, where he enjoyed considerable success, but returned to the Austrian countryside each summer in order to work. In 1908 he composed *Das Lied von der Erde* ('The Song of the Earth'), a song cycle of near symphonic proportions. The ninth symphony was completed in the same year and Mahler began to make sketches for a tenth symphony. In the Symphony No 8 (1906), known as 'The Symphony of a Thousand', Mahler abandoned completely the normal symphonic framework. He substituted what was in effect two choral movements. Requiring an orchestra and chorus of over a thousand people, it was a work on a truly awe-inspiring scale and received a standing ovation at its premiere in 1910 under the composer's baton. The ninth symphony which, together with *Das Lied von der Erde*, had its first performance after the composer's death, marked a return to a four-movement, purely orchestral work. The tenth symphony, which remained unfinished, is striking for its use of a nine-note chord of extreme dissonance that first occurs in the opening movement.

Working with orchestras of unprecedented size, Mahler pushed the symphonic structure of the late Romantic period to its limits. Despite the programmatic elements of much of his music he was both the heir to a tradition that stretched from Haydn to Bruckner and the forerunner of the musical revolution of the 20th century. In his experiments with tonality, sometimes ending a work in a different key from the one in which it began, he paved the way for Arnold Schoenberg and other members of the Second Viennese School, on whom he was to exercise a profound influence.

Symphonic music in Germany and France

Richard Strauss (1864–1949), Mahler's junior by only four years, was to find his inspiration in the symphonic music of Berlioz and Liszt. Born in Munich, he began writing music at the age of six and by the time he left school already had to his credit a symphony, songs, and orchestral and chamber works. After studying philosophy at Munich University, he decided to devote himself to music. Trained by Hans von Bülow, he embarked upon a career as a conductor in which he was to win great distinction. He held positions in Munich, Weimar and Berlin, eventually becoming director of the Vienna State Opera (1919–24).

His career as a composer was successfully launched with the first performance of his symphonic poem *Don Juan* (1889), in which his brilliant descriptive powers and skilled orchestration won immediate acclaim. *Tod und Verklärung* ('Death and Transfiguration', 1889) and *Also sprach Zarathustra* ('Thus Spoke Zarathustra', 1896) are more philosophical and reflective. His symphonic poems *Till Eulenspiegels lustige Streiche* ('Till Eulenspiegel's Merry Pranks', 1895) and *Don Quixote* (1897) are both descriptive, yet possess powerful psychological insight. *Ein Heldenleben* ('A Hero's Life', 1898) is generally considered to be autobiographical – the composer's struggle to achieve recognition in the face of hostile criticism. The *Sinfonia domestica* (1903) is an intimate depiction of everyday family life in the Strauss household. In 1915 *An Alpine Symphony*, his last symphonic poem, had its premiere in Berlin.

His final compositions were a horn concerto (1943), a work for solo strings, *Metamorphosen*, and an oboe concerto (both 1945), and his *Four Last Songs* (1948) for soprano and orchestra – the last a poignant reminder of his gifts as a song writer. Hailed as the successor to Wagner, to whom he paid due tribute, Strauss was also a devout admirer of Mozart and his love for the work of both composers can be seen in the contrasting styles of such operas as *Der Rosenkavalier* and *Die Frau ohne Schatten*. Using large orchestral forces to wonderful effect, he made a unique contribution to the development of the symphonic poem.

In late 19th-century France the symphonic tradition of Berlioz and Liszt was carried on by Saint-Saëns, Franck, D'Indy and others. César Franck (1822–90), who was born in Belgium, composed the richly chromatic Symphony in D minor (1888), notable for its use of the cyclic form in which thematic material from one movement is quoted in another. Other works by Franck include the *Symphonic Variations* (1885) for piano and orchestra, symphonic poems in the style of Liszt and the String Quartet in D major (1889). Vincent d'Indy (1851–1931) used folk song material in his *Symphony on a French Mountaineer's Song* (1886), which combines elements of both a piano concerto and a symphony. Ernest Chausson (1855–99) is remembered for his Symphony in B flat major (1891) and his *Poème* for violin and orchestra (1896).

Emmanuel Chabrier (1841–94) was strongly influenced by the music Spain and is best known for his colourful rhapsody for orchestra *España* (1883). He was, however, an ardent Wagnerite and his operas *Gwendoline* (1885) and *Le Roi malgré lui* (1887) show his debt to the master. He was also the composer of some important piano works, including the *Pièces pittoresques* (1881). Spanish influence is also present in the music of Edouard Lalo (1823–92). He achieved considerable success with his *Symphonie espagnole* for solo violin and orchestra (1875) and with his ce

Pencil drawing of Richard Strauss. Strauss made a notable contribution to the development of the symphonic poem, which he imbued with as much passion and warmth as he did his infamously scandalous operas.

concerto (1876), both of which have strong Spanish elements. Other notable works include the Symphony in G minor (1887), a violin concerto and the opera *Le Roi d'Ys* (1888), generally considered his masterpiece. The chief claim to fame of Paul Dukas (1865–1935) is his symphonic poem *The Sorcerer's Apprentice* (1897), but he also composed a Symphony in C major (1896) and an opera, *Ariane et Barbe-bleue* (1907).

The piano

Towards the end of the 18th century the piano began to replace the harpsichord as the leading keyboard instrument. Its most important features were its range of volume and the dramatic contrasts afforded by its sustaining power. The earliest exponents of the piano were Mozart and Haydn, but the instrument which they played underwent a considerable evolution in the early years of the 19th century. The keyboard was enlarged to seven octaves and an iron frame was introduced, permitting a considerable increase in tension on the strings and thus a vast improvement in both volume and sonority. Apart from the flexibility which these changes provided, they also had the practical advantage of enabling the instrument to be clearly heard in the large new concert halls. The piano rapidly became the most favoured solo instrument in such genres as the concerto and the sonata. Composers from Beethoven onwards used the piano to express some of their most intimate personal feelings and it soon acquired a vast repertoire.

…vertisement for a Steinweg …no, 1923: 'The genuine Grotrian …einweg is the result of German …ativity.' By the end of the 18th …tury, the piano had become the …ding keyboard instrument.

…opin in the salon of Prince …ton Radziwill', painted in 1887. …opin's delicate style of playing …s perfect for the rarefied …mosphere of the salon setting.

Among the first major composers of music for the piano were Chopin and Liszt, who were also accomplished players. Born in Warsaw, Frédéric Chopin (1810–49) eventually settled in Paris in 1831, where his attempts to pursue a career as a concert pianist were thwarted by the fact that his delicate touch on the keyboard was not at all suited to the ambience of large concert halls. However, the more restful atmosphere of the salon provided the ideal setting for his intimate style of piano playing. Chopin wrote almost exclusively for the piano and produced music of remarkable richness and melodic beauty, notable for its chromatic harmonies and ranging from major pieces such as polonaises, scherzos and ballades to preludes, mazurkas and waltzes. The mazurkas and polonaises reflected the dance rhythms of his native Poland. His etudes, such as the 'Revolutionary' etude in C minor, are among his greatest works. Much of his originality lies in his move away from Classical tonality, his bold experimentation with musical patterns and his skilful use of modulation. Among his other masterpieces are the two late sonatas, in B flat minor and B flat respectively, and the Fantasia in F minor. He also had an important role in the development of modern piano techniques.

Franz Liszt (1811– 86), born at Raiding in Hungary, made his debut as concert pianist at the age of nine. In 1824 he made his first appearance on the concert platform in Paris to a rapturous reception. It was in Paris that he met Berlioz and Chopin, who were to have a profound influence upon his subsequent musical development. When he heard Paganini perform he determined to apply his virtuoso techniques to the piano. In 1833 he made a piano transcription of Berlioz's *Symphonie fantastique*, the first of many arrangements of this kind which both demonstrated the versatility of the instrument and brought the music to the attention of a much wider audience.

At the end of the 1830s Liszt travelled around Europe to play and was enthusiastically received by audiences everywhere. In 1848 he accepted the post of director of music at the court of Weimar in Germany. He now found the time to compose and his work from these years, which includes the *Transcendental Studies* (1851), the *Années de Pèlerinage* (1854) and the first group of *Hungarian Rhapsodies* (1855), is both colourful and imaginative. Exploiting to the full the resources of the piano, it also makes great demands on the technical skills of the pianist. The outstanding pianist of his age, Liszt was the first to realise the full potential of the instrument. He made a supremely important contribution to the development of keyboard music and in his later works anticipated the harmonic language of the 20th century.

Other composers of the early Romantic period who wrote for the piano were Felix Mendelssohn, who is best known in this genre for his collection of pieces entitled *Lieder ohne Worte* ('Songs without Words') and Robert Schumann (1810–56), whose piano music forms, together with his songs, the most memorable part of his output. A love affair inspired two important piano works, *Etudes Symphoniques* (1834) and *Carnaval* (1835).

In 1834 Schumann also became co-founder and editor of the *Neue Zeitschrift für Musik*. He proved a perceptive critic and championed the work of the Romantic composers. During the 1830s Schumann continued to write piano music such as the Fantasy in C major (1836), *Kinderszenen* ('Scenes from Childhood') and *Kreisleriana* (both 1838). In 1840 he composed the song cycles *Dichterliebe* ('Poet's Love') and *Frauenliebe und Leben* ('Women's Life and Love'). The following year he wrote his first

The Hungarian pianist and composer Franz Liszt at a recital in Berlin, 1847. A particular favourite with the female portion of the audience, Liszt was a complex personality – temperamentally impulsive, notorious for his many love affairs yet with a strongly religious streak. He was the supreme pianist of his age.

symphony and began work on his piano concerto. In 1842 he turned his attention to chamber music, composing string quartets and a piano quintet. He finished his second symphony in 1846, wrote an opera, *Genoveva* (1847–50) and composed the overture to Byron's play *Manfred* (1848–9). In 1850 he composed his Cello Concerto in A minor and his third symphony, and in 1851 he published his drastically revised fourth symphony ('the Scottish').

N a t i o n a l i s m in music

The rise of nationalism in music in mid-19th century Europe was the result of an attempt on the part of composers to make their music reflect to a much greater degree the cultural heritage of their native countries. In so doing they sought to challenge the dominant position of German music. This reaction was most strongly seen in Russia which until the early 19th century had generally relied on the music of Italian and German composers to provide entertainment for the educated classes. Nationalism proved an equally potent force for the Bohemian composers Bedrich Smetana and (later) Antonín Dvořák, who found inspiration in their country's folk songs and legends. In Norway Edvard Grieg drew on traditional folk melodies and in Spain, where Italian opera had reigned supreme, Isaac Albéniz used his country's rich heritage of dance rhythms to create a distinctively Spanish style of music.

ntispiece of a piano score for a dred Serbian national dances, lished c.1900. In the mid-19th tury, composers began to llenge the dominant position of man music, which many saw as nical to the creation of a onal tradition of their own.

The Russian contribution

Mikhail Glinka (1804–57) was the first Russian composer to achieve
international recognition. The opera on which his fame rests, *A Life for the
Tsar*, had its first performance in 1836. Its use of folk music coupled with
a strongly nationalist plot undoubtedly contributed to its popularity. It was
followed in 1842 by *Ruslan and Lyudmila*, based on a poem by Pushkin.
This contained some fine music of considerable originality, but was less
successful. In 1844 Glinka travelled to France and then Spain, where he
wrote two colourful Spanish overtures. His orchestral piece *Kamarinskaya*
(1848) was again inspired by Russian folk melodies. He was also the
composer of a number of songs.

Alexander Dargomizhky (1813–69) devoted himself to the study of
Russian folk music. His two operas, *Rusalka* and *The Stone Guest* (the latter
unfinished), were nationalist in spirit and had a considerable influence
upon later composers.

The determination to create a self-consciously Russian idiom in music
was taken by a group of mostly self-taught composers based in St
Petersburg who reacted strongly against the German-orientated
academicism of the Conservatoire there. Known as 'The Mighty Handful' or
'The Five' (Balakirev, Borodin, Cui, Mussorgsky and Rimsky-Korsakov),
they sought inspiration in native folklore and popular music. The guiding
spirit of the group was Mily Balakirev (1837–1910), a pianist and teacher
at St Petersburg, who devoted his time to encouraging the others. In 1862
he founded the St Petersburg Free School of Music and later became
director of the Imperial Court Chapel. He is best known for his symphonic
poem *Tamara* (1867–82) and his oriental fantasy for piano, *Islamey* (1869)

Modest Mussorgsky (1839–81) began work on his opera *Boris Godunov*
in 1868, but the first version was rejected and the revised work did not
receive its first performance until 1874. Mussorgsky had already started
composing a second opera, *Khovanshchina*, and had supplied his own
libretto for both operas. *Khovanshchina* remained unfinished at the
composer's death, being completed by Rimsky-Korsakov. His other work
includes the symphonic poem *St John's Night on a Bare Mountain* (1867),
a series of song cycles – *The Nursery* (1868–72), *Sunless* (1872) and
Songs and Dances of Death (1875) – and the piano piece *Pictures at an
Exhibition* (1874), later orchestrated by Maurice Ravel. *Boris Godunov*
is a landmark in the history of Russian music. Depicting events in the
life of Tsar Boris who has usurped the Russian throne, it is
unconventional in its approach, lacking continuity but magnificent in its
realistic depiction of the guilty Boris and in its sympathetic portrayal of
ordinary Russian people.

Aleksandr Borodin (1833–87) completed his Symphony No 1 in E flat
major in 1867. His early enthusiasms were for Mendelssohn and
Schumann, but the influence of Balakirev and other members of 'The Five'
stimulated his desire to compose in a Russian idiom. In 1869 he began
work on his Symphony No 2 in B minor, one of his outstanding
achievements, and on his great opera *Prince Igor*. Completed
posthumously by Rimsky-Korsakov and Aleksandr Glazunov, it was not
performed until 1890. Infused with strongly nationalist sentiment, it
contains the famous 'Polovtsian Dances'. Like *Boris Godunov*, it is episodic
and lacking in dramatic continuity, but its colourful and melodic music,
unusual harmonies and exotic flavour have ensured its popularity.

A scene from a film of Modest
Mussorgsky's masterpiece 'Boris
Godunov', by the Bolshoi Company,
Moscow. Mussorgsky was one of
'The Five', a group of composers
who used popular folk music and
folk tales as their inspiration.

Borodin's other important work includes his tone poem *In the Steppes of Central Asia* (1880) and the Second String Quartet in D major (1885).

Nikolai Rimsky-Korsakov (1844–1908) was the first Russian ever to write a symphony, which was successfully performed in St Petersburg in 1865. He subsequently became a leading member of 'The Five'. In 1873 his first opera, *The Maid of Pskov*, received its premiere. The following year he conducted the first performance of his third symphony. He was, however, to be best known for his operas and symphonic poems, in which he included the themes of folk music remembered from his childhood. Taking his subject matter from Slavonic fairy tales and Russian history, he wrote some 15 operas, of which the most important are *The Snow Maiden* (1880–81), *Sadko* (1898), *The Legend of the Invisible City of Kitezh* (1907) and *The Golden Cockerel* (1909). A mixture of fantasy and the supernatural, they lack dramatic force but, with the use of chromaticism, the music skilfully conveys the distinction between the fairy-tale and the more naturalistic elements. His flair for colourful orchestration is shown in the symphonic suites *Capriccio espagnol* (1887) and *Scheherezade* (1888), and in the *Russian Easter Festival* overture (1888). He constantly revised his own early compositions and made far-reaching changes to Mussorgsky's work (not always with happy results) before submitting it for publication. Igor Stravinsky, Aleksandr Glazunov and Sergei Prokoviev were among Rimsky-Korsakov's pupils and through them the influence of the first generation of Russian composers made itself felt on the development of Russian music in the 20th century.

peter ilyich tchaikovsky
1840–1

Major Works

Operas
1869	*The Voyevoda*
1873	*The Snow Maiden*
1879	*Eugene Onegin*
1881	*The Maid of Orleans*
1890	*The Queen of Spades*

Ballets
1877	*Swan Lake*
1890	*The Sleeping Beauty*
1891	*The Nutcracker Suite*

Orchestral music
1872	Symphony No 2 in in C minor, 'Little Russian'
1875	Symphony No 3 in D major, 'Polish'
1878	Symphony No 4 in F minor
1888	Symphony No 5 in E minor
1893	Symphony No 6 in B minor, 'Pathéthique'
1885	*Manfred Symphony*
1870	*Romeo and Juliet*, fantasy-overture
1876	*Francesca da Rimini*, symphonic fantasy
1888	*Hamlet*, fantasy-overture
1875	Piano Concerto No 1 in B flat minor
1880	Piano Concerto No 2 in G major
1878	Violin Concerto in D major
1876	Variations on a Rococo Theme
1876	*Marche Slave*
1880	Serenade for Strings in C major
1880	*Capriccio italien*
1880	*1812 Overture*

Chamber music
1871–7	Three string quartets
1890	String sextet, 'Souvenir de Florence'

Vocal music
More than 100 songs, including:
1869	'None but the Lonely Heart'
1878	'Don Juan's Serenade'

Anton Rubinstein, director of the St Petersburg Conservatoire, conducting. The popular appeal of Tchaikovsky's music has led to much debate about its real worth. Rubinstein strongly criticised the composer's first piano concerto, but the public disagreed and it was enthusiastically received at its first performance in Boston in 1875.

ɔve: Throughout his life aikovsky was plagued with ɛp feelings of guilt over his mosexuality. His death from lera, supposedly from drinking poiled water, is now thought to ve been possibly self-inflicted.

t: Alicia Markova in haikovsky's 'Swan Lake', 1910. haikovsky is popularly known for ballets, which never fail to ɪch audiences through their otional poignancy and the ninous beauty of their music.

Tchaikovsky showed an aptitude for music from an early age. In 1862 he joined the St Petersburg Conservatoire, where he studied under Anton Rubinstein. In 1866 he moved to Moscow to take up the position of professor of harmony at the newly opened Conservatoire. His Symphony No 1 in G minor, which had its first performance in 1866, was quite well received but the effort he had put into it led to a nervous breakdown. About this time he made the acquaintance of Balakirev and the other members of 'The Five', and at Balakirev's suggestion he composed the fantasy-overture *Romeo and Juliet*. This was not a success at its first performance in 1869 and Tchaikovsky subsequently revised it. His opera *The Voyevoda*, which had its premiere the same year, was equally unsuccessful. In the early 1870s, however, with the completion of his second and third symphonies (1872 and 1875 respectively), two string quartets, his Piano Concerto No 1 in B flat minor (1875) and the ballet *Swan Lake* (first performed in 1877), Tchaikovsky's fortunes dramatically improved.

The opera *Eugene Onegin*, the Violin Concerto in D major and the Symphony No 4 in F minor were all completed in 1878. In 1880 there followed the *Capriccio italien*, the *1812 Overture*, the Serenade for Strings in C major and the Piano Concerto No 2 in G major. In the following year he relinquished his teaching post at the Moscow Conservatoire and now spent much time in foreign travel, making an international tour as a conductor in 1888, the year in which he finished his Symphony No 5 in E minor. He had completed his *Manfred Symphony* (a tone poem based on the work by Byron) two years earlier. His music for the ballets *The Sleeping Beauty* (1889) and *The Nutcracker* (1891–2) confirmed his mastery of this genre and his opera *The Queen of Spades* (1890) enjoyed immediate success. His final symphony, the No 6 in B flat Minor, known as the 'Pathéthique', received its first performance in 1893, just a few days before the composer's death.

Tchaikovsky's enormous popularity with audiences everywhere has led to heated debate about the real worth of his music. Its strongly emotional qualities have both alienated and attracted support. He was undoubtedly the first great Russian symphonist and, although his symphonies are uneven in quality, the fourth, for example, is notable for its brilliant scoring for all the instruments of the orchestra and its richness of melody. In his works for the theatre Tchaikovsky was particularly successful and his three ballet scores, *Swan Lake*, *The Sleeping Beauty* and *The Nutcracker Suite*, are acknowledged masterpieces. His operas *Eugene Onegin* and *The Queen of Spades* are notable for their dramatic intensity and sympathetic portrayal of the characters involved. The best of his other orchestral works includes the much revised *Romeo and Juliet* overture, the symphonic fantasy *Francesca da Rimini* and the Serenade for Strings.

Music in Bohemia

The music of Bohemia had for centuries reflected the influences of weste[r]
Europe, and it was not until the beginning of the 19th century that a nati[onal]
school of composers and musicians began to emerge. The most notable [of]
these were the pianist and composer Jan Ladislav Dussek (1760–1812)
and Frantisek Skroup (1801–62), who wrote the first Czech opera.
However, the founder of a truly national school of music was to be Bedri[ch]
Smetana (1824–84). In 1861 he took a leading role in establishing a
national opera house in Prague. He had already composed symphonic
poems but his music did not really come to public attention until his firs[t]
two operas, *The Brandenburgers in Bohemia* and *The Bartered Bride*, were
both performed in 1866 before enthusiastic audiences. Other operas,
including *Dalibor* (1868), were less successful.

He had always suffered from hearing difficulties, and in 1874 became
totally deaf. He nevertheless embarked upon a cycle of six symphonic
poems, *Ma Vlást* ('My Country'), which he completed in 1879. The best
known of these, *Vltava*, traces in wonderfully evocative music the course [of]
the country's chief river from its beginnings as a tiny stream to its majest[ic]
approach to Prague. Another fine work is the String Quartet No 2 in D
minor, *From my Life* (1876), a musical autobiography in which a repeated
high note in the last movement imitates the whistling noise in the ears
which preceded the onset of deafness. The characteristic nationalist flavo[ur]
of Smetana's music lies both in his choice of subject matter – Bohemian
history, legend and scenery – for his operas and symphonic poems and in
his use of melodies based on folk tunes and native dance rhythms.

Antonín Dvořák (1841–1904) was the first Bohemian composer to
achieve international recognition. By the end of the 1860s he had alread[y]
written two symphonies and some chamber music, and in 1875 he was
awarded a state grant by the Austrian government. This brought him to t[he]
attention of Johannes Brahms, who not only gave him advice and
encouragement, but also found a publisher for some of his works. The
Slavonic Dances (1878), commissioned by the publisher, proved
immensely popular and brought Dvořák to the attention of a much wider
public. His choral work, the *Stabat Mater* (1877), added to his
reputation, which by now had reached the United States. In 1885 he
completed the Symphony No 7 in D minor, generally considered his fines[t]
orchestral work, and conducted the first performance in London. The
Symphony No 8 in G major was composed in 1889 and the Requiem Mas[s]
in the following year.

In 1892 he accepted a post in New York, where he composed his mos[t]
popular symphony, the No 9 in E minor, 'From the New World' (1893).
Incorporating themes suggestive of American folk tunes, it yet remains
rooted in the traditional music of his own country. Other works from this
fruitful period were the String Quartet in F major, 'the American' (1893),
and the sublime Cello Concerto in B flat minor (1895), possibly the fines[t]
ever written for the instrument. Homesick, Dvořák returned to Bohemia
and devoted most of his energies to writing symphonic poems and the be[st]
known of his operas, *Rusalka* (1901), based on a fairytale. His most
memorable chamber music includes the Piano Quintet in A major (1887)
and the Piano Trio in E minor – the 'Dumky Trio' (1891). His strength as [a]
composer lay in his skills in adapting the folk music of his native country
to the Classical forms of both symphonic and chamber music.

Antonín Dvořák, 1879. Dvořák
successfully absorbed traditional
folk songs and dance music
into his compositions, in both his
native Bohemia, with works
such as the 'Slavonic Dances', and
in the United States, such as in
'From the New World'.

Music in northern Europe

Music in northern Europe was strongly influenced by the German tradition
but with the growth of nationalism in the 19th century Scandinavian
composers, too, began to look to their roots for inspiration. Edvard Grieg
(1843–1907) was born in Bergen, Norway, and as a young man studied at
Leipzig, where he was influenced by the early Romantic music of
Mendelssohn and Schumann. In 1863 he moved to Copenhagen, where a
meeting with the Norwegian nationalist composer Rikard Nordraak
(1842–66) altered the whole course of his musical development. The
Humoresques for piano (1865) are inspired by Norwegian folk tunes, as are
the *Lyric Pieces*, also for piano, the first of which were composed in 1867.
In the following year he wrote one of his best known works, the Piano
Concerto in A minor, which won the admiration of Liszt. At the request of
the dramatist Henrik Ibsen, he wrote the incidental music to the latter's
play *Peer Gynt*, the story of a character from Norwegian folklore. Its highly
successful first performance in 1876 established Grieg's position as his
country's leading composer. His orchestral work includes the *Holberg Suite*
(1884), although most of his music is on a small scale.

Carl Nielsen (1865–1931) was born near Odense in Denmark. His early
compositions show the influence of German romanticism but in his first
symphony (1892), while retaining the Classical structure, he introduces
progressive tonality, which allows the work to begin in one key but end in
another. This concept was to be repeated in his later symphonies
(particularly the Symphony No 5) which are notable for their bold use of
dissonant harmonies. His other works include an opera, *Saul and David*
(1902), chamber music, a violin concerto and a clarinet concerto.

Jean Sibelius (1885–1957), who was born at Tavastehus in Finland, rapidly made his mark as a composer. His strongly nationalist sentiments found expression in a series of symphonic poems, some based on Finnish legends, including *En Saga* (1892), the atmospheric *Karelia Suite* (1893) and *The Swan of Tuonela* (1895), with its immensely sad and brooding English horn solo. In 1899 he published his Symphony No 1 in E minor and his most famous tone poem, *Finlandia*. The symphony is generally conventional, but already bears the composer's individual stamp. His second symphony appeared in 1901, followed two years later by the lyrical Violin Concerto in D minor, which enjoyed immediate success. His three-movement third symphony, even more than the second, shows a departure from the traditional symphonic structure. The austere fourth symphony (1911) had a mixed reception but the fifth, which had its premiere in 1915, proved to be his most popular.

The sixth symphony was produced in 1923 and the seventh and last in the following year. The mournful symphonic poem *Tapiola*, inspired by Finnish mythology, was first performed in 1926. After this Sibelius wrote no more music of any significance. His originality lies in the structural innovations he made to the symphony: the virtual abandonment of the sonata form and the gradual exposition of the main theme, which sometimes appears as a series of motifs finally unified as a single entity. The one-movement seventh symphony, which forms an unbroken unit of sound, is in essence the logical culmination of all Sibelius's previous symphonic work.

Music in England

The revitalising of English musical life towards the end of the 19th century was largely the work of four men. Sir Arthur Sullivan (1842–1900) who, in partnership with his librettist, W.S. Gilbert, wrote a number of hugely popular operettas, including *Iolanthe* (1882), *The Mikado* (1885) and *The Gondoliers* (1889), was also the author of an oratorio, an opera and chamber works, but his serious music is now rarely heard. Sir Hubert Parry (1848–1918) composed oratorios, anthems and cantatas. The Irish-born Sir Charles Stanford (1852–1924), who was both a composer and a teacher, wrote much church music.

The most important of this group of English composers was Sir Edward Elgar (1857–1934). The son of a music dealer, Elgar was largely self-taught and learnt several musical instruments, including the violin, the bassoon and the organ. The *Enigma Variations* (1899), in which each variation is an attempt to capture in music the personality of a friend of the composer, was his first real success. His oratorio *The Dream of Gerontius* was not much appreciated at its first performance in Birmingham in 1900, but its triumphant reception in Düsseldorf in 1902 firmly established the composer's reputation on the international scene. The *Pomp and Circumstance* marches (1901–7) added immensely to Elgar's popularity, as did the profoundly lyrical *Introduction and Allegro* for strings (1905). His two symphonies (1908 and 1911 respectively) are late Romantic in idiom, yet possess a particular 'Englishness'. Other great works from his later period include his Violin Concerto (1910), the symphonic poem *Falstaff* (1913) and his final masterpiece, the supremely elegiac Cello Concerto (1919).

THE SORCERER

D'OYLY CARTE OPERA CO.

ht: Poster advertising Gilbert
Sullivan's operetta 'The
cerer', for a production in the
Os. The partnership of the
poser Arthur Sullivan and the
ettist William Schwenck Gilbert
ed to revitalise English music
ards the end of the 19th
tury. In all they produced 14
rettas together.

ow: The Spanish dance
ero was popular from the end of
18th century and throughout
19th century. Its colourful
hms have inspired many
posers, particularly in its
ve country, which witnessed a
ical resurgence at the end of
19th century.

Music in Spain

Spain possessed a musical tradition stretching back to the early centuries of Christianity, yet apart from Luis de Victoria and Antonio Soler had produced virtually no composers of any great significance. However, as in England, the latter part of the 19th century marked the beginning of a new creative period. Spain's national musical renaissance was to be based on its colourful native dance rhythms, which were also to inspire composers ranging from Rimsky-Korsakov to Debussy. Felipe Pedrell (1841–1922) wrote an opera entitled *Los Pirineos* ('The Pyrenees', 1890–1), but is best known for his writings on Spanish folk song. Enrique Granados (1867–1916), a pupil of Pedrell, composed the *Goyescas* (1911), a piano suite in a distinctly Spanish idiom, based on paintings by Goya. Isaac Albéniz (1860–1909), who became a gifted pianist at an early age, studied with Pedrell and Liszt. Most of his music was written for the piano and includes his masterwork, the four suites of piano pieces known as *Iberia* (1906–8), which deploy the rhythms and harmonies of Spanish folk music to marvellous effect.

the new music

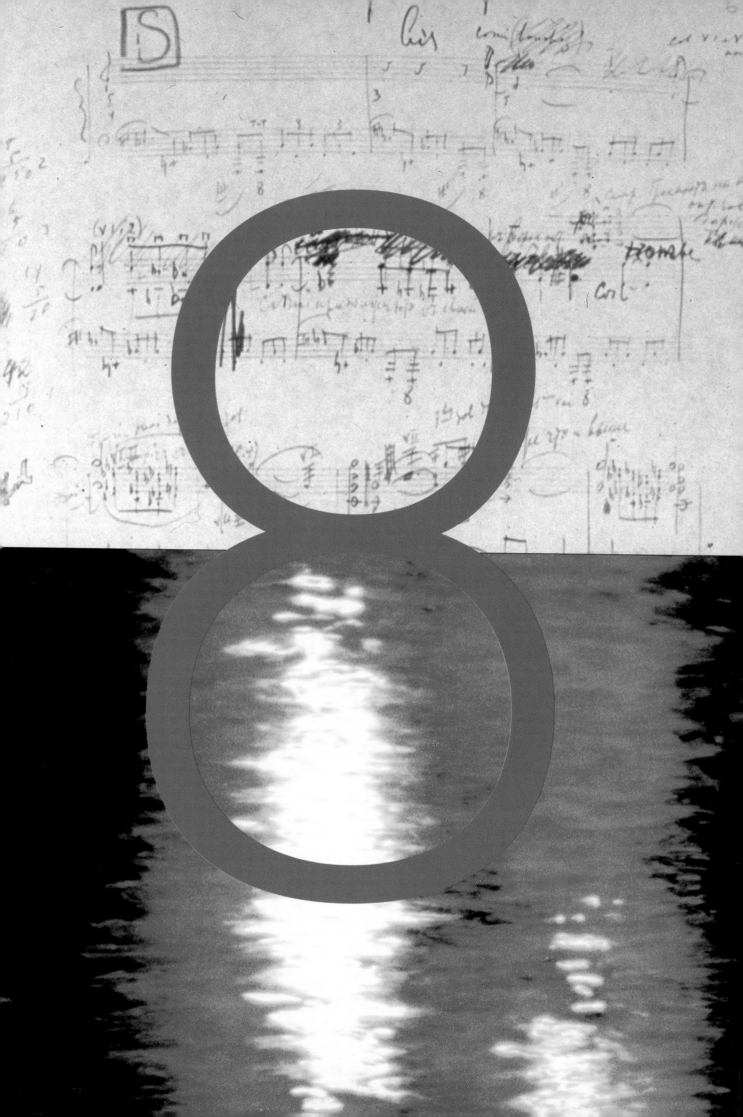

Western Europe enjoyed a period of relative stability in the first decade of the 20th century but in 1914 a series of entangling alliances brought all the great European nations into war. During the 1930s, a period of severe economic depression, the Nazis triumphed in Germany and the invasion of Poland by Germany in 1939 precipitated a truly global conflict. In the latter half of the century Europe began to create its own supernational institutions, and the collapse of Soviet Communism in the early 1990s provided a fresh impetus for a united Europe. The 20th century was a period of remarkable scientific and technological achievement. It was an era in which methods of communication were changed beyond recognition with the advent of radio, television and the computer.

20th century

The music of Claude-Achille Debussy (1862–1918) is often linked to the Impressionist movement in French painting. However, the associations are rather tenuous apart from, perhaps, the analogy between Monet's blurring of line and Debussy's breaking-up of directional harmonic movement. Debussy's influences come from different areas entirely. Earlier on in his career he was a great admirer of Wagner, visiting Bayreuth in 1888, and at the Paris Exhibition of 1889 he had his first encounter with Javanese gamelan music, an experience that would make a heavy imprint on his own music. He was also familiar with the work of Mussorgsky, an early exponent of a sort of non-functional harmony that is apparent in, amongst other works, the bell-ringing coronation scene from *Boris Godunov*.

Prélude à l'après-midi d'un faune (1894) is the first of Debussy's great orchestral pieces. It follows the slow-fast-slow form of the poem it was based upon while evoking the sensuous atmosphere of its subject. This work also shows the use of the whole-tone scale. This six-note scale became an important feature of Debussy's music and, although it is not dissonant in nature, its symmetrical form leads to the creation of melodies and harmonies that are effectively static. The three Nocturnes of 1899, *Nuages*, *Fêtes* and *Sirènes*, are based on paintings by Whistler. *Sirènes* in particular is notable for its use of a text-less female chorus whose function is to add colour rather than narrate a scenario. *La Mer* of 1905 is also in three parts and attempts to evoke the varying motions of the sea.

Right: Claude Debussy in 1916, photographed with his daughter Claude-Emma who was known by the nickname of Chouchou.

Below: A scene from the 1992 Welsh National Opera production of Debussy's one and only opera, 'Pélleas and Mélisande'.

Debussy's orchestration of often complex textures is remarkable. He makes extensive use of instrumental mutes in both strings and brass in order to produce a fullness of timbre at a subdued volume. There are also two harps present (instruments that are often associated with Debussy's orchestration), a large and varied percussion section and *sul ponticello* effects (bowing close to the bridge) on the strings. The focal point of the three *Images* of 1912 is the Spanish-influenced *Ibéria*, which is itself in three parts. *Jeux* of 1913 is a work with fleeting and constantly transforming motives and is notoriously resistant to musical analysis.

Debussy composed only one opera, *Pelléas et Mélisande* (1902). The central story involves a love triangle and is sung entirely in recitative. The opera is atmospheric rather than narrative and produces a strange other-worldly mood that is matched in the continuous orchestral backdrop of subtle colours and static harmonies.

Debussy was also active in the field of chamber music, especially that written for the piano. His piano pieces include the two books of *Préludes* (1910 and 1918), *Estampes* (1903), *Children's Corner* (1908) and the *Etudes* (1915). The piano writing mirrors the orchestral pieces in its mod and whole-tone harmonies, proliferation of non-developmental forms and use of flexible rhythmic figures. However, the first of the *Préludes, L'Isle joyeuse,* is in sonata form and looks forward to Debussy's return to a mo Classical idiom in his three chamber sonatas. Written for cello and piano (1915), flute, viola and harp (1915) and violin and piano (1917), these sonatas cast a glance backwards to Rameau and Couperin.

The music of Maurice Ravel (1875–1937) possesses many outward similarities to that of Debussy in as much as both display a gift for colourful orchestration and extensive use of whole-tone scales and modes. However, Ravel's music is somehow more precise and Classical in nature and his harmony less radical than that of Debussy owing to its basic functionalism. A rather sensuous brand of exoticism pervades many of his symphonic works such as *Shéhérazade* (1903) for singer and orchestra, *Rapsodie espagnole* (1908) and *Boléro* (1928), which despite its status as a popular classic exhibits quite a novel use of form where a large-scale orchestral crescendo is superimposed on to the simple repetition of a basic theme. Ravel wrote one opera, *L'Enfant et les sortilèges* (1925), and worked on the ballet *Daphnis et Chloé*, a masterpiece of impressionistic orchestration.

Ravel, himself a pianist, contributed considerably to the piano repertoire with his Piano Concerto for the Left Hand (1930), Piano Concerto in G (1931) and a number of solo pieces, the most famous of which are *Pavane pour une infante défunte* (1899), *Miroirs* (1905) and *Gaspard de la nuit* (1908). The solo works are more romantic in nature than those of Debussy. Ravel orchestrated many of his own piano pieces as well as *Pictures at an Exhibition*, the orchestrated version of Mussorgsky's collection of tableaux in fact becoming more popular than the piano one. The beginnings of Neoclassicism are apparent in *Sonatine* (1905) and *Le Tombeau de Couperin* (1917), while the orchestral work *La Valse* is a flamboyant and somewhat macabre portrait of that most celebrated 19th-century dance form.

The Spanish composer Manuel de Falla (1876–1946) composed the opera *La Vida breve* ('Life is short') in 1905. From 1907 to 1914 he lived in Paris where he met Debussy and Ravel. On his return to Spain he wrote the

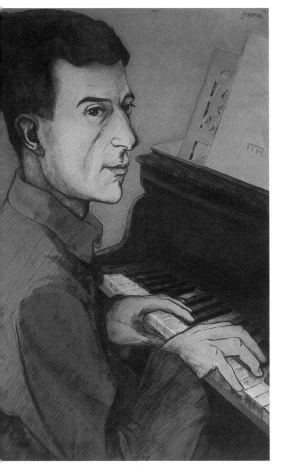

ow left: **A 1911 portrait of** ⠀rice Ravel playing the piano, by French artist Achille Ouvre. ⠀el's style was not limited by the ⠀ressionist aesthetic, drawing ⠀spects of Baroque, dance, jazz ⠀oriental music.

ow right: **The Spanish composer** ⠀uel de Falla, whose work, ⠀gh harmonically influenced by ⠀ressionism, never loses sight of ⠀native Spanish inspiration.

Right: A drawing by Jean Cocteau from 1920, inscribed 'à mon cher Erik Satie'. Cocteau's association with Satie from 1915 helped promote the latter's work, and included their collaboration with Diaghilev and Picasso on the 'realistic ballet' 'Parade' in 1917.

Below: The extraordinary Cubist-inspired costume by Pablo Picasso – who also designed the sets – for the character Slatkiewicz, 'The Manager from New York', in Erik Satie's 'Parade'.

music for a ballet, *El Amor brujo* ('Love the Magician', 1915). The music both opera and ballet are suffused with the primitive rhythms of the folk songs of southern Spain, an atmosphere which is again evoked in *Noche en los jardines de España* ('Nights in the Gardens of Spain', 1915), a suit of 'symphonic impressions' for piano and orchestra. In 1919 the ballet *El Sombrero de tres picos* ('The Three-Cornered Hat') was enthusiastically received and its vigorous and exciting music firmly established de Falla's international reputation. His last major work was a concerto for harpsichord and chamber orchestra (1926).

Erik Satie (1866–1925) represents the other side of French music during this period. A musical individualist, he displays in his work a disregard for accepted harmonic practices and a predisposition towards satire and comedy. The popular piano pieces *Gymnopédies* (1888, although later orchestrated by Debussy) are an early example of static, modal forms, while his *Socrate* (1920) for soprano and piano is more poised and Classical in nature. The influence of Satie was to be felt long after his death, most noticeably in the work of John Cage, who was famil with *Vexations* for solo piano, a piece where a section of music approximately two minutes long is repeated 840 times.

Another composer active at the turn of the century was the Czech, Le Janáček (1854–1928). For the greater part of his career he was to write a style reminiscent of Dvořák. Only in the final ten years of his life did he produce the works that he is now remembered for, including the two stri quartets (1923 and 1928), his *Sinfonietta* (1926) and operas such as *The Cunning Little Vixen* (1924) and *From the House of the Dead* (1928). It wa his understanding of the rhythm and stress of the Czech language that allowed him to develop a unique form of opera that placed a great emphasis on individual characterisation through the way the various parts were sung or spoken, while his interest in Moravian folk music introduced elements of repetition and non-resolution that were to infuse all his music with a subtle quality of modernity.

The Russian composer and pianist Aleksandr Skryabin (1872–1915) effectively approached what might be considered 'atonality' in his last piano sonatas (1912–13) through a strange compositional development that mixed the influences of Debussy and Liszt with his own preoccupation with mysticism in music. His first piano works were nocturnes and preludes written in the style of Chopin. However, he later developed an almost quasi-serial system of composition that involved deriving material from one large chord that often contained tritones and whole tones that would characterise the resulting music with a slightly wild Impressionistic flavour. As well as his ten piano sonatas, Skryabin also wrote two highly innovative and colourful orchestral works, *Poem of Ecstasy* (1908) and *Prometheus* (1910).

Skryabin's compatriot, the composer and pianist Sergei Rachmaninov (1873–1943), also added considerably to the piano repertoire. However, his music is of a distinctly post-Romantic style, with its focus on melodic writing and the exploitation of the more virtuosic elements of the idiom. He is best known for his piano concertos, especially the ever-popular second (1901), his symphonies and the *Rhapsody on a Theme of Paganini* for piano and orchestra (1935).

A 1917 pencil drawing of Arnold Schoenberg by the great Austrian Expressionist painter Egon Schiele. Schoenberg taught in Berlin until the rise of the Nazis compelled him, as a Jew, to leave the country.

The Second Viennese School

In many ways the composers that comprise the Second Viennese School, Arnold Schoenberg (1874–1935), Alban Berg (1885–1935) and Anton Webern (1883–1945), could be seen to have perpetuated the dominant Germanic trend of Western Classical music, despite what might be perceived as the radical nature of their music. The system of tonality was in a state of disintegration, mainly caused by the increasing chromaticism of the Romantics and the non-functioning ambiguity of Debussy's harmonies, a state of affairs that the Viennese School rapidly brought to its conclusion and then attempted to rebuild, albeit in a different manner.

Schoenberg sought to fuse the main tendencies of 19th-century music, encapsulated in the harmonic daring of Wagner and the rigorous motivic working of Brahms, into one unified style. His earlier works clearly betray his Romantic influences, most notably the string sextet *Verklärte Nacht* ('Transfigured Night', 1899). Other works of this period, the symphonic poem *Pelleas und Melisande* (1903) and the cantata *Gurrelieder* (finished in 1911), still display a taste for the large forces of 19th-century music, and it is interesting to note that as Schoenberg's music approached atonality, its instrumentation generally became smaller.

His First Chamber Symphony of 1906, while retaining the remnants of Classical form, displays a concentration of ideas that is clarified by the soloistic scoring (i.e. one player per part). The striking opening theme, consisting of a sequence of rising fourths, indicated the work's almost total surrender to atonality that can also be seen in the Opus 11 piano pieces of 1909. Schoenberg saw atonality as an inevitable step in the history of European music and invented the notion of 'the emancipation of the dissonance' to describe the fact that discordant intervals no longer needed to 'resolve'. They were sonorities in their own right.

The Second Viennese School was also linked with the Expressionist movement in German art. Expressionism represented a kind of corruption of the Romantic notion of personal expression, a need to display the distortion of inner experience, affected as it was by the anxiety and alienation of the modern condition. Schoenberg's affinity with Expressionism is perhaps best reflected in the monodrama *Erwartung* (1909) and in *Pierrot Lunaire* (1912). Both involve texts dealing with concepts of isolation and insanity, and *Pierrot Lunaire* in particular is macabre in tone, with its cabaret-like atmosphere and characteristic use of *Sprechgesang* ('speech-song').

In fact *Pierrot Lunaire* was to be the last of Schoenberg's 'freely atonal' works and it already betrays some of the composer's concerns with the structuring of music without the foundations of tonal harmony. The song cycle sees a return to set forms and regular counterpoint as well as metrical regularity. In the atonal works forms become smaller, or even miniature as in the Opus 19 piano pieces, unable to support larger musical structures unless a text is used to pull the music together. Other musical parameters become important, most notably timbre as in Schoenberg's theory of *Klangfarbenmelodie* ('melody of tone colours'). Timbre as structure is most clearly implemented in the strange shifting of sound in a virtually static harmonic field that defines number three of the Opus 16 orchestra pieces, entitled *Farben* ('Colours').

Schoenberg felt the need to develop a system that would incorporate the new atonality and yet order it to provide a framework analogous to the tonal system. The so-called 12-tone technique is most successfully used

Schoenberg's third and fourth string quartets, his Piano Suite of 1923 and the Variations for Orchestra of 1928. Briefly, the technique involves the use of a row consisting of all the 12 pitches of the chromatic scale that are placed in a fixed order. The row can be used both horizontally and vertically, that is as melody, counterpoint and harmony, and is translated into 48 versions through transposition and the writing of the row backwards, upside-down and both backwards and upside-down.

Schoenberg moved to the United States in 1934 and taught at the University of Southern California. As well as continuing with 12-tone music, he wrote some tonal works to be played by students. In the latter half of his career he also returned to larger forms as in the opera *Moses und Aron* (1932) and the choral work *A Survivor from Warsaw* of 1947. Schoenberg, however, was never to reach the same level of control and innovation in 12-tone technique that was mastered by his pupils.

Alban Berg first went to Schoenberg for composition lessons in 1904 with no significant background in playing music. His earliest works are the Opus 1 Piano Sonata (1908), the String Quartet (1910) and the Altenberg Songs for soprano and orchestra of 1912. The last of these especially reveals a gift for orchestration and a facility with the brief forms of free atonality. The last pre-serial works are The Chamber Concerto (1925) and the opera *Wozzeck* (1925). *Wozzeck* is a masterpiece of Expressionist music theatre. The music mixes atonality and tonality and skilfully blends contrasting Classical forms, such as passacaglias and a symphony, with distorted interpolations of popular music.

Berg adopted 12-tone techniques to his own ends and often broke the 'rules' by using more than one row in a single composition, as well as

ove: The front page of the rman 'Das Theater' review of nuary 1926, featuring a otograph from the Berlin emiere of Berg's 'Wozzeck' in cember 1925.

ght: The serialist pioneer Anton bern as painted by Max penheimer c.1908. Webern's luence on postwar developments serial language was profound.

varying rows through permutation. He also managed to incorporate his ongoing interest in the fusion of tonal and atonal into his music of this period through the structuring of the row so that it contained the potential for both types of material. The 12-tone row from Berg's Violin Concerto of 1935 contains not only triads, but also a whole-tone motif that is used to introduce the Bach chorale 'Es ist genug' at the end of the concerto. Berg's final opera, *Lulu*, remained incomplete at the time of his death.

Anton Webern approached the matter of atonality and serialism from a very different direction. The early atonal works such as the Five Pieces for Orchestra Opus 10 (1913) and Six Bagatelles for String Quartet (1913) display his predisposition for taking music to extremes. Not only do the pieces reveal Webern to be a master of the miniature form, but he compresses the material to produce music of extraordinary concentration and colour. However, Webern's main importance lies in his work with the 12-tone technique.

It is somewhat paradoxical that Webern's aims were very Classical and yet the resulting music was unlike anything that had ever been heard before. He wished to fuse the vertical and horizontal in music and create a level of complete formal coherence and 'connectedness'. Like Berg's, the structure of Webern's rows illustrates the nature of his objectives. They are often tiny structures within themselves, with sections of the row being palindromes, transpositions or inversions of other sections and the relationships often occurring on more than one level. The rows also contain only a limited number of intervals, such as thirds and minor seconds, that facilitate the structural relatedness.

The titles of his later works such as Symphony Opus 21 (1928), Concerto for Nine Instruments (1934) and Variations for Orchestra Opus 30 (1940) illustrate Webern's preoccupation with Classical forms. These pieces display what would later be considered a sort of purity of expression, devoid of anything approaching a melodic line and consisting of the passing of tiny fragments between the various instruments of an ensemble that are rarely used in 'tutti' fashion.

Stravinsky and Neoclassicism

If the Second Viennese School represents a continuation of the German Romantic tradition, then the work of the Russian Igor Stravinsky (1882–1971) can be seen as a reaction against it. Stravinsky's first ballet *The Firebird* (1910), exhibits a taste for colourful and sensuous orchestration with a touch of exoticism. The next two ballets, *Petrushka* (1911) and *Le Sacre du printemps* ('The Rite of Spring', 1913), represent the maturing of the first of Stravinsky's stylistic periods. Both employ Russian folk songs and an extended tonal language that includes the use of polytonal sonorities (the superimposing of two or more 'keys' that are often distantly related) and octatonicism (a scale of eight notes). However, the later score is much more abstract in its 'Russianness' than *Petrushka* and its brutal syncopated accents and motor rhythms in combination with a rather bold style of orchestration, which caused a riot at its premiere, have given rise to its association with primitivism.

From 1914 to 1920 Stravinsky lived in Switzerland where his music was to change considerably in both style and instrumentation. Strings are less important in the works of this period and the influence of jazz leans heavily on such pieces as *Ragtime* and *Piano Rag*, as well as in the scoring

Igor Stravinsky's three ballets – 'The Firebird', 'Petrushka' and 'Le Sacre du printemps' – were all staged by Sergei Diaghilev's Ballets Russes. This striking photograph shows the Russian dancer Tamara Karasavina as she appeared in 'Firebird', staged by the Ballets Russes in Paris in 1910.

of the music drama *L'Histoire du soldat* ('The Soldier's Tale', 1918).
Stravinsky's preference for a percussive rather than a lyrical employment
of the piano, first heard in *Petrushka*, continues to be important, especially
in the ballet *Les Noces* ('The Wedding', 1917–23) which has four in use in
addition to a battery of percussion. The most significant change, however,
was to come at the end of Stravinsky's stay in Switzerland with the ballet
Pulcinella (1919–20), a piece that ushers in the composer's involvement
with Neoclassicism.

Pulcinella is scored for a Baroque-type orchestra with concertino and
ripieno sections. The source of its material was the work of the 18th-
century composer Giovanni Pergolesi, which Stravinsky skilfully
manipulates, keeping melodies and bass lines intact while introducing
repetitions of phrases and an unbalancing of harmony that clearly alludes
to the modern origins of the work. Neoclassicism was a movement of a
dualistic nature, at once radical and highly conservative. Its radicalism
may be somehow due to its bypassing of Romantic ideals, slimming down
vast instrumentations and replacing 'expression' with a cooler objectivity.

Stravinsky's Neoclassical period was to last until 1951, with this
aesthetic taking most prominence in works such as the Wind Octet
(1922–3), the ballet *Apollon Musagète* (1928) and the Symphony in C
(1940). In 1951, by which time he had moved to the United States,
Stravinsky composed the opera *The Rake's Progress*, employing the forms
of 18th-century opera. Within this period Stravinsky also produced two
great vocal works, *Oedipus Rex* of 1927 and *Symphony of Psalms* of 1930.
His *Symphony in Three Movements* (1945) evokes the composer's Russian
period with its percussive piano writing and violent syncopation.

Right: 'Les Six' with (left to right) Francis Poulenc, Germaine Tailleferre, Louis Durey, a drawing of Georges Auric, their spokesman Jean Cocteau, Darius Milhaud and Arthur Honegger, in Milhaud's Paris flat in 1930.

Below: Part of a manuscript, signed by Béla Bartók, for a 1925 performance of his opera 'Duke Bluebeard's Castle'.

The last period of Stravinsky's life illustrates more than anything else the composer's openness to new ideas. Works such as the ballet *Agon* (1954–7), *In Memoriam Dylan Thomas* (1954) and Movements for Piano and Orchestra (1959) are examples of music using 12-tone techniques.

The influence of Stravinsky and Neoclassicism was to be felt most strongly by a group of French composers known as 'Les Six'. Most prolific among them was Darius Milhaud (1894–1974) who skilfully blended an eclectic mix of influences such as blues and Brazilian folk music with the sort of objective irony that is so characteristic of Neoclassicism. Among his works are several operas including *Les Malheurs d'Orphée* (1924) and *Médée* (1938), an opera-oratorio *Christophe Colomb* (1928), *La Création du monde* (1924) and *Le Boeuf sur le toit* (1919), which contains one of the most celebrated examples of polytonality in modern music.

Arthur Honegger (1892–1955) was the great orchestral composer among Les Six, writing five symphonies between 1931 and 1951 and *Pacific 231*, a work that evokes the movement of a locomotive-drawn train. He also achieved popularity with his opera-oratorio *King David*. Francis Poulenc (1899–1963) was perhaps the composer who most epitomised the Neoclassical style. He wrote a great deal of chamber music and songs that display his gift for melodic writing in addition to several operas including *Les Mamelles de Tirésias* (1940) and a piece for harpsichord or piano and small orchestra entitled 'Concert Champêtre' (1928). The other composers who constituted Les Six were Georges Auric (1899–1983), Germaine Tailleferre (1892–1983) and Louis Durey (1888–1979).

Bartók and folk music

The Hungarian Béla Bartók (1881–1945) approached the use of folk music in Classical composition in a more fundamental and methodical way than anyone before him. Together with Zoltán Kodály, he visited Hungarian, Romanian and Turkish villages and recorded the music of the people who lived there. The various tunes were ordered, catalogued and later published. However, although the folk music of eastern Europe is very often evident in Bartók's music, its use is never obvious or sentimental.

Bartók's output can be divided into roughly two periods. The music of the first period is more introverted and experimental in nature. He composed several works for the stage, the opera *Duke Bluebeard's Castle* (1918) and the ballets *The Wooden Prince* (1917) and *The Miraculous Mandarin* (1926). The last of these scores is remarkable for its impressive display of dazzling chromaticism and daring post-*Sacre* orchestration. He also began his cycle of six string quartets. The first two are more lyrical in style although the second contains a lively scherzo, while the third (1927) with its 'three movements in one' and the palindromic Fourth Quartet (1928) reveal Bartók's interest in structural innovation. The Fourth Quartet is possibly his most radical, containing two movements that are constituted exclusively by muted and plucked sounds and an opening chromatic theme that is used in a grating counterpoint.

Music for Percussion, Strings and Celeste (1936) effectively illustrates the change of Bartók's style between his first and second periods through the differences between its four movements. The odd-numbered movements are quiet, colourful and inward-looking and are characterised by the washes of sound provided by the celeste, while the second and

...ók (fourth from left) collecting ...ak folk songs in 1907 in the ...ge of Zobordarazs in Nyitra ...nty (now Drazovoce in the ...ch Republic). His research led ...to discover that the true ...yar folk music was significantly ...rent from the Gypsy style up ...hen regarded as authentic.

fourth movements are louder and rhythmically driven. A percussive style
piano writing is evident in this work and in the three piano concertos
(1926, 1931 and 1945, respectively).

The second period is perhaps more outward-looking and accessible b
does not contain the innovation of Bartók's earlier work. During this time
he composed the fifth and sixth string quartets (1934 and 1939), his
Second Violin Concerto (1938), the Divertimento for Strings (1939), his
popular Concerto for Orchestra (1943) and a Viola Concerto (1945).
Bartók also made a considerable contribution to the art of learning the
piano with his six volumes of *Mikrokosmos* (1926–39).

Zoltán Kodály (1882–1967) was also interested in educational music
and produced a complete course for use in schools entitled *Music for
Children* (1950–4). His interest in Hungarian music is evident in his
singspiel *Háry János* (1926) which uses the cymbalom, a traditional
Hungarian instrument, and *Psalmus Hungaricus* (1923) for a tenor soloist
chorus and orchestra.

Music in Germany

Paul Hindemith (1895–1963) represents a much more conservative side
of 20th-century Germanic music. His works of the 1920s are of a 'Neo-
Baroque' style and show the influence of Bach in both their form and
contrapuntal textures, although the modern context often requires an
ensemble that is less dominated by strings. Typical of this style are the
Kammermusik 1–7 (1922–7). Hindemith also wrote four string quartets
and two operas, *Cardillac* (1926) and *Neues vom Tage* (1929), during the
same period. The next decade saw Hindemith questioning the role of the

Above: A drawing of Paul
Hindemith by Milein Cosman. As a
result of Nazi disfavour Hindemith
left Germany in 1938, working in
the US from 1940 to 1951 before
settling in Switzerland.

Right: Kurt Weill's most celebrated
work was undoubtedly 'The
Threepenny Opera', written in
collaboration with playwright
Bertolt Brecht. The scene here is
from a production by the Welsh
National Opera company in 1984.

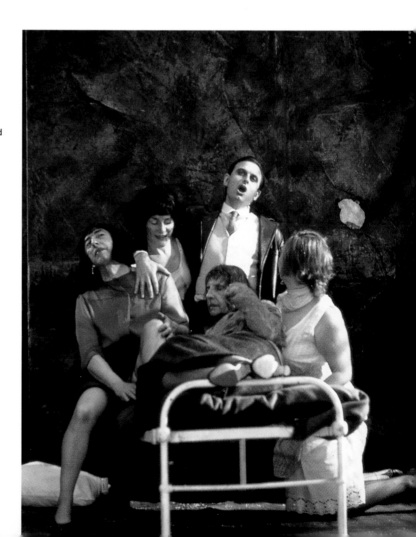

composer and music in the modern age. He believed that music should
have a function and that it should not be alienated from the public either
by excessive aesthetic or technical difficulty. *Lundas tonalis* (1942) for
piano is a set of pieces in every key based around Hindemith's theories
on extended tonal harmony, while the instrumental sonatas written
between 1936 and 1955 explore the possibilities of each orchestral
instrument in turn. His opera *Mathis der Maler* (1938) is a testament to
Hindemith's artistic concerns. Its central character, a painter, has to
decide between the relative 'usefulness' of artistic and political activity.

Hindemith's late works include a requiem, *When Lilacs Last in the Door-
yard Bloom'd*, *Symphonic Metamorphoses on Themes of Weber* (1943), an
opera, *Die Harmonie der Welt* (1957), and the last two string quartets.
Hindemith was also notable in the field of music theory, producing the
book *The Craft of Musical Composition*, which was published in 1957.

Kurt Weill (1900–50) went a stage further than Hindemith in his attempts
to reconcile the composer and his public. Concentrating mainly on opera,
Weill incorporated elements of American popular music into his
composition, both in terms of instrumentation and materials. His most
famous works are collaborations with the writer Bertolt Brecht (1898–1956),
with whom he produced *The Rise and Fall of the City of Mahagonny* (1929),
The Threepenny Opera (1928), which features the popular song 'Mack the
Knife', and *The Seven Deadly Sins* (1933). Brecht and Weill shared left-wing
beliefs, which manifested themselves in the subjects of their operas. In
addition to his stage works, Weill also wrote two symphonies (1921 and
1933) and a string quartet.

Weill was forced to leave Europe in 1935 both because of his Jewish
origins and the controversial and political nature of his work. He settled in
New York where he produced a series of Broadway musicals including
Knickerbocker Holiday (1938), *Lady in the Dark* (1940), *One Touch of Venus*
(1943) and *Street Scene* (1946).

Music in the United States

American music of the 20th century has veered between extreme innovation and conservatism. The music of Charles Ives (1874–1954) is significant for its highly original use of borrowed material and the presence of polytonality, atonality and even microtonality. Ives wrote fou symphonies, *The First Orchestral Set: Three Places in New England* (1914) and *The Second Orchestral Set* (1915), as well as *The Unanswered Questic* (1906), which is believed to predate Schoenberg in its use of atonality. H also composed around 200 songs and chamber music, including two pia sonatas, the quarter-tone piano piece *Tone Roads* (1911–15) and five vio sonatas. His music remained neglected until the 1930s.

Henry Cowell (1897–1965) was another American innovator. His mos well-known works were written for the piano and involve the use of tone clusters and effects obtained by playing inside the piano. His piano piec include *The Aeolian Harp* (1923), *Piano Piece* (1924) and *The Banshee* (1925). Cowell also used clusters in his orchestral writing and his *Mosaic Quartet* (1935) is an early example of indeterminacy, constructed from various sections whose order is left to the choice of the players.

The music of Aaron Copland (1900–90) represents the more accessib side of American composition. In an attempt to communicate with his audience, Copland incorporated traditional American songs and spiritua into his predominantly tonal style. *Appalachian Spring* (1944) for orches and the ballets *Billy the Kid* (1938) and *Rodeo* (1942) are examples of th style. Copland's later works are perhaps a little more complex in nature, such as the Third Symphony (1940), the 12-tone inspired Piano Quartet (1950) and *Inscape* (1967) for orchestra.

The mainstream of American composition was also contributed to by Samuel Barber (1910–81). Although he is best known for the perhaps over-exposed *Adagio for Strings* (1936), he also wrote songs, an opera, *Anthony and Cleopatra* (1936), and a violin concerto (1940), which is considered by many to be his best work.

A more experimental side of American music can be seen in the compositions of Elliott Carter (b.1908), Milton Babbitt (b.1916) and Conlon Nancarrow (1912–97). Carter forged a modernist style through h

Above: A study by Fred Dolbin of Charles Ives. Ives' career in insurance absolved him of the need to earn a living from music, which he felt would have compromised his artistic and ethical principles.

Below left: A 1950s 'long-play' album featuring Leonard Bernstein conducting the RCA Victor Symphony Orchestra, performing Gershwin's 'American in Paris' and Copland's 'Billy the Kid'.

Below right: Aaron Copland in 1940. Copland's work moved from the jazz and neoclassical influences of the 1920s, through an atonal serialism, to the tonal simplicity echoing American folk music which represents his best-known compositions.

manipulation of 'metric modulation' and quasi-serial technique. He is
particularly well known for his string quartets. Milton Babbitt followed a
more Classical, post-Webern course of inquiry, with his development of the
12-tone technique. Nancarrow forged a place in the modern repertoire
through an exploration of the possibilities of the player-piano, uniting an
interest in non-Western music with complex rhythmic ideas.

Music in England

During most of the 20th century English composers have mainly chosen to
follow their own, more conservative tradition. In accordance with English
music of the past, composers have stayed with musical genres such as
choral works, opera and the symphony. Ralph Vaughan Williams
(1872–1958) was the most important British composer of the first half of
the century. His output includes nine symphonies, a number of songs,
hymns and even film scores. His 'pastoral' and largely modal style of
music was influenced not only by his knowledge of his native folk song but
also by his interest in the music of the English Renaissance, especially
that of a sacred nature. His *Fantasia on a Theme by Thomas Tallis* (1910)
for strings divided into three orchestras and string quartet makes use of
the antiphonal effects often associated with 16th-century music. His
involvement in church music produced the opera *Pilgrim's Progress*
(1951), based on the work of the 17th-century Nonconformist John
Bunyan, and several oratorios. Vaughan Williams also edited the English

Hymnal between 1904 and 1906. One of his most popular works is *The Lark Ascending* (1914) for violin and orchestra, a piece that is the epitome of 20th-century English pastoralism.

William Walton (1902–82) also wrote symphonies in addition to a viola concerto, an opera, *Troilus and Cressida* (1954), and some chamber music. He is perhaps the most European of this generation of English composers. *Façade* (1921–2) for reciter and ensemble evokes the light irony of the French Neoclassicists, while the oratorio *Belshazzar's Feast* (1931) employs devices such as polytonality and syncopation that betray the influence of Stravinsky. Other composers of this period include Gustav Holst (1874–1934), who wrote the orchestral suite *The Planets* (1916), and Frederick Delius (1862–1934), known for his operas, orchestral pieces and tone poems.

Benjamin Britten (1913–76) is most renowned for his renewal of English opera. His musical language was based on an extended tonality with modal and sometimes chromatic inflections, much like the harmonic language of those composers from the previous generation. His output includes many fine operas such as *Peter Grimes* (1945), *Billy Budd* (1951) and *The Turn of the Screw* (1954), in addition to his *War Requiem* (1946).

The heir to Britten's crown was Michael Tippett (1905–98). His main works are the oratorio *A Child of our Time* (1941), the operas *The Midsummer Marriage* (1955) and *King Priam* (1962), in addition to three symphonies and a number of concertos. Peter Maxwell Davies (b.1934), part of Britain's avant-garde, has written three operas, including *Taverner* (1972).

Below left: Benjamin Britten (centre) inspecting a model of the stage set designs for the original production of his opera 'Peter Grimes' in 1945.

Below right: William Walton rehearsing the opera 'Troilus and Cressida' with Hungarian soprano Magda Laszlo at London's Royal Opera House, Covent Garden, 1954.

Music in R u s s i a : Prokofiev and Shostakovich

ove left: A still from the
ectacular 'battle on the ice'
quence in Sergei Eisenstein's
c film 'Alexander Nevsky',
which Sergei Prokofiev wrote
score.

ve right: Prokofiev in Nikopol in
10. Despite a clear loyalty to his
ssian homeland and the Soviet
tem, the composer avoided
nd obeisance with touches of
sical irony verging on satire.

The effect of living as a composer under a totalitarian regime is illustrated
in the careers of Sergei Prokofiev (1891–1953) and Dmitri Shostakovich
(1906–75). Prokofiev chose to leave his homeland in 1918, but decided to
return in 1936. During his earlier period he developed a strangely diverse
style of composition within the more traditional genres of symphony,
concerto and opera. His first symphony, *The Classical Symphony* (1917), is
an example of Neoclassicism predating Stravinsky and Les Six, while his
second symphony utilises the heavy, modern rhythmic drive that is
characteristic of *Le Sacre*. His opera *The Love for Three Oranges* (1921) is
sharp and ironic in style within its often bizarre narrative. Other works of
this period are more Romantic in nature, such as the early piano
concertos. However, he was still very much involved in the language of
complex tonality, using the occasional dissonant spice of polytonality.
Other works of his pre-Soviet period include two violin concertos (1917
and 1935) and the operas *The Fiery Angel* (1929) and *The Gambler* (1929).

After his return to the Soviet Union Prokofiev's music became more
conservative out of necessity, although not without some ironic moments.
His most interesting projects of this period were the music for the children's
piece *Peter and the Wolf* (1936) and his work on the film scores for Sergei
Eisenstein's *Alexander Nevsky* (1939) and *Ivan the Terrible* (1945). He also
completed the ballet music for *Romeo and Juliet* (1938), a score that was
initially judged as too modernist for Soviet purposes, and *Cinderella* (1945).

Shostakovich spent his entire career under the weighty influence of
Soviet artistic policy. His output is dominated by the two cycles of 15
symphonies and 15 string quartets. Although his musical language is
mainly that of tonality, Shostakovich, like Prokofiev, revealed a certain
modicum of subversion. His second and third symphonies entitled
'October' (1927) and 'The First of May' (1929) introduce into their
respective last movements choral sections that give praise to the
revolution. Shostakovich was obliged to withdraw his more daring Fourth
Symphony after a clamp-down by the government and instead offered his
Fifth Symphony, a grandiose work with its famous beginning in dotted
rhythms, but also not without moments of subtle irony.

Above left: A stage curtain designed for the Sergei Prokofiev ballet 'Chout' ('The Buffoon').

Below: Publicity material for the first performance in England of 'Lady Macbeth of Mtsensk' by Dmitri Shostakovich.

His Seventh Symphony ('The Leningrad', 1941) was so popular with the authorities that it was promoted abroad. However, the Eighth and Ninth Symphonies did not conform so well. After Stalin's death in 1953 Shostakovich produced perhaps his best symphony, the tenth, using a musical motive created from the translation of the composer's initials into German, a motive that also occurs in his Eighth String Quartet from the same period. The 13th Symphony is his most outspoken: it openly criticises the past actions of the Soviet government. In addition Shostakovich also composed operas, among them the celebrated *Lady Macbeth of Mtsensk* (1932), two piano concertos, violin concertos and cello concertos, and a collection of 24 Preludes and Fugues (1951) for piano, revealing perhaps more than any other works his ties with the European traditions of the past

Music from 1945 to the present day

The end of the Second World War provides the most convenient starting point in the classification of what might be termed contemporary Classical music. It is perhaps no surprise that the young composers of the first postwar generation wished in some way to 'wipe the slate clean' in terms of the development of a new musical language, and in many of the varied enterprises of contemporary music can be seen the common desire to reinvent both the role of the composer and the nature of his art.

Perhaps the most characteristic aspect of Classical music in the last 50 years has been the lack of a common style, methodology and aim among its protagonists. The plurality of music is indeed a reflection of the age in which we live. The following summary of music from the past 50 years is not intended as an exhaustive account of all the composers that have been active during this period. Instead, the main musical trends are summarised and accompanied by suitable examples of the composers working within the particular medium.

Integral s e r i a l i s m and the legacy of Webern

Of all the prewar composers it was, interestingly enough, Anton Webern who was to provide the inspiration behind the following period's first important compositional school of thought. The attraction of Webern's serial music lay in its sparse textures, its sense of enigmatic 'newness' and its apparent tendency towards total control and interrelation of materials and forms. However, it was the French composer Olivier Messiaen (1908–92) who made what is thought to be one of the first forays into total serialism with his piano piece *Mode de valeurs et d'intensités* (1949). The piece is constructed from three sets of 12 pitches, with each pitch having its own duration, dynamic and mode of attack. However, since the pitches are used in a relatively free manner the piece is not strictly speaking a serial one.

It was Messiaen's pupils Pierre Boulez (b.1925) and Karlheinz Stockhausen (b.1928) who were to exploit fully the notion of integral serialism. In Boulez's pieces for two pianos, *Structures I–II* (1952–6), every parameter of the composition is controlled. The work uses a 12-tone row that is transposed and inverted in the normal manner and then arranged into matrices. Since every specific pitch has a number allocated to it, series of dynamics, attacks and durations can be superimposed on to the matrix patterns. The different forms of the series are then basically presented in order, although the register, tempo and the number of different 'lines' present are varied. Stockhausen produced works of similar formal rigorousness in *Kreuzspiel* (1951) and *Punkte* (1952). However, both composers soon discovered that such music had its limitations.

Despite its formal radicalism and logical perfection, the processes of integral serialism produced music that was always similar in character. Isolated points of sound and a lack of melodic and thematic elements

Left: An album cover featuring music for the film 'The Gadfly', with compostions by Dmitri Shostakovich, whose photograph is repeated as part of the design.

Below left: Pierre Boulez in 1963. Boulez developed a totally serial musical language, has explored the relationship of poetry and music, and extended the range of his orchestral textures with elements of electronic music in later work.

Below right: Olivier Messiaen, whose work was much influenced by Indian music, Catholic mysticism and even, from the late 1950s, elements of birdsong as a source of melodic material.

created a style that came to be known as 'pointillism' which was both difficult for the audience to engage with and offered little in the way of future possibilities. Stockhausen began to solve the problem by organisin his material into groups – melodies, chords and textures – the result of which can be found in *Kontrapunkte* (1952–3). His tour de force, *Gruppen* (1957), for three spatially separated orchestras, includes freer sections among the more rigorously composed parts. Boulez also relaxed his compositional systems in order to produce *Le Marteau sans maître* (1955 The success of the music lies as much in its fragile, quasi-oriental and expressive musical lines as it does in the post-serial processes that created it. The music of the Italian Luigi Nono (1924–90) aimed at merging the musical language of integral serialism with political awareness. His *Il Canto sospreso* is a comment upon the atrocities of the Nazis and his opera *Intolleranza 1960* is a testament to his left-wing sympathies, possibly bringing into question the notion that musical avan gardism is of no importance other than to itself.

Hans Werner Henze (b.1926), despite his initial interest in serialism, soo turned to music theatre as his most prominent means of expression. Like We and Nono he sought to express socialist views in his work. His music contain quotations from both serious music of the past and more popular idioms. Hi operas include *König Hirsch* (1956) and *Das Floss der Medusa* (1968).

Electronic music

Perhaps the most important source of new timbres and compositional methods can be found in the realm of electronic and computer-aided music. New technology has not only provided the means for creating new sounds, but in recent times instrumental colours have been synthesised with increasing degrees of success. The pioneer of music in this field was Pierre Schaeffer (b.1910) who developed 'musique concrète' in his Paris studios. This earlier form of electronic music utilised prerecorded sounds that were manipulated in various basic ways through altering the direction or speed of the playback of the recording. Schaeffer's most famous work i his *Etude aux chemins de fer* of 1948, created from recordings of railway trains. Edgard Varèse had also successfully employed electronic music in combination with an instrumental ensemble in *Déserts* (1954), and in its own right in his *Poème électronique* (1958).

Electronic music was also to become possibly the ultimate expression the tendency towards determinacy found in the integral serialist movemer Karlheinz Stockhausen visited Schaeffer's studios, but found the methods of musique concrète not sophisticated enough for his purposes. If serialis could determine every parameter of a piece then the next step would be to build musical timbre itself in line with the structural principles of a composition. From his studios in Cologne, Stockhausen produced a numb of works, notably his Electronic Studies Nos 1 and 2 (1953), *Gesang der Jünglinge* (1956), in which 'concrète' sounds are also used, and *Kontakte* c 1960, with versions for tape alone and for tape, percussion and piano.

The development of the computer has greatly enhanced both the possibilities of non-instrumental music and the facility with which it is produced. Computers can generate the very material of composition as well as providing the means for live-processing and response in concert situations – so-called 'real-time' music.

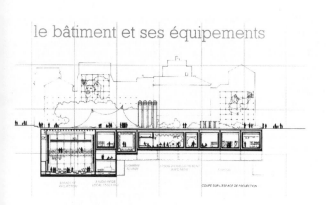

le bâtiment et ses équipements

Top: Karlheinz Stockhausen, 1960, working at the Studio for Electronic Music in Cologne. After his experiments in total serialism and electronic sound in the 50s, by the late 60s his work (partly influenced by eastern mysticism) left much to the actual performer's intuition.

Above: A plan of the building and facilities at the IRCAM music research institute in Paris.

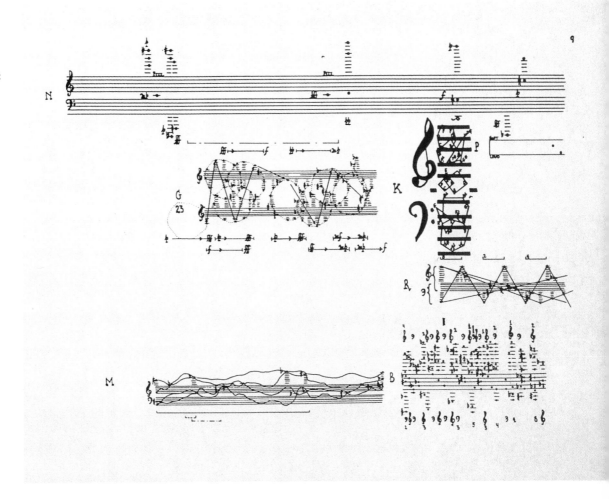

ht: A page from the John Cage
re of Concert for Piano and
hestra (1957–8). Influenced by
Iaism and Zen Buddhism,
e applied the principles of
domness current in visual art at
time to sound performances,
h unspecified instruments and
eterminate duration.

ow: John Cage (left) working in
recording studio with the
erican pianist and electronic
mposer David Tudor in 1965.

In the late 1970s the Institut de Recherche et de Coordination Acoustique/Musique (IRCAM) was established in Paris and has become the leading centre of research into electronic music, computer-generated music and the analysis/synthesis of sound. With the use of IRCAM's formidable technology, composers such as Tristan Murail (b.1947) and Kajia Saariaho (b.1952) have been able to develop methods of relating compositional structure to the structure of complex sounds to produce what is known as 'spectral music'.

Indeterminacy

The opposite side of the coin to the rigid determinacy of serialism can be found in the flowering of music incorporating chance compositional methods, improvisation and performer choice. Such music not only rejects the central tendencies of Romantic art and the concept of the creative genius, it also questions the very nature of Classical music and its relation to the world around it. The foremost philosopher in this area was the American composer John Cage (1912–92). Instead of baring his artistic soul to the public, Cage saw as his task the revelation of the sounds around us. The notorious 4' 33" consists entirely of four minutes and 33 seconds of what might at first be perceived as 'silence', but the inaction of which instead directs the audience to the ambient sounds around them. Cage also engaged in compositional activities that involved the production of musical material from chance processes such as the tossing of coins

(*Music of Changes*, 1951) and the inclusion of 12 radio sets tuned to whatever happens to be broadcast at the time of performance (*Imaginary Landscape No 4*).

Another aspect of indeterminate music was the concept of mobile forms. The musical work would differ at each performance either as a result of the reordering of its constituent parts, performer improvisation or the use of variable parameters. The resulting piece would be analogous to an object that can be viewed from many different angles, although essentially remaining the same. Stockhausen was to deal with this type of indeterminacy throughout the 1960s. His *Klavierstück XI* consists of a large sheet of paper scattered with various fragments of music. The performer is required to start at any fragment in any tempo, moving to the next fragment that catches his eye in the tempo marking specified at the end of the previous section. The piece eventually finishes when a fragment has been reached for the third time. Stockhausen's *Zyklus* (1959) for percussion and Boulez's Third Piano Sonata involve a similar variability as to the ordering of sections of music.

The inclusion of various kinds of improvisation is also prevalent in Stockhausen's music of this period. He created pieces using what he called a 'plus-minus' system where what was played next would be determined by an arrangement of + (more) and – (less) signs to indicate changes in musical parameters. The works *Plus-minus* (1963), *Prozession* (1967) and *Kurzwellen* (1968) are examples of this type of music. However, it is in *Aus den sieben Tagen* (1968) that the input of players and the scope of their improvisational skills are of greatest importance. The piece is a series of texts aimed at stimulating musical responses from the players.

In the United States composers were following the lead of Cage. In the 1950s Morton Feldman (1926–87) and Earle Brown (b.1926) engaged in graph compositions when one or more parameters of the composition would be left to the interpretation of various graphical elements by the performer. Feldman's *Projections and Intersections* indicate time through the spatial layout of the score while 'boxes' specify the instrumentation, register and number of sounds to be used, although pitch is not specified. Graph composition can be seen to reach perhaps its most ambiguous and enigmatic potential in works such as Brown's *December 1952* and Cornelius Cardew's *Treatise* (1963–7), which has no instructions and consists of about 200 pages of symbols and quasi-musical notation.

New sounds

It is not surprising that many of the postwar generation of composers decided to engage in musical activities that focused on timbre and texture. Perhaps the two most important composers in this field were the Greek-born Iannis Xenakis (b.1922) and the Hungarian composer György Ligeti (b.1923). Xenakis approached the art of composition from a somewhat fresh perspective. He was an architect and had a firm grasp of mathematics. The application of so-called 'stochastics' to the control of musical textures produced results of genuine artistic innovation and considerable musical power. *Metastasis* (1953–5) presents complex webs of string glissandi, while *Plithoprakta* (1955–6) includes a variety of new (and precisely computed) orchestral textures. His large output includes a considerable amount of string music, as well as percussion pieces (such

Below: Morton Feldman, whose music is characteristically slow, quiet and delicate.

Bottom: A page from the score of 'Aventures' (1962) by György Ligeti. His approach to sound masses in which shape is produced by a complex of submerged details is known as micropolyphony.

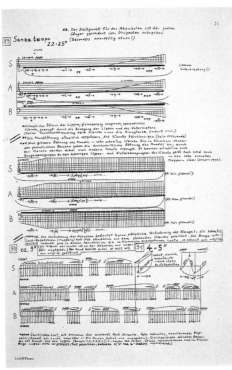

The Greek composer Iannis Xenakis (right) with the famed architect Le Corbusier, for whom he worked for some years after having studied both engineering and architecture.

as *Pleiades*) and electronic music. Ligeti's textural music is perhaps milder in tone and certainly less scientific in orientation. *Atmosphères* (1961) and *Lontano* (1967) consist of slow-moving clusters of sustained orchestral sound, while the Chamber Concerto for 13 Instrumentalists presents layers of ostinato-type material and contrasting pulses. It is perhaps noteworthy that Ligeti's music has reached a wider public than that of most other contemporary composers. It has been employed, for example, in the soundtracks for Stanley Kubrick's films *2001: A Space Odyssey* and *The Shining*.

The Polish composers Krzystoff Penderecki (b.1933) and Witold Lutoslawski (1913–94) have also engaged in the writing of textural music, often using sections where the players play material out of synchronisation with one another in order to produce dense textures. Penderecki's *Threnody for the Victims of Hiroshima* (1960) for string orchestra, despite its lack of refinement, must stand alone as perhaps the harshest and most grating piece of 20th-century music.

The exploration of sound was also the aim of Italian composer Giacinto Scelsi (1905–88). The limitations of pitch material and the concentration on timbral quality and microtonal variations are characteristic of his music. His *Quattro Pezzi for Chamber Orchestra* (1959) displays a powerful examination of sound, with the use of one dominant, static pitch. Scelsi's music was not widely played nor had it been 'discovered' in avant-garde circles until the last ten years of his life, and only recently has the importance and sheer originality of his compositions been recognised.

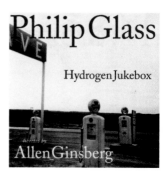

Above left: An album cover for 'Te Deum' and other religious pieces by Arvo Pärt, performed by the Estonian Philharmonic Chamber Choir and the Tallinn Chamber Orchestra, and conducted by Tõnu Kaljuste.

Above right: Philip Glass, well known for theatrical pieces in the field of opera, collaborated with the beat poet Allen Ginsberg for 'Hydrogen Jukebox'.

Minimalism

The reaction against what might be perceived as the increasing 'difficulty' of postwar music was inevitable. The beginnings of the movement, known as 'repetitive' or 'minimal' music, can be seen in the fluxus movement that started in New York in the early 1960s. The main protagonists of minimal music at this time were La Monte Young (b.1935) and Terry Riley (b.1935). Simple music was combined with other mediums in 'happening'-type events. Riley's *In C* (1964) involves the playing of a variety of motifs in C major with a constant and prominent pulse, whereas Young's *The Tortoise, His Dreams and Journeys*, for voices, mixers, amplifiers, drones and loudspeakers, stretches listeners as regards its duration and slow pacing.

Steve Reich (b.1936) and Philip Glass (b.1937) were to take minimal music to a new level of accomplishment through the use of audible processes. Reich initiated the idea of 'phase music' where simple musical ideas are gradually moved out of synchronisation with one another to produce what the composer describes as 'resulting patterns'. At first he used this method purely with taped excerpts of speech as in *Come Out* (1966), but later he developed the idea for instrumental music, such as in *Piano Phase* and *Violin Phase* (1967). Reich's work in the 1970s expanded on these basic ideas but grew in both duration and instrumentation. *Drumming* (1971), *Music for Mallet, Instruments, Voices and Organ* (1973) and *Music for 18 Musicians* (1974–6) are examples of works of this period. In more recent years Reich's music has perhaps been lacking in the radical flavour that it originally possessed. Pieces for increasingly larger ensembles such as *The Desert Music* (1982–3) and *The Four Sections* (1987) submerge processes in

Right: The Kronos Quartet, for whom Steve Reich wrote his 'Different Trains' in 1988. It was typical of his later work, which often reflected his Jewish heritage.

Far right: Philip Glass at the keyboard (right, foreground) in rehearsal with musicians in March 1977 at UCLA, Los Angeles.

the lush textures of an orchestral sound. He has also shown interest in writing music reflecting his Jewish heritage, for instance *Different Trains* (1988) for the Kronos string quartet and the multi-media work *The Cave* (1992).

Philip Glass began working with additive rhythmical processes in the late 1960s, probably influenced by his experiences of Indian music. He wrote several pieces using these types of processes for unspecified instrumentation such as *Music in Similar Motion* (1969) and later on varied this style to produce *Music with Changing Parts* (1970), which layers the additive processes with passages of sustained chords. However, Glass is best known for his forays into opera, including *Einstein on the Beach* (1975), a work lasting four and a half hours and containing no text or obvious narrative structure. Other minimalist composers have found opera an effective medium for their work. The American John Adams (b.1947) created *Nixon in China* (1987), a piece that reveals Adams' gift for refined orchestration. A more sophisticated and Stravinskian brand of minimalism can be seen in the work of Louis Andriessen (b.1939), who composed the opera *Rosa* (1992) in collaboration with Peter Greenaway.

Minimalism of a more religious and contemplative nature has been the goal of composers such as the Estonian Arvo Pärt (b.1935) and the English composer John Tavener (b.1944). Minimalism has had greater appeal for the general public than the other categories of postwar composition. The prime reasons seem obvious – more tunes, modal harmony and sonorous instrumentation.

Postmodernism and beyond

The term 'postmodernism' was first used in architecture to describe a style that rejected the harshness modernism of the international school and that instead began to incorporate or modify the architectural features of past ag in contemporary buildings. The effects of postmodernism in all mediums seems to have been manifold. Firstly, postmodernism reflects an age where history has halted, leaving a cultural free-for-all where material from any ag is available to the magpie artist. Indeed, the results are often witty and iron a true expression of the multi-layeredness of contemporary culture. In addition, postmodern art is more accessible to the public – indicating that perhaps humour is the most successful route to the public's imagination.

Two representatives of postmodern style in music are the Russian Alfred Schnittke (1934–98) and the American John Zorn (b.1953). Schnittke can in many ways be seen as continuing the traditions of the music of Shostakovich full of the irony that the distortion of 'other musics' can bring to a piece. In h *Concerto Grosso* of 1977 Schnittke mixes the Baroque with anachronous disruption of atonality and popular music. Zorn's music, on the other hand, much more directly linked to aspects and perhaps 'failings' of popular cultur *Forbidden Fruit* for string quartet and tape veers violently between various musics, resembling in a way the discontented 'channel-surfing' of modern consumers with their somewhat short attention spans.

Despite its apparent playfulness, postmodernism may be seen as pointing towards a rather nihilistic future. With no history and no force to propel us forward, where else is there to go if not backwards? Can such music ever have any real message and has it spelt the end for serious art music? The answer would seem to be 'no' according to the many composers who have not accepted the premises of postmodern theory.

Below left: The saxophonist and composer John Zorn, whose music is characterised by elements of jazz and rock, with his ex-wife Mori Ikue, who was his percussionist in many ensembles.

Below right: The composer Luciano Berio, whose 'Sinfonia' (1968) for voices and orchestra included fragments from other composers ranging from Ravel to Stockhausen, arranged around a framework of the scherzo from Mahler's Second Symphony. Direct quotation from other works has been a hallmark of postmodernism.

Many British composers can be seen to have kept the flag of modernism flying. Brian Ferneyhough (b.1943) has developed possibly the most extreme brand of post-serialism in a style that is often referred to as 'complexity'. Like that of his contemporary Michael Finnissy (b.1946), his music is characterised by a certain complexity of notation and the high demands made on the performer by extremely intricate rhythms and a great attention to the detail of instrumental technique and expression. Ferneyhough's *Transit* (1972–5) is for singers and ensemble and *Carceri d'invenzione* (1981–6) is a large cycle of works alternating between extremely virtuosic solo pieces and powerful, dense ensemble sections. Harrison Birtwistle (b.1934) occupies a place slightly nearer the mainstream of British music. His superb *Earth Dances* (1985–6) for orchestra and the operas *Gawain* (1991) and *The Mask of Orpheus* (1986) have done much to revitalise the more traditional genres of British music.

The German composer Helmut Lachenmann (b.1935) writes music that is concerned with extended instrumental techniques, and has developed tablature-type notation in order to achieve a more practical communication between the composer's intentions and the way the player might achieve them. In stark contrast, the music of his compatriot Wolfgang Rihm (b.1952) has been labelled 'neo-Romantic', forming yet another distinctive postwar aesthetic that has also found much favour in both the United States and Britain.

With such a plethora of often mutually exclusive aesthetics and styles in today's Classical music, it is difficult to imagine that there might ever be what would be considered a 'common practice' among composers, as was more or less the case in music before this century. However, perhaps this is not a necessary or even desirable state of affairs – the plurality of modern music is merely a reflection of our own times complicated by the accessibility of both past times and the rest of the world.

w left: The first recording of
d Schnittke's 'Sacred Hymns'
g with his Symphony No 4,
rmed by the Russian State
ohony Orchestra and
ucted by Valéry Polyansky.

w right: Schnittke in Berlin in
. His experimental work with
l procedures and electronic
c includes two symphonies,
 violin concertos, a piano
erto, an oratorio, a requiem
he celebrated 'Hymnus' series
amber works.

Index

Page numbers in *italic* refer to illustrations

Picture Acknowledgements

The Publisher wishes to thank the organizations listed below for their kind permission to reproduce the photographs in this book. Every effort has been made to acknowledge the pictures properly, however we apologize if there are any unintentional omissions which will be corrected in future editions. Thank you to Simon Scott for his help with our project.

AKG, London 29, 42 top, 45, 62, 72, 75, 79 right, 82 right, 96 right, 98 left, 99 left, 107, 108, 111 right, 115, 117, 124 top, 125, 126 top, 131, 132, 134 top, 135 left, 137 bottom, 138 bottom, 141 bottom, 142, 143 left, 143 right, 144 top, 147 bottom, 151 top, 154, 156 top, 157 bottom, 160, 162 right, 168, 170 bottom, 180 top, *Accaemia Rossini, Bologna* 76 bottom, *Akademie der Bildenden Kuenste, Vienna/Erich Lessing* 96 left, *Austrian Nationalbibliothek, Vienna* 42 bottom, *Bibliotheque Nationale* 28, *Biblioteca Governativa Statale* 23, *Bibliotheque Nationale, Paris* 30, 80 right, *Erich Lessing/Collection Schlo Ambras., Innsbruck* 41, *Fred Dolbin* 174 top, *Hamburgische Geschichte* 67, *Von der Heydt-Museum, Wuppertal, Germany/Erich Lessing* 167 bottom, *Histor. Museum des Stadt Wien, Vienna* 106, *Hosptial Tavera, Toledo/Joseph Martin* 77, *Erich Lessing /Kunsthistorisches Museum, Vienna* 36, *Erich Lessing* 16-17 top, *Liceo Musicale, Bologna* 98 right, *Moravska Museum, Bruenn* 165 top, *Erich Lessing/Musee du Louvre, Paris* 10, 12 bottom, *Musee du Louvre, Paris* 32, *Museo Bibliografico Musicale, Bologna* 82 left, 129 top, *National Gallery of Victoria, Melbourne* 100, *National Gallery, London/Erich Lessing* 93, *Osterr. Nationalbibliothek, Wien* 66 bottom, *Osterreichische Galerie im Belvedere, Vienna/Erich Lessing* 145, *Mauro Pagano* 65 top, *Royal College of Music, London* 103, *Schloss Schoenbrunn, Vienna/Erich Lessing* 56 top, *Staatsbibliothek, Munich* 48, *Staatl. Kunstslg., Schlo~Museum* 47, *Universitatsbibliothek, Hamburg* 86, *Versailles Musem* 79 left

Bridgeman Art Library, London/New York *Trustees of Berkeley Castle, Gloucs.* 54, *Biblioteca de el Escorial, Madrid/Index* 25, *Biblioteca Medicea-Laurenziana, Florence* 33 left, *Bibliotheque de L'Opera, Paris* 178 top left, *Bibliotheque Municipale, Laon/Giraudon* 18, *Bibliotheque Nationale, Paris/Artephot/Trela* 163 left, *Bibliotheque Nationale, Paris/Giraudon* 46, *Bibliotheque Royale de Belgique, Brussels* 22, *Biblitheque Nationale, Paris* 38, *Bonhams, London* 74, *British Library, London* 50 top, 87 bottom, 134 bottom, 165 bottom, *British Library, London/© Succession Picasso/DACS 1999* 169 bottom, *Chateau de Versailles/Giraudon* 104-105, *Chateau de Versailles/Peter Willi* 58, *Christie's Images, London* 85 right, *Christie's, London* 53, *Galleria dell' Accademia, Venice* 64, *Gemaldegalerie, Dresden* 122, *Guildhall Art Gallery, Corporation of London* 68, *Haags Gemeentemuseum, Netherlands* 112, 163 right, 179 right, *Haags Gemeentemuseum, Netherlands/photograph by G.L. Manuel Freres* 138 top, *Haags Gementemuseum, Netherlands* 141 main picture, *Ham House, Surrey* 55, *Historisches Museum der Stadt, Vienna* 102, 118, *Hotel Lallemand, Bourges/Giraudon* 51, *Louvre, Paris/Giraudon* 110 left, *Louvre, Paris/Lauros-Giraudon* 49 bottom, *Musee Conde, Chantilly/Giraudon* 80 left, *Museo di Goethe, Rome/Giraudon* 124 bottom, *Museo Real Academia de Bellas Artes, Madrid* 92, *Museum of London* 70, *National Gallery, London* 59, *Osterreichische Galerie, Vienna* 144 centre, *Osterreichische Nationalbibliothek, Vienna* 146, *Private Collection* 15, 43, 85 left, 87 top, 88, 95, 114, 137 top, 139, 153 right, 158-159 top, 166, *Private Collection/Peter Willi/© ADAGP, Paris and DACS, London 1999* 81, *Royal College of Music, London* 71, *Staatsbibliothek, Berlin* 109, *Stapleton Collection* 50 bottom, *Victoria & Albert Museum, London* 127, 157 Top, *Victoria & Albert Museum, London, UK* 69

Chandos 187 left

Corbis UK Ltd *Bettmann* arlin, 65 bottom, 119, 175 left, *UPI* 173, 175 right, *Gianni Dagli Orti* 14 top, *Kimbell Art Museum* 40

© 1993 ECM Records *cover photograph by Tonu Tormis/layout by Barbara Wojirsch* 184 top teft

© 1993 Elecktra Entertainment, *a division of Warner Communications Inc./design by James Victore Design Works/cover photograph © Robert Frank* 184 top right

EMI 178 top right

Hulton Getty Picture Collection 52 top, 94, 130, 156 bottom, *Erich Auerbach* 176 right, 181 bottom, *Alex Bender* 176 left

Alan King 6, 8-9 bottom, 16-17 bottom, 26-27 bottom, 34-35 bottom, 56 bottom, 90-91 centre right, 120-121 bottom, 158-159 bottom

Kobal Collection *Mosfilm* 177 left

Lebrecht Collection front arlin, 12 top, 13, 14 bottom, 20, 21, 26-27 top, 31, 33 right, 34-35 top, 39, 44, 49 top, 52 bottom, 61, 63, 66 top, 73, 76 top, 90-91 top, 99 right, 101, 110 right, 111 left, 120-121 top, 126 bottom, 128, 129 bottom, 133 top, 135 right, 136, 140 bottom, 140 top, 144 bottom, 147 top, 148, 149, 150, 151 bottom, 152, 153 left, 155 right, 155 left, 167 top, 170 top, 171, 174 bottom right, 177 right, 178 bottom, 183, © ADAGP, Paris and DACS, London 1999 164 top, 169 top, © Copyright 1964 by Henry Litolff's Verlag, Frankfurt. Reprinted by permission of Peters Edition Limited, London. 182 bottom, *Zdenek Chrapek* 184 bottom, *Milein Cosman* 172 top, *Betty Freeman* 185, 187 right, © Copyright 1960 by Henmar Press Inc., New York. Reprinted by permission of Peters Edition Limited, London. 181 top, *I.R.C.A.M.* 180 bottom, *Andre LeCoz* 179 left, *G. Newson* 182 top, © Succession Picasso/DACS 1999 164 bottom

Magnum Photos *Martine Franck* 5, 186 right, *Guy le Querrec* 161, 186 left

Performing Arts Library *Clive Barda* 162 left, 172 bottom, *Ron Scherl* 133 bottom

RCA 174 bottom left

Werner Forman Archive *Museo Nazionale Romano, Rome* 8-9 top